The Sign
of
Four Spirits

Sherlock Holmes Bookshop Mysteries
A Three Book Problem
A Curious Incident
There's a Murder Afoot
A Scandal in Scarlet
The Cat of the Baskervilles
Body on Baker Street
Elementary, She Read

Lighthouse Library Mysteries (writing as Eva Gates)
Death by Beach Read
Deadly Ever After
A Death Long Overdue
Read and Buried
Something Read, Something Dead
The Spook in the Stacks
Reading Up a Storm
Booked for Trouble
By Book or by Crook

Ashley Grant Mysteries
Coral Reef Views
Blue Water Hues
White Sand Blues

Year Round Christmas Mysteries
Have Yourself a Deadly Little Christmas
Dying in a Winter Wonderland
Silent Night, Deadly Night
Hark the Herald Angels Slay
We Wish You a Murderous Christmas
Rest Ye Murdered Gentlemen

Constable Molly Smith Mysteries
Unreasonable Doubt
Under Cold Stone
A Cold White Sun
Among the Departed
Negative Image
Winter of Secrets
Valley of the Lost
In the Shadow of the Glacier

Tea By the Sea Mysteries
Murder Spills the Tea
Murder in a Teacup
Tea & Treachery

Catskill Summer Resort Mystery
Deadly Director's Cut
Deadly Summer Nights

Also Available By Vicki Delany
More Than Sorrow
Burden of Memory
Scare the Light Away

The Sign of Four Spirits

A SHERLOCK HOLMES BOOKSHOP MYSTERY

Vicki Delany

CROOKED
LANE

NEW YORK

Published in the United States by Crooked Lane Books, an imprint of The Quick Brown Fox & Company LLC.

Crooked Lane Books and its logo are trademarks of The Quick Brown Fox & Company LLC.

Library of Congress Catalog-in-Publication data available upon request.

ISBN (hardcover): 978-1-63910-539-7
ISBN (ebook): 978-1-63910-540-3

Cover design by Joe Burleson

Printed in the United States.

www.crookedlanebooks.com

Crooked Lane Books
34 West 27th St., 10th Floor
New York, NY 10001

First Edition: January 2024

10 9 8 7 6 5 4 3 2 1

To Mom.

Chapter One

I consider myself to be a practical woman. I have no time for fantasies, visions, overactive imaginations, magic potions, ghosts, specters, or similar superstitious nonsense.

Therefore, I said, as firmly yet as politely as possible, "No. Absolutely not. It's out of the question."

"But, Gemma," Donald Morris replied, "as you well know, Sir Arthur was intensely interested in spiritualism. Any thorough academic study of the great man means—"

"I'm not engaging in an academic study of Sir Arthur Conan Doyle, thorough or otherwise. I'm not going with you to this thing, and that's final. You're welcome to attend if you want, but I suggest you ask yourself if a small-town New England psychic fair is of the order of seriousness Sir Arthur would have been interested in."

Moriarty perched on the counter between us, his amber eyes focused, his black head turning from one side to the other, his long tail twitching as he followed the conversation. Above his head hung a framed reproduction of the cover of *Beeton's Christmas Annual,* December 1887, and next to it was a small shelf holding the ugly glass statue awarded to my great-uncle Arthur

Doyle in recognition of his promotion of Sherlock Holmes beyond England's shores.

"Sir Arthur was interested in a great many things," Donald said, not knowing when to give up. "I would have thought, Gemma, you would be also with that intense inquiring mind of yours. You don't have to *believe*. You simply have to have an open mind."

I gave my friend a smile. "Nice try, but no luck. You can't flatter me into agreeing to come with you. Now, if you'll excuse me, it's opening time."

It was five minutes early, but I was getting uncomfortable with the direction this conversation was taking and wanted to put a stop to it. It's true I have no interest in the sort of fortune-telling and amateur spiritualism one can find at a so-called psychic fair. It wasn't entirely true that my "inquiring mind" wasn't interested. I'd had a brief (fortunately, extremely brief) brush with the possibility of the supernatural over the winter. It was not an experience I intended to ever repeat.

That incident was something my "inquiring mind" had firmly locked away, never to be thought of again. So far, I'd managed quite successfully.

Moriarty leaped off the counter and followed me to the entrance to the shop, ready to greet the first of the day's customers. I unlocked the door and flipped the sign to Open. It was the first Friday in July, the start of what the weather forecast predicted would be a glorious Cape Cod weekend, and I expected the Sherlock Holmes Bookshop and Emporium would have a busy—and hopefully profitable—day.

I didn't expect the first person through our doors to be Bunny Leigh, former teenage pop sensation, now middle-aged resident of West London. She wiggled her ring-encrusted fingers at me and gave me a big grin. "Good morning, Gemma. Another lovely day in our fair town."

"Morning. Ashleigh isn't scheduled to start work until noon today."

She waved one hand in the air. "I'm not here to see Ashleigh." When Bunny first arrived in West London in January of this year, she'd been the talk of the town. The talk of the now-forties age group who'd been her rabid teenage fans in her glory days, anyway. Over the spring, she'd made herself at home, rented a small apartment close to Baker Street, reunited with her long-lost daughter, and gradually became nothing more (or less) than a regular West London fixture. It had been months since I'd heard her talk about the contract for the major motion picture of her life story, to be signed any day now, or the progress of her comeback album. "Ready to go, Donald?" she asked.

I cocked one eyebrow at Donald. He smiled sheepishly. "Almost ready. I've been trying to convince Gemma to come with us, but she says she's not interested."

"She says that," I said, "because she's not interested. Are you two going together to this . . . thing?"

Moriarty peered out the door. Seeing no one approaching who might be more inclined to fuss over him, he headed for his bed under the center table and the first of the day's naps.

Bunny held her arms out and twirled around. She normally dressed in some version of fashionable shredded jeans and sky-high boots in an attempt to add some height to her diminutive frame, but today she was looking very 1960s hippie in a swirling, ankle-length, multicolored skirt; loose, flowery, lace-trimmed blouse; and miles of brightly colored, clattering beads wrapped around her wrists and neck. All she was missing was the flowers in her hair. In contrast, Donald, a keen Sherlockian, wore a long black overcoat, a black waistcoat trimmed with gold embroidery, black trousers, and black shoes polished to a brilliant shine. He even had an imitation gold pocket watch attached by an imitation gold chain tucked into the front of his waistcoat. Donald sometimes forgets that clothes suited for a Victorian gentleman during a rainy London winter might be too warm for a New England summer.

The two of them made quite a study in contrast.

"We are," Bunny said in answer to my question. "Isn't it exciting?"

"I suppose you could say that. I wasn't aware you knew each other."

"We got to chatting a couple of days ago," Donald said, "when Miss Leigh came to get Ashleigh at closing. I happened to mention that Sir Arthur had a keen interest in spiritualism."

"In return, I told him about the fair this weekend," Bunny said. "Ready to go, Donnie?"

Donnie?

"I am," *Donnie* said.

"It's only nine-thirty," I said. "Jayne hung a poster in the window of the tearoom, and it says the fair doesn't open until noon today."

Bunny waved a cheaply printed booklet in my direction. "Donnie and I want to go over the things we'd like to see first. Some of the better-known palm readers will be booked instantly, so I want to be sure and get my chance." She clapped her hands together. "I'm so excited!"

"How big is this event anyway?" I asked.

"Huge," Bunny said. "They've taken the entire West London Community Center, both floors, as well as meeting rooms at some of the hotels, where they'll conduct seminars and the like.

People have come from all over the eastern United States and Canada. That's why I need to get a good idea of what I want to see and do. I can't leave it to chance."

"Have you been to several of these things?"

"Oh, yes," she said. "Many times. I went to a gypsy fortune teller when I was in high school, just for a lark, with some of my friends. That experience opened a whole new world to me, Gemma." Her intense green eyes sparkled at the memory. "And I mean that literally. It led directly to my music career. Who knows what would have happened to me without the benefit of that gypsy woman's wise advice?"

I didn't bother to tell her that real gypsies preferred to be called Roma people these days. It's highly unlikely any fortune teller who visited Lincoln, Nebraska, in the late 1990s was a genuine traveler, and even less likely they were a genuine fortune teller.

Not that there is such a thing as a genuine fortune teller.

"I told Donnie all about it," Bunny said. "The old gypsy woman who read my cards foretold that I had a big career ahead of me, and all I had to do was be bold enough to grab it. Fortune favors the brave, she told me. She said I was wasting my time singing in a high school band and bigger things were waiting for me as soon as I could make my escape from the confines of my life and my family's expectations for me." The smile she gave us lit up her face, and I caught a glimpse of the young woman who rose to stardom largely because of sheer personality, as well as good luck. "And she was right! My parents were so skeptical. They outright forbade me to quit school and go to LA in pursuit of my dreams, but I went anyway. And see how it all turned out! How'd she even know I was a singer? Tell me that, I asked my parents, and they couldn't answer."

Young Bunny, real name Leigh Saunderson, would have had naked ambition written all over her pretty face. Singer, actress, dancer. Take your pick, and the "fortune teller" had. It was entirely possible Leigh's band put up posters around town advertising their next gig at some local bar, and the fortune teller mentally filed the information for future reference if needed.

"I've had my cards read many times over the years," Bunny continued, "particularly since Rupert, who became my manager and got me my big break, died. No one's told me anything as groundbreaking as she did that first time, but their advice has always been helpful. I was working a job in Atlantic City last year." Her face tightened at the memory, and I surmised it hadn't been a job she was particularly happy with. "A palm reader suggested it was time for me to reunite with Ashleigh. And here I am!" The big smile and dancing eyes returned. After initially distrusting her, I decided I liked Bunny Leigh. The end of her glory days had been a crushing disappointment to her, and she openly craved a return to her time in the spotlight, but she was generally a bouncy, cheerful woman. Her reappearance in my shop assistant's life had made Ashleigh very happy.

"That's nice," I said. "Don't let me keep you."

"Let's have a coffee while we go over the outline for the day." Bunny took Donald's arm and led him toward the sliding door joining the Emporium to Mrs. Hudson's Tea Room. "Ashleigh said she has to work this weekend, but I'm hoping Gemma will give her time off to come with me tomorrow. Maybe someone can tell Ashleigh how to direct her focus to make the right moves in life. The way it happened to me."

Ashleigh, I knew, had plans to own a bookstore empire one day. For the moment, she contented herself with being my assistant, but she was always coming up with ideas as to how I could also have a bookstore empire.

Which is something I wanted about as much as I wanted to have my cards read by a "gypsy" fortune teller.

* * *

Jayne Wilson is half owner, manager, and head baker at Mrs. Hudson's Tea Room, located at 220 Baker Street. Great-uncle Arthur and I own the other half of the restaurant as well as the Emporium, which is at number 222. Every day at 3:40 PM, Jayne and I meet in the tearoom for a cup of tea, what remains of the day's offerings, and a business meeting. Because she's my best friend as well as my partner, our meeting is usually more of a girlfriends' chat and gossip session than a professional consultation. Uncle Arthur is strictly a silent partner in our enterprise. He was currently visiting friends in Peru. Or was it Portugal? Maybe Pennsylvania? One of the *P*'s, anyway. I tend to lose track of where Great-uncle Arthur is at any given time. No, not Pennsylvania. If he'd gone anywhere on the east coast of North America, he would have driven, but his beloved 1977 Triumph Spitfire was currently parked in our garage. Wouldn't be Paraguay: no coastline. Uncle Arthur never ventures far from the sea.

Mentally drawing up a list of costal countries beginning with a *P*, I headed for the day's partners' meeting. The tearoom closes at four o'clock, so it's normally almost empty when I come in, but today many of the tables were still occupied with women relaxing over a late lunch or enjoying a full afternoon tea. As part of the tearoom's name and to match the decor, Jayne serves a proper afternoon tea from one o'clock until closing. Every time I'd glanced through the joining door, I'd seen a full restaurant, with take-out lines winding through the room.

"You've been busy today," I said to Jocelyn, one of Jayne's assistants.

"Totally run off our feet," she said with a hearty sigh. "As well as the usual tourist crowds, tons of people are in town for the psychic fair. I've seen them consulting their program books."

"You sound as though being busy isn't a good thing."

"Not many people tip less than middle-aged women attending a psychic fair. Unless it's elderly men also going to the fair but pretending their interest is for research purposes only. What they're researching, I have no idea. I considered asking if they don't believe in karma, but Jayne said hinting for better tips might not be a good idea."

A young woman dressed in the tearoom uniform—black skirt, white blouse, and white apron featuring the Mrs. Hudson's logo of a steaming cup next to a deerstalker hat—passed us. She gave me a quick, nervous smile before ducking her head and turning her attention to clearing a recently vacated table.

"How's Miranda working out?" I asked Jocelyn in a low voice.

Jocelyn's face puckered, which told me a heck of a lot. "I'm glad we have her. We need her. We've been so busy."

"But . . ."

Jocelyn leaned toward me and whispered. "Miranda's nice and all, and she does an okay job, but she needs to be not quite so nervous."

"She'll get into it," I said. "Give her time." Miranda only started working at the tearoom that week. Jayne had needed additional help all through the spring but, ever frugal, she insisted she could manage. This summer turned out to be so busy, she needed to have her other permanent assistant, Fiona, working full-time in the kitchen, and thus she hired Miranda to wait tables alongside Jocelyn. Miranda was quiet and shy, and she always slipped nervously past me as though fearing I'd leap on her and take a bite.

"I'll tell Jayne you're here," Jocelyn said. "Your table's free."

Jayne and I like to sit in the window alcove and watch the activity on Baker Street while we have our meeting.

I slipped into the bench seat against the window, facing into the room. A moment later, Jayne dropped into the chair opposite. "You have flour on your nose," I said.

She groaned and wiped at it. "I'm absolutely beat, Gemma. I don't know how I'm going to get through the rest of the summer. It's only the beginning of July."

"You need more than one new fresh-faced young waitress. Hire an assistant baker. We can afford it, particularly if we're going to be as busy as expected."

She freed her long blond hair from its scraggly ponytail and shook it out. Jayne might protest she was tired, but her blue eyes sparkled, her hair shone, and her face (under the flour) was tinged a healthy pink. "Have someone baking in my kitchen? Never!"

"Suit yourself," I said. And it did—suit her, I mean. Jayne's always a bundle of energy, and she loves nothing more than to pour that energy into her baking. That and spending time with her fiancé, Andy Whitehall. Andy's a chef and owner of his own hugely popular restaurant, the Blue Water Café. He'd be as busy as Jayne, and everyone else in town who catered to the tourist crowd, over the summer. We'd taken advantage of the slow winter season to start making plans for Jayne and Andy's wedding, which would be held next January. The date had been set, the church booked for the ceremony and the Cape Cod Yacht Club for the reception, but Jayne's mother, Leslie, was getting impatient that the final details, including the guest list and Jayne's dress, weren't being attended to quickly enough. Jayne simply smiled in that so-casual Jayne way and said, "There's plenty of time, Mom."

"Moot point," Jayne said now. "I'd have trouble finding someone available to take the job this far into the tourist season. When poor Lorraine broke her wrist, I was darn lucky to snag Miranda. She was looking for work late in the season because she only just arrived on the Cape to spend the rest of the summer with family."

On the far side of the room, Jocelyn whispered to Miranda and pointed toward our table. Miranda wiped her hands on her apron and approached, a frozen smile fixed on her face, her cheeks so red I feared she was about to burst into flames. She was not long out of her teens. Taller than my five foot eight, slim without being skinny, with thick black hair cut very short, large dark eyes, a long neck, and the sort of clear skin and perfect teeth that indicates she, or her family, has money to spend. "Tea?" she said.

"I feel like Darjeeling today," I said. "Jayne?"

"Fine for me too. I put aside a plate of sandwiches and some tarts. Can you bring us that also, please?"

Miranda's head bobbed once, and she almost dropped into a curtsy before she fled.

"You scare her," Jayne said.

"Me? What does that mean? I've scarcely ever spoken to her. Come to think of it, I've never spoken to her other than to order tea."

"You're getting a reputation around town, Gemma. Some people think you can read their minds."

"Perish the thought. Even if I could do such a thing, I have not the slightest interest in what goes on in anyone's mind."

"Speaking of mind reading, that psychic fair this weekend is looking to be a bigger deal than I expected. Jocelyn said almost everyone who came in for lunch today was talking about it."

The door opened, and a man and a woman walked in. They were in their midforties, well-groomed, expensively dressed for their seaside vacation. He wore blue trousers and a white cap trimmed with gold braid. She was in white capris with a loose-fitting blue silk shirt. The tip of her nose was tinged pink where the big sun hat with a wide ribbon in the same shade as her blouse had failed to protect it. They both wore boat shoes. Straight off a sailboat was my guess. Although I insist I never guess.

"Good afternoon," Jocelyn said. "We're about to close, so table service is finished for the day, but you're welcome to order something to take with you."

"Thanks," the man said. They approached the counter.

Miranda came out of the back carrying a tray with the tea for Jayne and me. She froze. All but her hands, which shook so much I feared she'd drop the tray. I started to stand, and Jayne, catching the direction of my gaze, half-turned.

Then, like a dog coming out of the ocean, Miranda shook herself off, tightened her grip on the tray, and rapidly crossed the room. Her face, which moments before had been pink with shyness, had turned pure white.

"Are you okay?" I asked her.

"I'm fine."

"You don't look fine."

Her hands continued to shake as she put the china teapot on the table.

"What's the matter?" I asked. "Do you know those people?"

"Nothing's the matter." Miranda dropped a plate of sandwiches and lemon squares in front of us.

11

"I—"

"Gemma." Jayne tightened her lips and threw me a look. "Miranda said nothing's the matter."

"But—"

"They . . . those people . . . reminded me of someone, that's all." Miranda hurried back to the kitchen as fast as she could go without breaking into a sprint. At the counter, the couple paid Jocelyn and waited while she made their lattes. They didn't spare a glance for Miranda as she scurried past them, head down.

"That's odd," I said.

"Nothing odd about it." Jayne picked up the teapot and poured for us both. "You're looking for mysteries where none exist, Gemma."

"I suppose you're right. Is Miranda working out okay?"

"I wish she had a bit more confidence in herself. She's always apologizing to everyone, even when she's done nothing wrong. Still, early days yet. She only started on Wednesday, so she hasn't experienced a weekend yet, and this is her first restaurant job."

"Was it wise to hire someone with no experience?" I added a splash of milk and took a sip of tea. Hot and fragrant and delicious. I then helped myself to a perfect little circle of a sandwich: cucumber with the slightest hint of curry powder arranged on thinly sliced white bread.

"Wise? Probably not, but you know what it's like around here in the summer, Gemma. Everyone's desperate for seasonal staff. Miranda had a good reference from the store she worked at last summer. They closed, so she couldn't go back this year."

"Last summer? Is she in university?"

"Yes," Jayne took a salmon sandwich cut into a triangle. She's a business major at Harvard."

"That must be incredibly boring. Perhaps that explains the aura of sadness surrounding her."

"Sadness? What do you mean by that? I haven't noticed her being sad."

"She's not expressing her feelings, certainly not to people she works with and hardly knows. Her nails are bitten to the quick, leaving a few ragged hangnails, and considering how well-groomed she is otherwise, I suspect that's a recent development. There's a tightness to her smile that's covering up a deeper sadness and fresh lines appearing under her eyes. She did badly on her exams this year, I suspect, and she's worrying about her future. That would explain why she didn't look for a summer job until July—she had to do extra classes."

"Good thing you're not interested in reading minds," Jayne said as she helped herself to a second sandwich.

Chapter Two

B ack at the Emporium, Ashleigh was helping customers find what they wanted (or what they didn't know they wanted until she told them) while Gale, my other assistant, rang up purchases. Moriarty's full length was stretched across the sales counter, allowing customers to stroke his belly. Like the tearoom, the shop had been busy all day, and I had high hopes for a prosperous summer season.

I ran my eyes over the shelves as I came in. I'd been away for half an hour and two Sherlock Holmes jigsaw puzzles had been removed from the merchandise table, as had four of the "I am Sher-locked" mugs, and one brain puzzle game. Several copies of the latest Daniel Pitt mystery by Anne Perry were gone from the new books display, as were a couple of editions of the short-story collections edited by Laurie R. King and Leslie S. Klinger, and one of *Gaslight Ghouls: Uneasy Tales of Sherlock Holmes*, edited by J. R. Campbell and Charles Prepolec. Several volumes had been removed from the YA shelves, where the Enola Holmes books by Nancy Springer were prominently placed.

Large gaps in the nonfiction shelf were visible. From this angle, I couldn't see exactly what was missing, but the space was where we kept the nonfiction works of Sir Arthur Conan Doyle as well as biographies about him and books to do with his life and times. Those have a select readership, so we don't normally sell many of them on an average day.

"Did one person take all those nonfiction books?" I asked Gale when she finished with another satisfied customer.

"We had a run on them shortly after you left. Several women arrived in a pack and immediately charged for the nonfiction section. Some of them bought more than one book. They completely cleared us out of *The History of Spiritualism* and *The Coming of the Fairies*. Do you have any more in stock?"

I shook my head.

"They're with the psychic fair." Ashleigh pulled a flyer out of her skirt pocket and showed me. "One of them gave me this. If I show it at the door, I'll get twenty-five percent off the entrance fee."

"There's an entrance fee?"

"It's a big deal, Gemma," Gale said. "You must have seen the various posters popping up all over the place. The town's expecting hundreds, maybe thousands, of people to attend. They've rented the entire community center for the weekend."

"There's a sucker born every minute." Then, realizing my comment might have been a mite imprudent, I glanced at my employees. "But if people want to go to the fair, that's none of my business. Are you going?"

"Not me," Gale said firmly. "Bunch of total nonsense in my opinion."

"Bunny suggested it," Ashleigh said. "She has some story about how advice from a fortune teller led her to her career, and she wants me to have a consultation. But I'm not sure I want to."

Ashleigh was Bunny Leigh's daughter. When Bunny had been on the verge of becoming a major teen pop star, she returned to her hometown of Lincoln, Nebraska, to drop the baby off with her own parents. She didn't see any of them again for another twenty-two years. Not until this past winter when she popped up in West London wanting to build a relationship with her only child.

They were doing okay, I thought. That was mostly down to Ashleigh, wise enough not to rush into things and to take each day as it came to slowly get to know her mother. They'd made a trip to Lincoln together in the spring so Bunny could reconnect with her own parents. Neither of them told me how that had gone, and I hadn't asked. Their identical smiles and happy chatter when they talked about the trip were enough.

"I suppose there's no harm in going to the silly thing," Gale said. "You don't have to believe any of it." She took the flyer out of Ashleigh's hand. "According to this, they're having séances with some famous medium. So famous I've never heard of her, but then again, I'm hardly their intended audience. You wouldn't catch me dead at one of those."

"You made a joke," Ashleigh said.

"So I did!"

We broke off our conversation as the chimes over the door tinkled and three women came in.

"Do you have anything about Sir Arthur Conan Doyle?" one of them asked us.

"He's an English writer. Best known for being the creator of Sherlock Holmes," her friend added helpfully.

"We have an extensive selection," Ashleigh said. "Right over here."

"He was prominent in Victorian spiritualism," the third woman said. "We're from Raleigh, and we've come for the psychic fair. Have you heard about that?"

"Oh, yes," I said.

"We met this nice man earlier, and he told us all about Mr. Conan Doyle."

"Sir Arthur," I said.

"What?"

"He's called Sir Arthur, being a knight. Not Mr. . . . . Never mind."

"Okay. Sir Doyle, this nice man told us, was very involved in spiritualism. He was an early member of the Society for Psychical Research in London, England. Isn't that amazing! He wrote lots about spirits, and he even wrote about fairies. He spent a good part of his life investigating those things. Imagine that! He said you had his books here."

"Mr. Arthur's books. Not the nice man's," her friend added. "He was a hoot. Dressed just like him."

"Dressed like Sir Doyle, not himself."

My head spun. Obviously, they'd met Donald. Donald was never shy about promoting his passion, and, incidentally, the Sherlock Holmes Bookshop and Emporium.

"He, the nice man, told us to get *The History of Spiritualism* as the best place to start. Do you have that one?"

"We're sold out of that particular volume at the moment, but we can order it for you," Ashleigh said. "In the meantime, I'll show you what we do have."

"What a lovely cat," the third woman said as Moriarty wound himself around her legs.

I headed for the computer to place a rush order.

* * *

That night, I enjoyed a late dinner date with my boyfriend, Ryan Ashburton. We had a lovely, relaxing meal at the Blue Water

Café, Andy's place, sitting out on the deck perched above the calm waters of the harbor. After dinner, we bought ice creams and strolled along the crowded boardwalk, licking our cones and watching the tourists, also licking and strolling and watching the tourists. Ryan's the lead detective for the West London police, and I asked him if they had any reason to be interested in the goings on at the psychic fair.

"We're keeping an eye on it," he said. "But I wouldn't say we're interested. I might think crystal ball reading and tarot cards and the like are a whole lot of nonsense, but if people want to fork over good money to hear what they hope the future holds for them, that's not a crime. If they want to buy a pack of crystals or so-called fairy dust to keep them safe or to attend a lecture on what supposedly happens after death, that's not a crime either. There are plenty of people who prey on the believers to the point of extortion or who take advantage of the elderly and confused to bilk them out of their life savings, but you don't usually get that sort at a heavily advertised public event like this one." He licked his triple chocolate explosion ice cream. "The real criminals prefer to keep themselves far away from the limelight." We reached the lighthouse at the end of the boardwalk and turned and retraced our steps. "As for the attendees, we can only wish all the tourists who come to town are as well-behaved as them."

Chapter Three

I'd once been talked, against my better judgment, into sitting up all night in a drafty old house waiting for a ghost to appear. After that experience, I vowed I'd never do anything like that again.

"I'd kinda like it if you came, Gemma," Ashleigh said.

"You want me to come to a séance?"

"Yes, I do. I'm nervous about it, and I'd feel better if you were there."

"Are you responsible for this?" I glowered at Donald.

"In a way, I suppose I am. Bunny and I had a fascinating time at the fair yesterday. I, of course, approached it purely as a matter of research, but Bunny insisted some of the exhibitors were legitimate. She had her palm read." He turned to Ashleigh. "The palmist knew she'd recently reconnected with a long-lost object. Isn't that fascinating?"

"Gosh, yes."

I mentally rolled my eyes. "It would be more fascinating if she'd known the long-lost object was a daughter. These people know how to make generic statements of the sort everyone can relate to. If Bunny hadn't reacted to that, they would have come up with something else. Did Bunny react?"

"She sort of squealed and clapped her hands," Donald admitted.

"My point exactly."

"I'm okay with the palm reading stuff, I guess," Ashleigh said. "But I don't know about going to a real séance. It's kinda . . . spooky, don't you think?"

"I must follow," Donald pronounced pretentiously, "where Sir Arthur leads."

Donald was a kind and gentle man, a good and loyal friend, but sometimes he could go a mite over the top in pursuit of his passion. This morning he was dressed in normal, for him, clothes of ironed jeans and a T-shirt proclaiming, "You Know My Methods."

I attempted to change the subject. "Donald, have a look at the nonfiction section."

He glanced to where I'd indicated. "Where have all the books gone?"

The shelves were almost bare.

"You did such a good job of talking up Sir Arthur yesterday, we've been cleaned out of most of the biographies on him as well as his own nonfiction books. Not that I'd call *The New Revelation* nonfiction, more like imaginative rubbish, but that's how it's classified. However, I digress. I've paid extra for a rush shipment of *The History of Spiritualism* and *The Coming of the Fairies* and some of the others, and I'm expecting them to get here by noon. If you happen to be going back to the community center this afternoon, you can continue pushing them."

His eyes gleamed as a thought occurred to him. "I might do that, Gemma. Then again, I might not go back today. Although, if you agreed to come to the séance . . ."

"Nice try," I said.

Despite my protesting instincts, I allowed my curiosity to get the better of me. "Okay, Donald. Tell me about this intended séance. How did it come about? Was it Bunny's idea?"

"I'm not entirely sure," Donald said. "Bunny and I separated at one point when she went in search of healing crystals." He peered at me. "Do you know what those are, Gemma?"

"No, and no one else does either. Someone polished up chunks of scrap glass and stuck a hefty price tag on them."

"Your skepticism does you no credit," he said sadly.

"I'll live with that, if I must. Please continue."

"While Bunny was searching for her crystals, I fell into conversation with a group of women who were fascinated to hear that the creator of Sherlock Holmes had been a prominent figure in the world of spiritualism in the Victorian and Edwardian eras. I mentioned to them that his books could be found at this very establishment."

"Thank you for that."

"When Bunny and I met up later at the snack bar, she told me she'd met a prominent medium—or perhaps the medium's assistant. I'm not entirely sure on that point. Anyway, this medium's offering private sessions this weekend for select attendees."

I assumed "select" meant wealthy. Or vulnerable. Or, best of all, wealthy *and* vulnerable. Although neither Bunny nor Donald were that. Wealthy, I mean. They might both be vulnerable.

Moriarty yawned and leaped off the counter, going in search of more interesting conversation.

"The medium—or her assistant—offered to set up a special séance tonight, specifically for Bunny and any friends she'd like to invite."

I snorted. "Special. Yeah, I'm sure."

"The woman said she's a huge fan of Bunny's and was thrilled at the chance to do something specifically for Bunny."

"Donald, surely you don't buy that? Bunny's blended into life here in West London, but it's not hard to find out about her background. This woman's flattering her in order to use her."

"Perhaps you're right, Gemma. But really, what can it hurt? Bunny's excited about it, and after telling me about the arrangement, she rushed off to phone Ashleigh and ask her to come."

"Which she did," Ashleigh said, "and, without thinking about whether or not I really wanted to go, I agreed."

"Once she'd gone to do that, and I finished my coffee," Donald continued, "I spotted a booth selling material about the history of spiritualism and went to see if they had anything on Sir Arthur I might not have read."

"Like that's remotely possible," I mumbled. "Sorry. Carry on with your story."

"To my surprise, they had nothing at all on or by Sir Arthur. Most of their books were more in the overly sensational line." He sniffed in disappointment. "Whereupon I got to chatting with some of the people browsing the booth and told them about Sir Arthur and the wealth of information on his life and times, with a particular emphasis on his involvement in the spiritualism of the Victorian era, which is available at this very store."

"I'm sure the book vendor loved you for that."

"He did ask me to leave. Quite forcefully. I told him I could make some suggestions as to how he could improve the quality of his stock, but he seemed to be uninterested in my advice."

"Imagine that."

"Did Bunny say why she wanted to go to a séance?" Ashleigh asked.

"I didn't ask her," Donald said. "I assume she's simply curious, as am I. Think it over, Gemma. I'm sure it will be a fascinating evening."

"How much are you paying for this?" I knew Donald didn't have much in the way of excess money. On his father's death, he'd been left a small inheritance, enough so he could abandon his family law practice and devote his life to the study of the Great Detective and his creator. Being a Sherlock enthusiast doesn't exactly pay well, but Donald's happy with his lot, and I believe that's good enough for anyone.

"Bunny's treat," he replied. "She'll pay for herself and any guests she wants to invite. Meaning, so far, me and Ashleigh. Plus you, if you want to come, Gemma. Nine o'clock tonight, at a private home in West London."

I groaned inwardly. If this medium invited Bunny, it might be because she knew her history and suspected Bunny was wealthy. Such was not the case. Bunny Leigh had been a big star and had made a great deal of money in her glory days, but most of that was gone: bad investments, bad men, too many failed attempts to get her career back on track.

Still, if Bunny wanted to waste what limited funds she had treating her daughter and friend, that was her business.

"Count me out," I said. "But you two enjoy yourselves."

The bells over the door chimed, and more customers came in.

"I spoke to those ladies yesterday," Donald said. "Allow me to assist them." He bustled over to greet the new arrivals.

I turned to Ashleigh, ready to suggest we get back to work. The color had drained out of her face and her eyes were wide.

"Ashleigh?"

She took a deep breath and spoke in a low voice. "I think I've figured out the answer to my question, Gemma. Why Bunny . . . Mom wants to go to the séance, I mean."

"Why?"

"She wants to see my dad. One more time."

I kept my voice down to match hers. "Your father?"

"I'm guessing that's it. My dad died before I was born. She decided she couldn't raise me by herself and at the same time continue to build her career, so she took me to Grandma and Granddad in Nebraska. She didn't intend to . . . to not come back, but her career took off and . . . Anyway, he was the love of her life. They were totally wrapped up in each other and so looking forward to the future and raising a family together." Tears filled Ashleigh's eyes. She swallowed hard and glanced away.

"Donald!" I called. "Ashleigh and I are taking a break. Can you watch the shop?"

"Happy to," he called back.

"Come on," I said to my assistant. "Upstairs. You can have a good cry if you need one."

She nodded, unable to speak. I led the way up the seventeen steps to my office. I settled Ashleigh into the visitor's chair and went for a glass of water while she scrambled through her pockets in search of a tissue. When I returned, I pressed the glass into her free hand. "I'll leave you, if you want to be alone for a while. Come down when you're ready."

She sniffled, blew her nose, and wiped her eyes. "I'm okay. It kinda hit me out of the blue when I realized why Bunny . . . Mom . . . arranged this séance. She loved him, my dad, so much. His name was James. She called him Jimmy. She never found true love again."

When Bunny first arrived in Ashleigh's life, I'd been suspicious of her intentions, and I checked into the history of the once-upon-a-time pop star. Bunny's name had been linked with plenty of men over the years, but she'd only been married once, when she was in her thirties, and that marriage hadn't lasted more than a year. She had no other children. My investigation hadn't turned up anyone named James or Jimmy. It was possible, if they'd been together before she became famous, his name had been left out of the gossip columns and her biographies. Possible, but I had my doubts.

"Would you like to see a picture of him?" Ashleigh asked me. She took out her phone without waiting for an answer and scrolled through the photos app. She held the screen up to me.

I saw a photo of a photo of a good-looking man in his early twenties, deeply tanned, with chiseled cheekbones, wavy dark hair tumbling to his shoulders, and large brown eyes under thick black lashes. He stood against a plain background, just a beige wall, and there was nothing to identify where, or when, the picture had been taken. I could see no resemblance between him and Ashleigh, but that didn't always mean anything. Ashleigh looked very much like her mother at that age: the same fine-boned frame, heart-shaped face, cleft chin, and expressive green eyes.

"She must be hoping this medium can put her in touch with him," Ashleigh said. "If that's the case, I . . . I want to go too. I've always wanted to have a dad. I knew my mom was out there somewhere. Grandma and Granddad told me that, but they never said anything about my father. I loved Granddad to bits. You know that, Gemma. He tried hard, but he wasn't a real dad." She drained the water glass, wiped her eyes once more, and stood up.

I had no idea if Bunny's story was true or not. She wouldn't likely tell her only child she was the product of a one-night stand. But that didn't matter, and it was none of my business. If it helped Ashleigh, and Bunny, to believe it, that was all that counted.

"We'd better get back downstairs. Donald means well, but he's likely to give those customers free books to apologize for not having the volumes they came in for." That, I knew, was true. Donald didn't exactly have a head for business. "If you're sure you're okay."

"I am. Thanks. Gemma?"

"Yes?"

"I'm scared, but I don't know what I'm scared of. Of meeting my dad? Of not meeting my dad if the thing's a flop?"

"Bunny will be with you," I said.

"Yeah, but she'll be sort of preoccupied, don't you think? I mean, you know what she's like, Gemma. Bunny . . . Mom . . . isn't all that practical. Sometimes she doesn't think things through. If she pins her hopes on seeing him, and he doesn't come . . . or if he comes and it's not what she's expecting, she'll be a mess. I need to be there for her." She looked at me. Her green eyes sparkled with tears. "Will you come, Gemma? Please. Will you be there for me?"

Chapter Four

I told Ashleigh I'd give some thought to attending the séance, although I had to admit to myself, I didn't have all that much to think about. She'd asked me—how could I say no? I could have made up some excuse—an important business meeting tonight, a date with the love of my life, the urgent need to rush to Great-uncle Arthur's hospital bedside. Unfortunately, I'd previously told her I had nothing planned for tonight other than a walk with the dogs, a quiet dinner, catching up on some Netflix programming, and going to bed early with two dogs and a good book.

The shop was busy the rest of the day, and we sold most of the copies of *The History of Spiritualism* and other books I'd rush ordered. Who knew a psychic fair would be so profitable for a Sherlock Holmes-themed bookshop? I had Donald to thank for that. Midafternoon, he called me, whispering into the phone that he'd been invited to give an impromptu lecture on Sir Arthur and Victorian spiritualism and would be mentioning the names of various books on the subject and where one could purchase them.

Shortly before closing, a man and a woman I didn't recognize came into the shop. Late thirties, nicely dressed in a version of upper-crust New England or West Coast holiday attire. He wore a short-sleeved, blue-and-white check cotton shirt, untucked; slim-fitting, ankle-length khaki trousers; and Italian loafers without socks. She was in a sleeveless, causally flowing, mid-thigh-length flower-patterned dress and leather sandals. She was of average, height thin to the point of scrawny. The thick, luscious black hair tumbling around her shoulders, flawless olive skin, large dark eyes, and strong nose told me that somewhere in her past she had Southern European ancestors. A tiny diamond pierced her left nostril, diamond studs were in her ears, rivers of silver were draped around her neck, and silver rings adorned every finger.

Ashleigh was busy behind the counter, ringing up purchases, so I approached the new arrivals and gave them a smile. "Welcome. Please let me know if you need any assistance."

"Thanks," she said, not bothering to look at me, a portrait of well-crafted boredom on her pretty face.

"You're in town this weekend for the psychic fair," I said. "We're almost out of most of the books we have on Victoria-era spiritualism, but I'm expecting more to come in on Monday."

"How'd you know—?" he began.

I smiled. Her giant canvas tote bag was open, and it was stuffed full of the same products I'd seen yesterday and earlier today carried by fair attendees.

"You're right," he continued. "My wife insisted on going to a lecture by this old guy on Sir Arthur Conan Doyle, and he told us about this store." His accent was pure New England. Most likely, he'd been educated at a private school in Boston. He gave the woman with him a warm smile, but she didn't return it.

"Don't be so patronizing, Daniel," she said. "You don't have to pretend you only went to that talk because I wanted to. You were interested too." Her accent, in contrast, was straight from the West Coast and rougher around the edges.

"Just commenting, honey. Don't get all offended now."

She forced her face into a smile. "Sorry." She looked at me for the first time. "You know what men are like. They always have to pretend they're indulging us little women, but I could tell he was interested too. I only know Conan Doyle from the Sherlock Holmes stories, like most people, I guess. It was fascinating to hear how important spiritualism was to him. Did you know he dedicated much of his life attempting to prove the validity of spirits, and even fairies and the like? Did you know he was actually friends with Harry Houdini?"

Of course I knew that. I also knew Houdini eventually got so fed up with Conan Doyle's insistence on the validity of the paranormal they fell out and never spoke again. On several occasions, Houdini went so far as to show Conan Doyle how he did his tricks, yet even then Sir Arthur refused to believe him.

"To tell you the truth," she went on, "we're visiting family, and I was absolutely thrilled when I heard a psychic fair was going to be here at the same time. I find that sort of thing so interesting, don't you? Only small-minded people dismiss things they don't understand out of hand." She gave me a wink and tilted her head to indicate the man standing behind her. "We're going to a séance tonight, and I'm really excited about it. Word around town is that Madame Lavalier is fairly new to the world of spiritualism, but she's making a strong impression. She was late finding her talent, but she's the real deal and they say she's very powerful."

Behind her, Daniel pulled a face.

"I'm hoping to contact my nona. I miss her so much. Daniel, look at those mugs. Aren't they the sweetest!" She wandered over to the merchandise display.

"The books?" Daniel asked me.

"Let me show you what we have. Like I said, I can do special orders if you want anything in particular." I led the way to the decimated nonfiction shelves.

"Just browsing for now," he said.

"Oh, look at this adorable cat." Before the woman could get to the items she was interested in, Moriarty, stretching and yawning, had come out from under the table. She crouched down and held out her hand. Her nails were polished a fresh light pink, the perfect manicure marred only by the faint trace of a healing hangnail on the index finger of her right hand. Moriarty, always eager to be admired, purred and rubbed himself against her.

Daniel smiled affectionately at the scene. "Eleanor would love nothing more than to have a cat," he said to me. "But I'm far too allergic to have one in the house." He turned back to me. "I should introduce myself. I gather you know my step-mother, Rebecca. I'm Daniel Stanton, and that's Eleanor, my wife."

"Rebecca. Yes, of course. She was in here only the other day. Your wife said you're visiting family?"

"For a few days. To my eternal regret, I don't get out to the Cape as much as I did when my dad was alive. Dad sure loved Cape Cod. Pressure of being a small business owner, you must know how that is."

"What does your company do?" I asked politely.

"Men's wear. I . . . I mean, we . . . have a line of men's leisure clothing." He flashed a row of brilliant white teeth. "I noticed you admiring my shirt. It's from this season's new collection."

"Very attractive." I didn't correct him to say I hadn't been admiring it—just observing.

"Our focus has previously been on athletic wear, workout clothes, the sort of things your middle-income guy would wear to go golfing with pals or kick the ball around with his kids in the driveway. We're branching out into vacation wear this year."

I felt my smile cracking. I'm interested in a great many things in this world. Men's clothing isn't one of them.

"It's a big step for the company. A crowded field, but I think we're going to make a go of it. Right, Eleanor?"

"You got it, babe." Eleanor was ferrying a set of I-am-Sherlocked mugs and a throw pillow embossed with the saying to the sales counter.

"My wife's not a trained designer or anything, but she has a great eye and the most fabulous taste, and she's been a big help."

"How nice."

The chimes over the door tinkled and a group came in.

"I'll leave you to browse." I made my escape.

Chapter Five

"I don't know how you talk me into these things," Jayne said.

"I don't know how I get talked into these things," I replied as I pulled my Miata off Harbor Road and drove down the long driveway between two rows of stately old pine trees toward our destination.

The Emporium closes at six on Saturdays, so I'd had time to go home, take Violet and Peony, my dogs, for a long walk, gulp down a quickly reheated dinner, make an attempt to reassure myself I didn't mind going to a séance, and pick up Jayne, all in plenty of time for us to be at the meeting place by ten to nine as instructed.

"I would have expected this to start at midnight," Jayne said. She'd gone home after the tearoom closed to have a quick nap and changed for the night out into a short pink dress with spaghetti straps clinched with a thin black belt and strappy sandals with substantial heels.

"It'll be dark enough in a short while," I said. "I wonder if we're but the first of a number of exclusive private events to be held tonight."

A thick bank of clouds blocked the setting sun in the western sky, and to the east the ocean was a stretch of black velvet. A flock of starlings flew overhead, heading for their nightly refuge. The first drops of rain pattered against the car windows, and a bolt of lightning flashed in the distance. Too far away, so far, for thunder to follow.

In one of those coincidences that make life interesting, when Donald called to tell me where the séance was to be held, he said a name I'd heard within the past half hour. The event would be at the oceanside home of Rebecca Stanton.

Jayne and I had been to this property before, when Mrs. Hudson's catered a fundraising event for the West London Theater Festival prior to their performance of *The Hound of the Baskervilles.*

"I wouldn't have thought Rebecca Stanton's the sort to get involved in spiritualism," Jayne said when I told her where we were going for tonight's gathering.

"Takes all kinds," I said, although it had come as a surprise to me too. As well as her participation in the theatrical community, Rebecca was heavily involved with various charities in the Lower Cape.

The house and grounds were particularly impressive. Behind and to either side of us stretched perfectly maintained lawns and perfectly groomed flower beds, white geraniums glowing in the day's dying light. The house was a substantial one, two stories of pale-gray siding, a dark-gray roof, and multiple windows. Soft yellow lights spilled out from behind the drapes of the tall windows on the ground floor and the imitation-gas lanterns burning on either side of the main entrance. The doors to the three-car garage were all closed, and a cluster of cars were parked in front of the house. A lamp shone behind the curtains in a room above the garage.

"Did you tell Ryan we're coming to this?" Jayne asked me.

"I did not. Sometimes what he doesn't know won't hurt him. Did you tell Andy?"

"Heavens, no. I'd worry he'd hurt himself laughing. At least it's not costing us anything. I wonder what the medium charges."

"No idea," I said. "Probably a heck of a lot as it's not the sort of thing she's likely to do every night."

I parked next to the other vehicles, and we got out of the car as the rain increased. We climbed the wide, sweeping staircase between rows of huge iron urns containing masses of colorful annuals, tall ornamental grasses, and tumbling variegated vines. The property was to the east of Harbor Road, and from the other side of the house came the murmur of waves crashing against the rocks. The night air was full of scents from the sea and the lawns and flower beds, all overlaid by thick ozone heralding the approaching storm.

"Do you think the medium arranged this weather herself?" Jayne asked me. "If that thunder arrives, it'll help with the atmosphere."

"If she was able to do that," I said, "I'll become a true believer."

I rang the bell, and Rebecca herself opened the front door. Her highlighted blond hair fell in sleek waves to her shoulders, a gold necklace was around her throat, and she wore a perfectly tailored white pantsuit over an orange silk blouse. Her sharply pointed orange shoes had two-inch heels. She gave us a broad smile. "Gemma, Jayne. I was so pleased when I saw your names on the guest list." She stepped back. "Please come in."

The spectacular red-and-gold glass Chihuly chandelier I'd admired on my previous visit still hung in the front hall, suspended from the twenty-foot-high ceiling. I didn't have much chance to admire it this time, as Rebecca quickly hustled us into the house. "She's not quite ready yet, so we're enjoying a drink while we wait. Isn't this exciting?"

"Is spiritualism an interest of yours, Rebecca?" Jayne asked.

"I try to have an open mind about many things. Ron, my late husband, would have laughed himself silly to see me indulging in this, but . . . I do miss him so." The smile died and her eyes filled with tears as she lost focus. "I sometimes find myself in need of his sage advice and wishing . . . hoping . . ." She swallowed and turned the smile back on. "What's the harm, right? Let's regard it as a pleasant evening's entertainment and a chance to get together with dear friends we don't see nearly often enough. I'm glad you came, Gemma and Jayne. My stepson, Daniel, tells me he and Eleanor visited your shop this afternoon."

"And they bought handsomely, I'm happy to say."

Her face briefly tightened. "More, perhaps, than was wise, considering . . . Never mind that. Come in, please. Most of the others have arrived."

English homes are often criticized for being cold in the winter. They can be, particularly if it's damp as well. For reasons unknown to me, Americans appear to want to compete with us, but in the summer. It was a warm night, but Rebecca had turned the air-conditioning up far too high, and I was glad I'd slipped a light jacket over my summer clothes. Jayne would be freezing in her bare arms and thin dress.

The others were gathered in the living room, a nervous little group. Bunny Leigh wore a loose-fitting, calf-length black dress with black flats and no jewelry. She bounced on the couch, trying to release an excess of energy. Ashleigh sat next to her, hunched in on herself. Ashleigh tells me she dresses as her mood dictates. Such was not the case tonight. Rather than reflecting her mood, she'd attempted to lighten it by dressing in a riot of color. She'd first adopted the punk rock persona—tight, sparkly T-shirt; short, colorful skirt; stripped socks pulled up to the knees; pink hair tied in bouncing bunches—when Bunny came to town, before she knew of their relationship. She'd put it on tonight, and it looked completely out of place. The relieved smile she gave us as Jayne and I entered the room made me glad I'd come despite all my reservations.

Donald was in full Victorian costume: Inverness cape over black trousers, gray waistcoat, white shirt with black collar, gold pocket watch with matching chain. He looked ready to bound across the moors in pursuit of the great spectral hound, and certainly ready for a true Victorian spiritual experience. He alone didn't look at all apprehensive but was clearly excited at the prospect of participating in a séance of the sort so beloved by his idol.

The couple I'd noticed in the tearoom yesterday was sitting to one side, still looking nautical in blue jackets with gold buttons. He wore pressed white trousers, and she was in a white skirt and espadrilles. The diamonds in her ears and around her neck looked genuine, as did his gold Rolex watch. They sat close together, not touching, also nervous. They didn't look up as Jayne and I came in, and Rebecca did not introduce us.

"Hi, there." Daniel Stanton raised a crystal tumbler full of a smokey liquid toward me. "Nice to see you again." He wore white jeans and what was probably another one of his company's leisure wear shirts in a pattern of pink and white under a white blazer. Eleanor was in a short white dress and a badly wrinkled blue linen jacket. She'd been so bouncy and friendly in the shop earlier, but tonight she barely acknowledged our arrival. Her eyes were narrow and her face pinched. She clutched an almost-empty glass of red wine, the knuckles of her right hand white with tension. Rebecca might have tried to laugh off the séance as harmless entertainment, but Eleanor appeared to be taking it seriously indeed.

I introduced Daniel and Eleanor to Jayne. Daniel leaped to his feet and pumped my friend's hand with enthusiasm. His eyes might have lingered on her lovely face a moment longer than was polite but, as usual, she didn't notice. Eleanor barely gave Jayne a nod and sipped her drink.

"Are you looking forward to the séance?" Jayne asked politely.

"I heard she was good, but we'll have to see what she can do," Eleanor said. "Some mediums have more talent than others, and some have absolutely none at all. I'm prepared to take it however it comes and have fun with it." That was clearly a lie. She was coiled as tightly as a spring.

"I regard it as a night's entertainment," Daniel said. "I believe in keeping an open mind. Let people believe what they want to, although I would have thought Rebecca had more sense." He glanced at his stepmother. "Then again, maybe not." He headed for the bar to get a refill.

The look on Rebecca's face as she watched him was not friendly.

"Takes all kinds," Donald said. "I'm sure we all have different reasons for coming tonight."

"So we do," Jayne said.

As further introductions didn't seem to be forthcoming, I went up to the people I didn't know. "Good evening. I'm Gemma, and that lady is my friend and colleague, Jayne. You were in Jayne's tearoom yesterday. I'm sorry you weren't able to be seated, but we close at four, as we explained."

"That's fine. We know for next time. I'm Max and this is my wife, Larissa."

"Pleased to meet you," Larissa said, not meaning it. She crossed her legs, uncrossed them, crossed them again. All the while, she rubbed her fingers across the fabric of the couch on which she sat. She radiated so much nervousness it was almost visible. He was tense also, but he managed to hide it better.

Fair enough. They had come here to commune with the dearly departed.

He put his hand on her shoulder, and she managed to give him a weak smile. They both had pronounced Southern accents. Louisiana, I guessed.

"We're from New Orleans originally," Max said. "But we live in Boston now."

"Are you berthed at the Cape Cod Yacht Club or West London?" I asked.

"We've left the boat at the Cape Cod Club. Did you see us there? Are you a member?" His eyes showed a flicker of interest at the idea I might be a fellow boating enthusiast.

"Not a member, no," I said, and the interest died. "Are you in town for the psychic fair?"

"Didn't even know about it until yesterday. We're enjoying a short holiday on the Cape. We like to get the boat out for a run now and again." He shifted his weight, and his wife crossed her legs again.

"Are you also here for the séance?" I asked them, as if there'd be another reason they were in Rebecca's living room at nine o'clock tonight.

"Yes, we are. The club hung a poster on their bulletin board advertising the extra features being offered as part of the fair, and Larissa managed to wrangle us an invitation. You?"

"As an observer only."

"Drinks are self-serve tonight," Rebecca said. "Please help yourself while we wait."

I turned away from Max and Larissa. "Nothing for me, thanks."

The expansive living room was much the same as the last time I'd been in here, perfectly decorated in shades of cream with discreet gold accents. A glass wall overlooked the floodlit lawns to the wild Atlantic Ocean beyond, and the interior walls were decorated with tasteful, not to mention expensive, art. The rich voice of Diana Krall, low and throaty, came from concealed speakers.

A bar cart had been set up in a corner of the room. Jayne poured herself a small glass of wine and then took a seat next to Donald. He held a glass of what looked like whiskey, untouched. Daniel's drink was not untouched, and he poured himself another generous serving. Rebecca watched him, her expression disapproving. She caught me looking and gave me an embarrassed shrug.

Max and Larissa had red wine; Bunny a glass of white. She finished it in one gulp and got up to serve herself another.

Ashleigh twisted her hands together.

I took a seat next to Jayne.

And we waited.

Diana Krall continued to sing. Ashleigh and Daniel scrolled through the screens on their phones, their expressions indicating they weren't taking anything in. Bunny shifted in her seat, finished her wine, got herself another. Donald put his untouched whiskey on a side table and pulled a folded copy of *Canadian Holmes* magazine out of the pocket of his Inverness cape. Donald could always be counted on to have something to read on him at any time. I wished I'd brought a book. Max tapped his foot and checked his watch every minute or so. Larissa alternately drank her wine and chewed her nails. Eleanor had crossed to the windows and pulled back the drapes, looking out into the night as the storm moved closer.

Rebecca tried to make conversation, as a good hostess should, but eventually her voice trailed off as she realized no one was responding as good guests should.

About fifteen minutes of this passed before Ashleigh glanced up from her phone and said, "Not that I mind, but I thought this was going to be a private event, Bunny. Just us, I mean." She glanced at Max and Larissa and Daniel and Eleanor.

Bunny shrugged. "The medium's assistant arranged this for me, yes, but they need more people to make up the optimal numbers."

Optimal numbers in terms of dollars, I thought, but didn't say.

The doorbell rang. Everyone jumped. "Finally," Rebecca said. "The last member of our little gathering. I'll get it."

I heard voices in the hallway, and someone I hadn't expected came in. Miranda, Jayne's new employee, had changed into jeans and a loose sweater. She'd recently dragged her hands through her short black hair, and tufts were standing on end. The strength of rain hitting the wide windows had increased in the time we'd been here, and the first rumblings of thunder could be heard, coming closer. Miranda's head and shoulders were dotted with rainwater.

She stepped into the living room, glanced around, and froze. She stared at Max and Larissa, but they didn't so much as blink in return. Miranda almost visibly pulled herself together and dropped into a spindly-legged chair upholstered in cream and brown damask. Yesterday, Jayne suggested the couple might have reminded Miranda of someone she knew. Her reaction tonight was too strong for that, I thought, but I didn't know what it meant.

"Hi," she said to Jayne in a strangled voice. "I didn't know you and Ms. Doyle were coming to this."

"We get around," I said.

"Miranda tells me she enjoys working at the tearoom." Rebecca smiled at Jayne, but her eyes darted around the room. She was as nervous as the rest of them.

"That's nice," Jayne said. "We work hard, but we try to have fun too."

"You and Miranda know each other?" I asked.

"Oh, yes," Rebecca said. "She's my sister's girl. Miranda loves the Cape and likes to spend her summers here." She smiled at her niece. "Don't you, dear?" Miranda nodded. "She's living in what used to be the chauffeur's quarters, now a little guest apartment above the garage."

I wouldn't have said the two women looked alike, but there was a resemblance in the shape of the eyes and the small chin.

I checked my watch. Nine thirty. "Is our . . . leader this evening delayed?"

"No," Rebecca said. "She's here."

"Here? What are we waiting for then?"

"She'll call us when she's ready."

"I hope it's not going to be too much longer," Ashleigh said. Beside me, Jayne shifted. Donald turned a page. Max put a hand on top of his wife's. Calming her down or telling her to be patient, I wondered.

"It takes time to prepare," Bunny said. "Isn't that right, Rebecca?"

"So she said."

"I knew this house would be perfect," Bunny said. "Not only because not everyone has a room big enough for a table to seat us all, but the atmosphere is so good. Don't you just love this house, Ashleigh?"

"It seems . . . nice," Ashleigh said.

A flash of lightning lit up the room, and two seconds later thunder roared outside. Larissa yelped, and Jayne said, "That was close." The promised storm had arrived. Eleanor watched for a few minutes as another bolt of lightning came fast on the heels of the previous one. This time, the thunder was little more than a second after. As the sound faded away, she turned from the window, allowing the drapes to drop shut behind her, and helped herself to another drink. Her husband carried on doomscrolling with one hand while the other kept a firm hold on his glass. He lifted it to his mouth and then realized the glass was empty. He put his phone down, stood up, and headed for the bar.

Rebecca stepped in front of him. "I think it best if we all have clear heads tonight, Daniel."

"I think I can decide how clear my head needs to be, Rebecca."

They stared at each other for a long time. Eleanor watched, a spark of interest lighting up her eyes, but she didn't take sides. Eventually, Rebecca stepped aside. "As you like."

He grinned at her, not ready to graciously accept his victory. "I've been meaning to have a word with you about that, Rebecca. That bottle's not very good. Dad had better taste than to buy that stuff."

"Your father," she snapped, "enjoyed a glass of good whiskey on occasion. As a treat. He didn't drink it like water."

Daniel pushed past her, heading for the bar.

Eleanor lifted her own glass in a toast and said in a low voice. "One point for Rebecca."

"Not another word out of you," Daniel growled.

His wife only grinned in response.

Rebecca and her stepson, I gathered, didn't get on all that well.

Another peal of thunder sounded. This one was close, very close.

"You've been here before?" Jayne asked Bunny in a desperate attempt to clear the air after the recent unpleasantness.

"Oh yes," Rebecca said, glad of the distraction. "Bunny and I got to know each other when she was renting that house near here over the winter. As soon as I realized who she was, I was anxious to meet her. Her music was after my time, but my younger sister, Miranda's mother, was a great fan, as I recall."

"Music?" Larissa's ears perked up for the first time tonight. "Are you a musician? Might I have heard of you? I don't recognize the name."

Bunny didn't reply. Once, she would never have had to tell people who she was. I wondered if it stung having to do so now.

"My mom's Bunny Leigh," Ashleigh said. "You must remember her. 'Baby, I Can't Live Without You.'"

Larissa's expression indicated she'd never heard of the song. I have to confess (although not out loud), I'd never heard of it either.

"The song?" Ashleigh said. "Went platinum? 2001? That was Bunny."

"Oh, right. Of course." Larissa let out a strangled sort of laugh. "How silly of me to forget."

Bunny's ears burned with embarrassment, but she pretended not to be paying any attention to the conversation.

Next to me, Jayne yawned. She'd woken up this morning, as she usually does, at four in order to get the baking started and then worked until five in the afternoon. She'd gone home for a nap before I picked her up, but she'd need to be up early again tomorrow. I decided to give this charade another fifteen minutes and then suggest we take our leave.

Fourteen and a half minutes later, a woman slipped silently into the living room. Everyone's eyes immediately turned to her. She was short and round, about forty. Her cheeks were plump and pink, her eyes small and dark, her lifeless brown hair pulled back into a tight bun. She wore a cheap, mass-produced, below-the-knee black dress with black tights and thick-soled black shoes. No jewelry. I don't know what I'd been expecting a medium to look like, but it wasn't this. I'd have thought she'd have more flair, more pizzazz, more presence. She stood in place, back straight, hands folded in front of her. She tried to keep her face impassive, but when her eyes landed on Bunny Leigh, she couldn't help a smile touching the edges of her mouth.

I was the first to stand up. Donald shoved his magazine in his pocket and did the same. Ashleigh sucked in a breath. Bunny was still holding a wine glass; the other hand shot out, and she gripped her daughter's arm so tightly Ashleigh's skin turned white. Eleanor Stanton let out a nervous chuckle. Miranda, Larissa, and Max said nothing. Daniel ostentatiously pretended to smother a fake yawn, but he failed to hide the spark of interest in his eyes.

"Is it time?" Rebecca asked.

"Madame Lavalier will see you now," the woman proclaimed in an unexpectedly high, squeaky voice. Clearly, this was not the medium, but her assistant. "She apologizes for the delay, but you understand how these things work. It took some additional time for the atmosphere in the room to be made perfect."

"Of course, of course." Rebecca clapped her hands. "This is so exciting, but I have to admit, I'm very nervous."

"And so you should be," the assistant intoned. "Contact with the world beyond the mirror is not to be trifled with."

One by one, everyone stood. Some were eager, some nervous, some simply curious as to what would happen next.

"The world is a double-sided mirror," the medium's assistant said. "What you and I see is but one side of it. We do not cease to exist after what is called death. We but pass through the mirror to the other side. Madame Lavalier has been granted a great and unique gift—she can see this side and the other."

"Cool," Ashleigh said. Bunny clutched her daughter's arm tighter.

"The strain of seeing the two worlds together at one time is immense. It can be dangerous for Madame Lavalier. Many who make the attempt do not survive. To ensure the safety of all participants, Madame most of all, you must do as I tell you at all times. Is that understood?"

"Yes," almost everyone chorused.

"You, sir." She addressed Daniel Stanton, who had not spoken. "Do you understand what I am saying?"

"Yeah. Got it."

She next fixed her eyes on me.

"I'm not here to cause trouble," I said.

"Glad to hear it. Please pay attention to the rules. Miss Leigh, put that drink down. I'm sorry, but you cannot take it in."

Bunny almost dropped her glass.

The woman cracked another smile. "I'm so pleased you came, Bunny. It's such an honor to have you here tonight." She almost giggled before remembering her place, clearing her throat, and settling back into the steady monotone. "There is to be no talking unless you are spoken to. No laughing. No moving of furniture."

"No breathing," Jayne whispered nervously to me.

The assistant glared at her until Jayne mumbled, "sorry." She continued. "Once seated, you are not to stand up. Sir, you must remove that cape."

"Me?" Donald said.

"Yes."

"I'm not wearing a wire." He attempted to make a joke. The woman did not laugh, and Donald slipped the cape off, folded it carefully, and put it over the back of his chair.

"Is my sweater okay?" Miranda asked, wrapping the wool tighter around herself.

The woman studied it. "The room might get unexpectedly cool. You may keep it, and the others can keep their jackets. But ladies' purses must remain here." Larissa and Jayne put theirs down. I expected her to order us to leave our phones behind, but she didn't mention them.

She turned her unblinking stare on each of us in turn. I wondered if she perfected that look in front of the mirror. Ashleigh, Miranda, and Jayne dipped their heads. Bunny and Rebecca tittered with embarrassment. Donald cleared his throat. Larissa let out a long breath, and her husband grunted, their hands clenched tightly together. Daniel Stanton glanced at Eleanor. Her eyes were round with excitement and what might have been a touch of fear. I watched the medium's assistant. Her gaze turned on me, and she gave me a small nod. Then she stepped to one side, made a sweeping gesture with her right hand, and said, "Please, follow me, and take your seats."

She led the way down the hallway to the library. The last time I'd been in this room, I'd thought it would be the perfect place to film a scene set at Baskerville Hall. Tonight it made the ideal setting for a horror movie. Floor-to-ceiling shelving, crammed with hardcover books, filled two walls. A third wall was occupied by a wood-burning fireplace. On a July night, the logs were not lit, and instead the hearth was filled with a glass candelabra bearing tall white candles, freshly lit by matches, not a lighter. The air carried the scent of sulfur and smoke. Heavy red drapes were pulled across the windows. The drapes were thick enough to keep out the lightning, but outside thunder pealed, wind hammered the house, rain threw itself against the windows, and the house creaked under the force of the storm.

A red-and-gold Aubusson carpet covered the center of the wide-planked red cedar floor; the paint on the walls was a shade of soft gold that glimmered in the candlelight. A coffee table, a well-seasoned brown leather couch punctured with brass hob-nails, and one of the red-and-gold wingback chairs had been pushed against the walls, and a large round wooden table brought in. Twelve dining room chairs surrounded the table. Counting the medium and her assistant, we were thirteen. I doubted they'd counted wrong, and I couldn't see the assistant being asked to leave. She'd be essential for making subtle movements at the medium's unspoken request. Perhaps she would stand up the entire time.

The ceiling was twenty feet high, and tonight a plain white sheet had been suspended across it.

"The Chihuly?" I whispered to Rebecca, referring to the enormous glass fixture, a multitude of sweeping, intertwining yellow-and-green strands that dominated the room and thoroughly destroyed the illusion we might be at Baskerville Hall.

"Madame Lavalier inspected the room earlier, and she said the chandelier reflects too much light. Her visitors would be repelled by it."

I understood. So pure was the glass and so brilliant the colors that made it, the chandelier barely needed electricity; it caught the ambient light and glowed from within.

One chair, a match to the wingback that had been pushed against the far wall, was occupied. The figure sitting there did not move as we filed into the room. It was a woman, dressed all in black. Long black hair fell across her shoulders. Gold bangles covered both arms almost to the elbows, and a cascade of gold necklaces was wrapped around her throat. Her face was so pale I suspected she'd applied white powder to it. Her eyes were black—not simply dark brown but a genuine black. Contact lenses obviously. She watched me. I watched her. Outside, the ferocity of the storm increased.

I broke eye contact first, turning my head to study the layout of the room. I saw the medium's assistant give a jerk of the head in my direction.

"Ms. Doyle," said the medium in a deep, rolling voice. "If you'll leave us, *s'vous plais.*" Her accent was Quebecois, not French, but I detected a false note behind it. It was not her real accent.

Jayne threw me a look.

Madame Lavalier's hands rested on the table in front of her, and the mass of candles blazed behind her. Her chair was about two feet out from the fireplace, its back to it.

"I'm here as Ms. Leigh's guest," I said.

"That may be, but your skepticism is not wanted here. It will . . . disturb . . . some of my visitors."

"But I want Gemma to stay," Ashleigh said. "She came because I asked her to."

"You have Ms. Wilson and your mother for moral support, Ashleigh."

"But—"

"Please, everyone. Take your seats. We will begin once Ms. Doyle has left us."

The assistant was behind me, standing too close, her breath hot on my neck. Was she going to manhandle me out the door if I refused? Judging by the scent of her breath, she'd consumed a beer, and recently too. No doubt while we waited restlessly in the living room and they drew out the wait as long as they dared.

I wasn't surprised Madame Lavalier knew our names and could match names to faces. Bunny had been asked to provide a list of people she'd invited, and I had no doubt the medium spent the earlier part of the evening reading up on us. I wondered what she learned about me that made me *persona non grata*.

Then again, maybe I shouldn't take it personally. They might simply not have wanted a supposedly unlucky thirteen gathered around the table. Maybe Rebecca could only provide twelve chairs.

"You can wait in the living room, Gemma," Rebecca said, her tone apologetic. "Feel free to help yourself to a drink or get something from the kitchen."

"I'll do that. Thank you."

"Gemma?" Jayne said.

"I haven't yet had a chance to read the current issue of *Canadian Holmes*," I said. "Donald, may I take it out of your pocket?"

"What? I mean, yes. Help yourself."

I'd only come to this thing because Ashleigh asked me to. I gave her a smile and touched her arm lightly as I passed. "I'll be right outside," I said in a whisper meant only for her to hear. "If you start to feel uncomfortable, get up and walk out."

She didn't return my smile, but something lit up behind her eyes.

I left the library. The door shut quietly behind me. Thunder shook the house.

Chapter Six

I located Rebecca's iPad next to the speakers and switched off the music. Then I got the magazine out of Donald's pocket and poured myself a glass of white wine, but I didn't take a seat in the living room. Instead, I took a cushion off the couch and dropped onto the floor outside the library doors, next to a nicely crafted wooden stand bearing a wide-mouthed porcelain vase in the Chinese style, showing goldfish swimming through green and blue seaweed against a white background.

Madame Lavalier would have realized I'd do precisely that. If she'd truly wanted me gone, she would have had Rebecca order me off the premises. Her banishing me from the library was nothing more than an amateurish power play intended to start the proceedings off with a dramatic gesture. Her initial research on the séance attendees would have revealed that I've earned a small reputation in West London as someone who sometimes knows what others do not. I had not come here with the intention of exposing the medium as a fake—why spoil everyone's fun? I'd accompanied Ashleigh, as asked, and as long as Madame Lavalier didn't make any attempt to extort the attendees, beyond the price of admission, I regarded it as nothing more than an evening's entertainment, although not the sort of entertainment I normally sought.

Which was a moot point, as I was outside the door, sitting on the floor, alternately eavesdropping and reading.

Parts of this house, the library in particular, might look as though they were built in centuries past, but it was thoroughly modern, including the impressive-looking but flimsily constructed double doors leading to the library.

Madame Lavalier might not have had the powers to arrange the storm, but I had to admit, her timing was excellent. Lightning flashed, thunder roared, rain pounded against the roof, and wind rattled the windows.

At first, above the racket raging outside, all I could hear from inside the library was the creak of chairs and shifting of bodies. The assistant told everyone to take the hands of the people next to them and repeated the rules about not talking and not standing up. "Do not," she said in a tone that reminded me of the headmistress at my exclusive English boarding school when I'd done something she didn't approve of (which, come to think of it, was often), "under any circumstances release your neighbor's hand. Breaking the chain without warning can do immeasurable harm to Madame Lavalier if she is in the midst of establishing contact."

"Got it," Daniel Stanton said in a voice pitched to hide his nervousness.

"Shush," Rebecca snapped.

The thin line of light leaking from under the doors was gradually extinguished as the candles were snuffed out. Miranda gasped. Max cleared his throat. "It's sure dark in here," Daniel said, and Rebecca shushed him once again. A floorboard creaked as the medium's assistant took her own seat. All fell silent for several minutes. A man cleared his throat. A woman coughed. A chair scraped against the floor.

Finally, Madame Lavalier said, her voice low and soft and full of sympathy, "Miranda, *ma petite*. You've suffered a great loss."

Miranda sobbed and replied in a muffled voice, "My mom."

"My sister, Amy," Rebecca said. "We lost her a few short months ago."

"A car accident," Madame Lavalier said. "Such a tragedy. Amy, your daughter and your sister are here. They miss you very much and would love to have the chance to speak with you."

Silence once again. No one moved. Then a bark, so unexpected, I started.

"Freddy!" Miranda cried. "Freddy, is that you? Is Mom with you?"

More barking as though coming from a small, overly excited dog.

Larissa cried, "Please, no!"

Max said, "What the—"

"Silence!" The assistant's voice was low, the command unmistakable. "One more interruption, unless you are being addressed directly, and the guilty party will be instructed to leave."

"Please," Madame Lavalier said, "Stay with us awhile longer, Amy."

I could almost hear Rebecca and Miranda holding their breath.

"I'm here, Miranda, my darling girl," said an unfamiliar voice. It was a woman, speaking with a Boston accent, faint and muffled as though the person was talking from beneath a pillow. "My faithful companion is here with me. In death as in life. We're fine. We're both fine. Please don't worry."

"I don't know what to do, Mom." Miranda's voice broke. "I'm barely passing my courses. I don't want to go back to college in the fall. Tell me what to do."

"You know what to do. Study hard. Work hard. Rely on your father and your aunt Rebecca. You know Harvard was my dream for you."

"But—"

"I must go. Goodbye, my beloved. Goodbye, my darling sister. Know that I am well here, and we will meet again in the fullness of time." The voice faded. The dog barked once more, also sounding as though it was moving away. Miranda and Rebecca sobbed. The others around the table murmured words of shock and sympathy.

"Surely it can't be—" Larissa said.

Max snapped, "It's not."

If there'd been anyone to observe me, I would have rolled my eyes. The dog, Freddy, must have died in the car accident with Miranda's mother. Rebecca was a well-known person in the Lower Cape; her sister's sudden death had been reported in the paper and talked about. I myself had seen a mention in the *West London Star* and offered my sympathies the next time I saw Rebecca. The story mentioned the demise of the family dog, which gave it a tragic angle so beloved of newspapers and social media.

Silence again fell over the room except for the sounds of clearing throats and bodies shifting. Then Madame Lavalier spoke again. "Mr. Morris, *je suis désolât*, but Sir Arthur is unable to appear tonight."

Donald sucked in a breath so loudly even I heard it. "How did you know—"

"Sir Arthur knows. He extends his regrets. He thanks you for, and is humbled by, your continued devotion, but this is not a good night for him. Another time perhaps; he tells me he'll be delighted to speak with you on a more opportune occasion."

"Oh, yes," Donald said. "Any time. Any place. I can't believe it!" *Neither could I.*

I wondered what sort of specter she'd drum up for Jayne. Jayne's father had died some years ago. She'd loved him very much, and she missed him greatly, but she was no longer mourning him. I thought it unlikely she'd want to seek him out.

Madame Lavalier let out a long moan. Her chair squeaked.

"Something's happening," Larissa cried. "Granddad, are you there?"

"Quiet," Madame Lavalier's assistant shouted. "The next spirit is arriving."

"Where is it?" Larissa yelled. "You have to tell me."

"Hey, honeybunny," said a new voice. It was a man, an older man with a strong California accent tinged with good humor. "It's been a heck of a long time."

"Rupert," Bunny said. "Is that really you?"

"In the flesh, honeybunny, although I guess that's not exactly right. Not any longer." He chuckled. I sat up straight. My skin crawled. This voice was good—all traces of a woman with a Quebecois accent were gone.

"Who's Rupert?" Ashleigh asked.

I knew who Rupert was. Or was supposed to be, at any rate. Rupert McNamee had been Bunny Leigh's manager in her glory years. He'd guided the fresh-faced young thing off the bus from Lincoln, Nebraska, straight to the top. A lot of things had contributed to her decline—which came as quicky as her rise— ever-changing teenage tastes most of all. But it probably hadn't helped that Rupert died of lung cancer, leaving Bunny without the firm hand on her career she needed.

"What can I do you for?" the voice asked.

"Things aren't going well for me these days," Bunny said. "The new album's not going to happen. The producer dropped it, and no one else is interested. They say I'm washed up. Finished. I need you, Rupert."

"Sorry to have to tell you this, honeybunny, but I'm dead."

"I know. I know. I thought you might still have some influence with the old crowd. You could help me from . . . behind the scenes, so to speak."

"You think you're finished, Bunny? What about me?" He laughed. "Yeah, okay, kid. I hear you. I can try and pull a few strings. From beyond the grave, like. Give me a couple of weeks. We'll talk again."

"Rupert! Don't go. How will I know what to do? Who should I talk to?"

"I'll be in touch." The voice faded away.

Ashleigh broke the silence. "I thought you wanted to reach my dad."

"Why would you think that?" Bunny asked.

"That was so creepy," Rebecca said. "Did you recognize the voice, Bunny? Are you sure it was the person you knew?"

"Quiet," Madame Lavalier snapped. "You people talk too much."

The dark hallway in which I sat was suddenly filled with light as a bolt of lightning flashed across the sky. At the same instant, a rolling peal of thunder shook the house. Bunny squealed, and Daniel nervously said, "Close one."

"I'm very tired all of a sudden," the medium said. "I . . . I . . . need rest. You must go."

"But what about Grandfather?" Larissa yelled. "I haven't spoken to my grandfather. I have to know—"

56

"Another time. I . . . I . . ." The medium's voice was so weary she struggled to get the words out. "No! Wait! Someone is coming. He insists on being heard. It's a man, a younger man. He's not happy. He's angry. I see darkness. I see fury. His anger is filling the space. I—What do you want?"

"What do I want?" said a man's voice. I couldn't detect the slightest trace of Madame Lavalier's voice, fake accent or not. He sounded as though he was in his thirties or forties. His English was perfect but overlaid with a slight Spanish accent, full of rage and the possibility of violence. "You know who I am. You know what I want. I want what you stole from me. You took my life. So I am here for yours. I want everyone to know you lied. I—" There was a loud crash as something inside the library fell over.

Rebecca and Larissa screamed.

Jayne said, "This is getting to be too much."

Max said, "What the—"

Miranda started to cry.

"Leave us, spirit!" the assistant yelled. "You have not been called. You are not wanted here! Madame, Madame, come back. Iris, for heaven's sake this is going too far."

Another flash of lightning, another roll of thunder directly overhead. Sheets of rain pounded against the steel roof. Someone, it sounded like Eleanor Stanton, shrieked in terror. A floorboard creaked, a footstep stumbled, someone grunted in surprise.

Ashleigh said, "She's dropped my hand. The circle is broken."

"Everyone stay where you are!" the assistant shouted. "Don't let go of those hands. We must remain together to give Madame our combined strength so she can fight this unwanted specter and return to us."

Her plea came too late. I heard people yelling and crying, chairs being shoved back, everyone jumping to their feet. I leaped up myself, unsure whether or not to open the door. If this was part of the show, Madame and her assistant were giving the audience their money's worth.

The medium let out a loud cry, suddenly cut off. Something hard and solid hit the table.

"Madame?" the assistant whispered. "Are you there? Iris?"

I came to a decision: time to put an end to this. I reached for the door handle, and at that moment, Rebecca screamed.

"What's happening?" Larissa cried.

"Daniel," Eleanor yelled. "Daniel, where are you? I can't find you."

"I can't see a blasted thing," he said.

"Light! Someone turn on the lights," Donald shouted.

"Gemma!" Jayne yelled.

I threw open the door and hit the switch. A dim light filled the room. The brilliant colors of the Chihuly chandelier glowed faintly from behind the cover that had been pulled over it.

Bunny and Ashleigh had their backs pressed against a bookshelf, huddled together, their eyes wide and hands over their mouths. Miranda sat in a corner on the floor, head buried in the arms wrapped around her knees, weeping. Daniel Stanton was attempting to drag the heavy drapes open, to let some light into the room, panic making him clumsy. Eleanor slumped in a chair, breathing heavily. Rebecca wrung her hands together and kept saying, "What's happened here? What's happened?" The medium's assistant was frozen in place, moaning.

Donald and Jayne stood at the head of the table, on either side of Madame Lavalier, hands in the air, both of them unsure what to do.

As I stood in the doorway, taking in the scene, Max rushed past me, dragging his wife behind him.

"What's going on?" Rebecca looked up. "Is she sick?"

Madame Lavalier was slumped facedown on the table, not moving. Jayne reached out a hand and ineffectually patted the woman's back. Donald said, "Should I call an ambulance?"

"Yes," I ordered. "Tell them to send the police as well, and quickly. Jayne, you stay with her. Everyone else out of this room. Donald get them out of here. Now. We need to secure the scene."

A small, thin object was imbedded in the back of the medium's neck, precisely placed between two vertebrae at the base of her skull.

Chapter Seven

"The rest of you, move," I ordered. "Now! Into the living room." I turned and ran down the hallway to find Max in the act of opening the front door.

"You need to stay here," I said to him.

"I don't know or care who you are, but I don't take orders from you." Max threw the door open and started out. A bucket of rain hit him full in the face. Lightning flashed, but thunder was slow to follow. The storm was moving away.

"The police have been called," I said.

Larissa turned her pale face and wide frightened eyes toward me. "The police?"

"Look, lady, I don't know why you did that," her husband said, "but if that crazy woman took sick, that's nothing to do with us. We're only going to be in the way."

"The police will want to talk to you," I said. "It will be better if you're here when they arrive."

His eyes narrowed, and he looked at me. "Better for who?"

"You. The police don't like having to go in search of witnesses. They will ask, and it will save them some time if I have your last name."

Max hesitated before spitting out, "Greenwood."

"Thanks. Suit yourself." I turned and walked away. I had no more time to waste on them.

I found the rest of the group, aside from Jayne and Rebecca, in the living room, collapsed into chairs or pacing the room. Ashleigh stood at the window, staring into the night. Lights in the garden tastefully illuminated statuary and bushes. Donald gave me a quick nod and indicated the phone he held to his ear, telling me help had been summoned. The calm voice of the 911 operator leaked out. Someone had turned the music back on, and Mozart's *Requiem* emerged softly from the Bose speakers. Not, I thought, a tasteful choice, considering the circumstances.

"The emergency services have been called," I said to the group. "We need to stay here and stay together until they arrive. All of us."

The Greenwoods slipped in behind me. Max gave me a poisonous look while he said to his wife, "Nothing to worry about. I know the type; she's trying to make herself seem important. Easier to go along with it, for now."

I ignored him and went back to the library. Jayne and Rebecca hovered over the unmoving form of Madame Lavalier, unsure of what to do.

The medium was slumped in her chair, arms thrown out, head back, eyes open wide, staring straight at us. The object I'd seen in her neck lay on the table. "I took it out," Jayne said. "I . . . thought it might help, but . . . it didn't."

"It was the right thing to do." The object looked to be made of silver, thin and about seven inches long. One end came to a sharp point, the other topped by a silver filigree cup cradling a large luminous pearl. A hat pin, possibly antique or a good imitation. Hat pins had been widely available in the days when elegant women wore enormous hats over elaborate hairstyles, and something had to keep the whole construction fastened firmly in place. But they weren't used at all these days, apart from on theatrical or movie sets. No one in this house had been wearing a hat tonight, not even Madame Lavalier or her assistant.

There should be no reason anyone would be carrying such a thing around in their pocket.

The sounds of sirens could be heard coming down the driveway. "Can you get the door, please, Rebecca?" I said. She lifted her head and looked at me. She nodded and then slipped away.

"Are you okay?" I put my hand lightly on Jayne's arm and stared into her face, giving her what I hoped was an encouraging smile.

She swallowed. "I will be. What do you think happened here, Gemma?"

"That's for the police to find out." I heard voices and footsteps, and two medics ran into the library. I pointed out the hat pin to them, and then I took my friend's arm, and we left them to do their jobs.

Chapter Eight

The police arrived not long after the ambulance.

Officer Stella Johnson found us gathered in the living room, a shocked, stunned, silent group. Bunny, Max, Larissa, Daniel, and the still-unnamed assistant, however, were not so stunned as to fail to take the opportunity to make full use of Rebecca's bar.

Johnson's eyes widened when she saw Jayne and me among the group. I gave her a "What can I say?" shrug, and she shook her head. "I've called the detectives."

"What on earth for?" Max said. "The woman had a heart attack. Maybe an aneurysm. Sad, but nothing that requires a police investigation."

"Let them do their jobs, Max," Larissa said in a low voice.

I said nothing, and neither did Officer Johnson. We could hear the medics working in the library and police talking in low voices in the hallway. Notably, Madame Lavalier had not been rushed away under full lights and sirens.

"My wife and I would like to be on our way." Max drained the contents of his glass and pulled out his phone. "I'll give you my number. Your detectives can contact us in the morning if they need a statement."

I wondered why he was in such a rush. Was he throwing his weight around, making sure we all knew how important he was? Or did he have more specific reasons to want to avoid police attention?

Larissa put her hand lightly on his arm. "It's okay, honey. We can wait."

He sighed heavily, making sure we all knew what a great sacrifice he was making. "In that case . . ." He reached for the whiskey bottle.

When they did try to leave, I might have a quiet word with Officer Johnson. Max should not be driving anywhere tonight, and Larissa herself had enjoyed a couple of drinks.

Bunny held her own glass out toward Max. "As long as you have the bottle there."

"You okay, babe?" Daniel asked Eleanor. "You don't look too good. You want a drink?"

She looked up, gave him a weak smile, and shook her head. Some of her long, dark hair had come loose, and tendrils caressed her face. Her rings caught the light from the lamps when she brushed a lock back. "I'll be fine. Just give me a few minutes. I'm sorry, everyone, if I overreacted in there. It's . . . I've been absolutely terrified of thunder ever since I was a little girl." She gave a choked laugh. "Product of an overactive imagination, my mom used to say."

Daniel gave her a questioning look and started to say something, but then he shrugged and turned away.

"Don't blame yourself," Ashleigh said. "It was terrifying."

At that moment, an all-too familiar voice came from the hallway. Jayne threw me a frightened look. I might have winced in return.

"We'll check out the scene first," Detective Ryan Ashburton was saying. "Tell the witnesses to stay put in the meantime."

Max finished pouring for Bunny and held up the bottle. "Anyone else?"

"As long as you're offering," Donald said. "A wee tipple might help calm the nerves. Gemma, what did you observe once you entered the library following the, uh, incident?"

I didn't answer. I'd observed a great deal in the short time I'd been in the room, but nothing that led me to any conclusions. I leaned back in my chair, crossed my legs, and watched the people in the room while Officer Johnson studied my face.

Rebecca Stanton didn't react to Max taking advantage of her bar. A touch of color had returned to her perfectly-put-together face, and she sat silently, one arm loosely draped around Miranda's shoulders. The younger woman played with her phone, but I didn't get the sense she was typing important messages or spreading the news on social media. Pointedly, she ignored Max and Larissa. Ignored them so much, it was obvious she was paying close attention to them at all times. I wondered why she was so disturbed by them, considering they didn't seem to even know her.

The medium's assistant threw back her drink and without another word held her glass out for a refill. The expression on her face was somber, but I saw none of the signs of grief or sorrow I might have expected, and she had not asked to be allowed to stay with Madame Lavalier. An employee, I decided, hired to do a job, not a close friend. And likely not a longtime employee at that. Once she had her drink, she dropped onto the couch next to Bunny and gave the other woman a warm smile. She said something I didn't catch; Bunny's mouth turned up in a smile, but the smile didn't reach her eyes and she shifted, ever so slightly, away.

"We're staying here, as guests of Mrs. Stanton, my father's widow," Daniel said. "My wife and I would prefer to go to our room to wait until we're needed."

"I'd prefer if you don't," Johnson said. "The detectives will be here soon."

"In that case," Daniel said, "top me up, buddy. Eleanor?"

She shook her head.

I found it interesting that Daniel referred to Rebecca as "my father's widow" not "my stepmother," but I brushed the thought aside. Rebecca had married Ron Stanton late in his life. She'd never been a mother to his son, and I'd earlier noticed a considerable degree of tension between them.

I continued to study the people gathered in the room. Emotions varied between shock, sorrow, disbelief, and not particularly concerned. No one stood out as having stabbed the woman with a hat pin. But then again, it took a cold-blooded person to commit such a cold-blooded act.

A few minutes later, Ryan and his partner, Detective Louise Estrada, walked into the living room. Ryan was dressed in jeans and a freshly ironed white shirt under a denim jacket. His curly black hair, slightly longer than he normally wore it, needed a trim, but he'd shaved recently. He was on call tonight, so he didn't look too much as though he'd been dragged into work. Estrada, on the other hand, wore a sleek, elegant, and probably expensive, knee-length blue dress under a black leather jacket that didn't suit the outfit. She had grass-stained trainers, what Americans call sneakers, on her feet. The shoes, I surmised, had been grabbed out of the trunk of her car to replace the heels that would have been selected to match the dress after much consideration. Her long, dark hair was pulled hastily back into a rough ponytail and secured with a pink elastic band. Her eye makeup was perfect, but she'd missed a spot where she'd dragged a tissue across her mouth in an attempt to remove the bright red lipstick. Her pierced ears were empty. She'd been on a date when she received the call to attend a murder scene. She would not be in a good mood tonight.

The look Estrada gave Jayne and me wasn't so much angry as simply resigned. "When they told me you lot were here, I thought they were joking. I should have known better."

"Sorry," Jayne said.

"Good evening, Detectives," Donald said. "I hope you weren't interrupted while doing anything important."

"Detective Ashburton." Rebecca, once more the perfect hostess, rose to her feet. "I'd say it's nice to see you again, but not under these circumstances."

"Hi, Ryan." Ashleigh waved from the far side of the room where she was standing next to Bunny.

"What is this?" Max growled. "Old home week?"

"Small towns," his wife said.

Ryan cleared his throat. "Ms. Doyle, I'll talk to you first and the rest in turn."

Max put his glass on a side table and stepped forward. "You can talk to me first. Then my wife and I will be on our way. As you all seem to know each other—"

"I don't know these people," Eleanor said softly.

"We don't want to be caught up in your gossip session," Max finished.

"In your turn, like the detective said," Estrada snapped. Yup, not in a good mood.

Larissa put her hand on her husband's back. He glared once more at Estrada, and then his shoulders slumped ever so slightly. The detective nodded her thanks to Larissa.

Interesting. That was the second time within a few minutes Larissa had calmed her husband down with nothing but a touch. Was he really that highly strung, and did it happen often, or was it an act they played? Did he have a particular reason to be so on edge tonight?

"Mrs. Stanton, do you have a room where we can chat privately?" Estrada asked.

"I'd normally say the library, but . . ." Rebecca's voice trailed off. "You can use the dining room. Miranda, dear, will you show them—"

"I know the way," I said.

"Officer Johnson, please keep these people company," Estrada said, meaning keep them from fleeing the scene. "Refrain from speculating among yourselves until we've taken statements from you all."

"I have nothing to speculate about," Eleanor said. "I've absolutely no idea what happened. One minute we were sitting around the table holding hands, and then everyone was jumping up and down and yelling, and her —Gemma—was ordering us all out of the library as if this was her house and—"

"When I said no speculating," Estrada said, "I meant no speculating. Do you want to wait for us down at the police station?"

"That won't be necessary," Rebecca said. "Eleanor will be quiet."

"See that she is," Estrada said to Officer Johnson. "See that they all are."

Max snapped his heels together and saluted smartly. His wife dug an elbow into his ribs. With his cheerful nautical attire, the salute made him look as though he were performing in an amateur production of the *Pirates of Penzance*.

Probably not the look he was going for.

"Kind of an odd dining room," Estrada said as we walked into the room. "No table or chairs?"

The dining room was large and formal and, like the rest of this house, beautifully and tastefully decorated. The top three-quarters of the walls were painted a deep blue, and the wainscoting was white, as was the baseboard and ceiling trim. A glass-fronted cabinet, also painted white, containing glass figurines and fine china, was set at an angle in one corner. The drawn curtains were beige silk shot with blue thread selected to match the paint, and ink drawings of flowers in bright shades of blue, pink, and green hung on the walls. A blue-and-red rug filled the center of the room. The rug was the only thing in the center of the room, as there was no table. Two chairs that matched the ones in the library had been pushed to one side.

"They were moved into the library for the occasion," I said. "The furniture in there's also been rearranged."

"Do you deliberately seek out trouble, or does it find you all by itself?" Estrada said to me once she'd shut the door.

"Considering I came here this evening not knowing someone would be murdered, I can't claim to have sought it," I replied as I settled myself comfortably into one of the two chairs. Both detectives remained standing. "Trouble seems to find me."

"Don't I know it," Ryan groaned.

"I hope your date is the understanding type," I said to Detective Estrada in an attempt to be friendly.

Her eyes narrowed, not looking at all friendly. "What's that supposed to mean?"

"Nothing. You were on a date when you were called into work. Considering it's now well after ten, the date would have been underway, getting over the initial awkwardness and moving into the comfortable stage. Then you up and left, after making profuse apologies, I'll assume. Some men are okay with that. Some are not. Ryan doesn't mind when I have an emergency at the store, although I suppose a failed book delivery doesn't equal a homicide."

"It does not. And yes, I was on a date and, not that it's any of your business, Gemma, I don't know him well enough to know how he's going to take being left alone at the restaurant in the middle of dessert. I won't ask how you know all that, because I truly do not want to know."

"Sure you do."

"Shall we begin?" Ryan said. "You used the word murdered, Gemma. I assume you saw what happened?"

"No, I didn't. I was the only person in this house tonight not in the room when it—whatever it was—happened."

"I didn't see that one coming," Estrada said.

"Where were you then?" Ryan asked.

"Listening at the door. I'd been, uh, evicted from the room."

"What does that mean?" Estrada asked.

"First things first," Ryan said. "Before we get to the specifics, what was going on here tonight? The 911 operator says Donald told her a woman collapsed during a séance? Of all the things I'd never expect to find you at that's got to be top of the list. I saw the draping over the chandelier, an out-of-place table in the library, twelve chairs round the table, a mass of recently extinguished candles in the fireplace. The place did look like a setup for something like a séance."

I explained the situation quickly, why Jayne and I were involved, and what I'd heard and observed, and they didn't interrupt.

"Why did this so-called medium ask you to leave the room, do you think?" Estrada asked when I'd finished.

"As a way of heightening the drama, probably. Or not wanting an unlucky number thirteen around the table. I originally considered they might not have had enough chairs for us all." I indicated the two dining room chairs that had been left behind. "Obviously that was not the case. I don't know why she singled me out. I'd never seen her or her assistant before."

"The most obvious question to ask you," Ryan said, "is if you happened to see anyone toting that sharp object around. It was pointed out to me, but I haven't examined it yet. Do you know what it is?"

"A hat pin," Estrada and I chorused.

"You mean like the souvenir state pins my dad puts into his fishing hat to show off all the places he's been?"

"Not the same. Think about the last big-budget historical drama you saw."

He gave me a blank look. Not one for historical dramas, Ryan.

"Okay. Hat pins were originally used to keep nuns' wimples or veils in place in case of a strong wind. By Victorian times, ladies' hats could be so large and ornate," I illustrated my point by holding my hands about a foot away on either side of my head and then lifting them up, "and their hair so elaborately fashioned, women needed a pile of pins to keep everything firmly in place. The pins had to be long—sometimes as much as ten or twelve inches—to secure the hat and their hair. And they were sharp in order to pierce the fabric easily. Plus, because the Victorians were never restrained in their sense of decoration or eagerness to display their wealth, the heads of the pins could be elaborately decorated, sometimes with jewels. Such as a nice fat pearl."

"Gemma's right," Estrada said, as though that might possibly be in doubt. "Antique pins are popular collectors' items these days."

"That, and they're used by theatrical costume companies, movie sets, and the like. As an aside, it's because of the ornateness of women's headwear that women are still not required to remove their hats on certain occasions, such as the singing of the national anthem. Far too difficult to get off and on, although—"

"I said you were right," Estrada said. "That doesn't mean I want to hear a lecture on the origin and customs of women's hats."

"Never hurts to have knowledge," I said. But I refrained from adding any more details that might be of interest.

"I didn't see a hat in the library," Ryan said. "Was the dead woman, or anyone else, wearing a big hat?"

"No, and that's the point. Whoever had the pin brought it with them, and it's not the sort of thing someone normally carries around in their pocket or purse these days."

"Can you get protectors for them?" Estrada asked. "Because they're so sharp?"

"When they were common, hat pins often came with protective covers. In the days before plastic, something as simple as a piece of potato or a cork would do the trick. Hat pins were popular weapons in their time. As a matter of historical interest, the length of the pins was legislated in America in 1908 in an attempt to stop women from using them as weapons during suffrage demonstrations and the like, and a couple of years later, covers became mandatory to avoid accidents."

Ryan stared at me. "I shouldn't be amazed at the things you know, Gemma, but sometimes I am."

"I'm sometimes amazed at the things she doesn't know," Estrada said. "All that is beside the point. You didn't see anything like that pin before the incident?"

"No. Such a thing wouldn't be hard to conceal." I didn't particularly want to, but I summed up an image of the hat pin when I'd seen it. Long and thin and extremely sharp, embedded in the medium's neck. "The air-conditioning in this house is turned up mighty high. About the only person who doesn't have room to hide anything on themselves is Jayne. Also Ashleigh, perhaps. Max and Larissa Greenwood, the couple who look like they've just stepped off their private yacht, are wearing blazers; Rebecca and Eleanor, her stepdaughter-in-law, each have a jacket; Bunny's dress is, uncharacteristically for her, roomy enough to conceal a baby elephant; Miranda, Rebecca's niece, is in jeans with loose pockets; and Daniel, Rebecca's stepson, has a pocket on his shirt, and he's wearing the usual men's trousers with roomy pockets. The women were told not to bring handbags into the library, and Donald had to remove his Inverness cape. I assume that was so we couldn't conceal anything we might have employed in an attempt to disrupt the séance."

"Disrupt," Estrada muttered, "is the word."

"Anyone wearing gloves?" Ryan asked.

I grinned at him. "No. The house is chilly but not freezing. Gloves would have stood out."

"We might get prints off the hat pin then."

"Unlikely, but possible. Anyone who went to the trouble to plan this ahead of time would know about fingerprints. Unfortunately, the situation was such that everyone, except for Jayne and Rebecca, left the library before the police arrived. You'll likely find a pair of gloves in a plant pot somewhere or stuffed down the back of the couch."

"You couldn't keep the suspects together in the library?" Estrada asked.

"I debated doing that. At the time, I decided that preserving the scene was more important. One other thing you have to consider—"

"Only one? Estrada asked.

"One of many. The hat pin pierced the exact spot between the vertebrae which would cause death to be instantaneous. A couple of inches further up or down, to one side or the other, and the result wouldn't have been guaranteed. Yet all the lights were off in the room. As I said, I wasn't there, but Jayne should be able to fill you in about that."

"The drapes were partially open," Estrada pointed out. "It's a dark night, with that storm blowing through, but lights at the back of the house are on and they would have shone into the library."

"Daniel Stanton opened the drapes after I ran in at Jayne's call. I couldn't stop him. Sorry. Check with the others as to how dark it was, but I'd say almost totally."

"Eyes get accustomed to the dark over time," Estrada said.

"Yes, provided there's some ambient light for them to work with. No light – no improvement in vision. However, the light in the hall was on, and strong enough for me to read by. You need to ask them if they could make out much of what was going on."

Estrada was taking notes. I was pleased to see her jotting my suggestions (instructions? orders?) down. "The question then is, was it a lucky strike or did the killer know exactly where to insert the pin to do the optimum amount of damage?"

"You seem to know," Estrada said. Once, I would have bristled at the apparent accusation. The first time we met, the good detective wanted to arrest me for murder. On the second and third occasions, I was high on her suspect list. Lately, she seemed to be coming around to trusting my instincts. Tonight, I just grinned at her. "Proving you don't have to be a medical professional to know where to strike. Just a well-read person with a wide variety of interests. As it happens, I read a historical mystery recently, set during the Klondike Gold Rush, if memory serves, in which a hat pin was the weapon. Nothing similar appears in the Holmes Canon though, which seems to be an oversight on Sir Arthur Conan Doyle's part, considering how suspicious Holmes was regarding women, and how every woman of any social status would have had—"

"A subject for another day," Ryan said.

"Not if I can help it," Estrada muttered.

Ryan pretended not to hear that. "Any possibility the killer came from outside?"

"Crawled through the window and went out that way when the deed was done? Impossible. The carpet beneath the window is still dry and considering the amount of rain that has fallen over the last hour, someone hiding in the shrubbery waiting for the opportune moment would be soaked through. Regardless, I doubt anyone could move so silently as to open the window, reach in and pull back the drapes, climb over the windowsill, cross the floor, wield the hat pin, and then leave by the same route, no matter how dark it might be, without being noticed."

"Agreed," Ryan said, and Estrada nodded.

"What can you tell us about that bunch?" he asked me.

"Very little. Bunny, Donald, Jayne, and Ashleigh you know. Rebecca also. Miranda is Rebecca's niece; she's staying here for the summer and has a job at Mrs. Hudson's. Daniel and Eleanor Stanton are Rebecca's stepson and his wife. I get the feeling they're not close, but Rebecca's husband was an older man when they married, so she likely didn't have much involvement in Daniel's childhood, if any. Maybe he resents her for his parents' divorce. That's common even if the new wife or husband had nothing to do with it. Max and Larissa Greenwood, the couple who look like they stepped out of a community theater production of Gilbert and Sullivan—"

"Who?" Estrada asked.

"Don't ask," Ryan said.

"Despite their accents, they now live in Boston and sailed here on their own boat, which is docked at the Cape Cod Yacht Club, conveniently situated not far from here. Larissa attended this séance in an attempt to get in touch with her grandfather, as she's looking for something and she believes he knows where it is."

Estrada began to make a note. "Is her grandfather in town?"

"Her late grandfather. Through the medium of the medium."

"Oh, that. Right."

"The first thing the Greenwoods did, when the lights came on and we saw what had happened, was attempt to leave. I ran after them and managed to persuade them to stay until you could talk to them."

"Do you read anything into that?" Ryan asked.

"I'd need to know more about them, but initially I'm inclined to say no. Never mind the way it ended, the séance was an intense experience. They might have regretted attending and decided to take the first opportunity to get out of here. As for the other persons present, I'd never met Madame Lavalier, that's the late medium, before, nor her assistant. Come to think of it, I don't even know the assistant's name. They weren't close."

"The assistant wasn't in the room at the time?" Ryan said.

"I mean not close as in not friends. She's noticeably not mourning her loss or even pretending to."

"My head's spinning," Estrada said.

"They're going to be getting restless out there," Ryan said. "I can't keep them waiting forever. Let's get statements from the rest of them. But one more thing. How did this séance come about and why are you—of all people—here?"

"Bunny Leigh organized part of it. You'll have to ask her and Donald for the specifics, but that's what they told me. Donald was," I coughed, "hoping to have a chat with Sir Arthur Conan Doyle."

Ryan rolled his eyes to the ornate plasterwork on the ceiling.

"It would appear Bunny wanted to get in touch with her manager, now deceased, and ask for his help in getting her career back on track."

"This case is not going to be simple," Estrada said in a classic understatement.

"Daniel and Eleanor had little to say during the séance and didn't ask to get in contact with anyone, although, of course, the evening was cut short. So to speak. They may have attended only out of casual interest, because they're staying in the house in which it was being held. Eleanor seemed to be quite keen on it, but Daniel was skeptical. As for me, I came, reluctantly I must point out, because Ashleigh asked me to. She was afraid she'd be emotionally distraught and wanted the companionship. I asked Jayne."

"Okay, thanks," Ryan said. "I'll leave Donald and Jayne till the end and ask them to sum up."

"You both know what Jayne's work schedule's like," I said. "She can't sit here twiddling her thumbs all night. Let her go home, and get the finer details about what happened in the library from Donald. You can talk to Jayne in the morning." I rubbed my hands together and stood up. "Good, that's settled nicely. Since Jayne came with me, and I've been asked to stay, I'll find an officer to take her home."

"Last I looked," Estrada said, "you don't run this investigation."

"I never mind assisting the police with their inquiries." I opened the door before she could remember that I hadn't actually been asked to stay. "Shall I send Rebecca in? It is her house, and you can ask her how this all came about before getting details about the dead woman from her assistant."

"Might as well," Estrada said.

The storm had moved on, leaving nothing behind but a light rain caressing the windows. Back in the living room, the music had been switched off and everyone sat quietly, either scrolling through their phones or staring into space. Everyone except for Donald, happily immersed in his magazine. The bar things had been put away. Ryan's orders, Officer Johnson told me.

"Rebecca," I said. "You're next."

She stood up slowly. Her eyes were wet, rimmed red, and I gave her an encouraging smile.

"I hate that this happened here, in my home," she said.

"Madame Lavalier hates it more," Eleanor said.

Rebecca flushed. "That's not what I meant."

"I know," Eleanor said. "I'm sorry."

"Detective Ashburton says Jayne can leave," I told Johnson. "Call a ride for her, will you?"

She nodded and touched the radio at her shoulder.

"What about us?" Max Greenwood asked.

"He didn't mention you. Come along, Jayne, don't dawdle."

I walked with Jayne to the front hall and we stood together, bathed in the gorgeous light from the chandelier hanging above us.

"Are you going to be okay, Gemma?" she asked me.

"I'll be fine. But I'm more concerned about you. You stayed with Madame while I chased after Max and Larissa and everyone else fled."

"Rebecca was with me. It wasn't nice, but I didn't know her . . . Madame Lavalier. Do you think that was her real name?"

"Probably not. The police will get the info from the assistant. Did you get her name, by the way?"

"I did. It's Mary Moffat. She didn't seem overly upset about what happened. She said she and Madame Lavalier haven't worked together for long."

Jayne opened the door, and we peered outside. The rain had almost finished, leaving everything thoroughly drenched. Rainwater dripped from the leaves on the trees and the potted plants, wet grass sparkled in the lights from emergency vehicles scattered everywhere. As we watched, the summoned patrol car splashed through puddles and pulled up to the steps in a spray of water. The air was moist and fresh, the light drops welcome on my face. Jayne ran to the car and hopped into the front passenger seat. I waved and then shut the door. Rebecca's voice leaked from the dining room; more voices were coming from the library. No one had shut the door so I popped my head in.

"Excuse me, ma'am," a man in a white boilersuit and booties bent over the body on the table gave me a stern look. "You can't come in here."

"Carry on," I said. "Don't mind me."

Another man waved a small brush used for gathering fingerprints at me. "Ms. Doyle, do I have to call Detective Ashburton to remove you?"

"Not necessary." I backed away.

The decor in this home is not entirely to my taste, but obviously carefully chosen. And expensive, such as the two Chihuly light fittings. The furniture was a combined arrangement of comfortable modern and valuable antiques. Outside the library, a small, exquisitely crafted mahogany table, probably Federal, held a tall, slim, blue-and-white Ming vase. My knowledge of Chinese ceramics isn't extensive, so I wasn't sure if the vase was an original, but it was beautiful. I peered inside. It was obviously dark in there, so I pulled out my phone and switched on the flashlight app. I shone the light inside and stared down. Something was in there, stuffed at the bottom. I didn't have any gloves on me nor a handkerchief, so I couldn't lift the vase to shake it out. I could probably use the sleeves of my jacket, but if my fingers slipped I might destroy a piece of art worth several thousands of dollars. Not to mention render any evidence within useless in court.

I stuck my head back into the library. "Hi there. Me again. Sorry to bother you, but if no one has checked the vase outside this door for clues, you might want to do that."

"We'll get around to it in due course, thank you," the first man said.

"Make her happy, Eddie, or we'll never hear the end of it," the second said.

They exchanged resigned glances. Eddie muttered something unintelligible, and they came into the hallway. The three of us formed a circle, staring down at the vase. "Probably Ming," I said. "Worth thousands, maybe even tens of thousands."

"It's nothing more than a piece of evidence to me." Eddie leaned over and peered into the depths. "Okay, I see what you're talking about. There's something in there and, judging by the way this house is maintained, there shouldn't be. Better call one of the detectives before we fish it out."

"I heard that!" Rebecca burst out of the dining room, a look of horror on her face. "Don't you dare touch that." Daniel and Eleanor had come out of the living room, the rest of the motley crew peering over their shoulders.

"We'll be careful, Mrs. Stanton," Ryan said. "But if it is evidence, I have to check it out."

"That's a genuine Ming vase," Eleanor Stanton said. "It's worth more than a small-town cop will earn in a lifetime."

The forensic techs hesitated, looking at Ryan for instructions.

"I can't—" he began.

"Actually," Rebecca said, "it's a knockoff worth about twenty bucks, maybe forty on a good day."

Eleanor's face was a picture of shock. She threw a questioning look at her husband and he shrugged in return.

"That vase has great sentimental value to me," Rebecca said. "My late husband bought it from a street vendor in Beijing on our honeymoon because I admired it. It has a hairline crack in the back, and with rough handling it might break."

"We'll be careful," Ryan repeated.

"Thank you."

"In the meantime, can the rest of you return to what you were doing? Officer Johnson?"

"Back we go, folks. You'll have your turn to tell your stories soon enough." Johnson shepherded everyone into the living room.

"What else in this house is fake?" Eleanor said to Daniel as they walked away.

"My dad never cared much for spending money on collectibles."

"Maybe he should have," she snapped.

"Mrs. Stanton," Ryan said, "there appears to be something inside that vase. Do you know what it is?"

"I do not. I don't keep anything in it."

Ryan pulled a pair of latex gloves out of his pocket and slipped them on. The forensic techs gathered around. Rebecca peered over their shoulders. No one had asked me to leave, so I didn't. I attempted to blend in with the wallpaper while still trying to observe what was going on.

Ryan picked up the knockoff Ming vase and, taking great care, turned it upside down over the table. He gave it a small, gentle shake, and something fell out. We all eagerly leaned forward. A crumpled-up, coarse-textured white cloth and a tiny lump of clear plastic about half the size of a golf ball fell out. Earlier, I'd thought we might find gloves stuffed down the back of a couch. It appeared this cloth had been used instead of gloves.

"Get these items to the lab ASAP and this vase and table printed right away," Ryan said. "Whoever handled these things might have inadvertently touched something. Mrs. Stanton, do you recognize this cloth?"

"I don't see anything special about it, Detective. It looks like an ordinary cleaning rag to me."

"I agree," I said. "We use much the same at the Emporium. Everyone probably does."

"I'll need your prints for elimination purposes," he said. "As well as the others."

Ryan would know any of the guests in this house tonight might have touched the vase and table on their way between the living room and the library. The vase was attractive—I'd admired it myself, although I hadn't touched it. Still, it could be one of the mundane details used to slowly and painstakingly build a case.

"Detective Estrada, can you ask Miranda Oberton to join us, please." Ryan said. His eyes flicked toward me, and he gave me the briefest of nods and a private smile before returning to the dining room.

Chapter Nine

Ryan, Detective Estrada, and the forensics team had still been at the Stanton home when I left around one in the morning. I waited with Rebecca Stanton while one by one the police interviewed her guests and then allowed them to leave. I'd attempted to talk to the medium's assistant, Mary Moffat, but Stella Johnson snapped at me and reminded me we'd been ordered not to speak of what had happened.

Finally, I could think of no other pretext to stay any longer, so I'd headed home, none the wiser about who killed Madame Lavalier and why. I let the dogs out for a quick romp before rolling into bed, where I slept soundly, unbothered by dreams of lethal hat pins and raging thunderstorms (although I might have dreamed of ocean-blue eyes and a wicked smile from a certain police detective).

On Sundays, the Emporium opens at noon, so in the busy summer season, it's the one day of the week when I can enjoy a leisurely morning. I let the dogs into the yard and then fixed a proper English breakfast for myself—two fried eggs, crispy bacon, toast, sautéed tomatoes and mushrooms, a giant pot of tea—and dug in. As I ate, I texted Uncle Arthur with an update. Update on the dogs that is. He trusted me to take care of myself (foolish man), and as long as the shop didn't burn to the ground, he trusted me to mind our businesses too.

Me: *All well here. P cornered a squirrel. Didn't know what to do with it.*

Arthur: *Lucky squirrel. Lucky Peony*

Me: *Big storm last night*

Uncle Arthur: *Damage report*

Me: *None to house. A few trees down on Harbor Road*

Uncle Arthur: *Heading to Ecuador later today*

Me: *Safe travels*

Uncle Arthur: 👍

Ecuador! He must be in Peru. Then again, for Uncle Arthur, Ecuador is a quick jaunt from Portugal. Or even Pennsylvania.

I switched on the radio to catch the local news, interested to learn if there'd been an arrest in last night's murder. The chief of police had made a short, terse statement first thing this morning. As usual, no fuss, no muss. No speculation. An arrest, he'd said, is imminent. That's usually cop code for "haven't got a clue." I switched off the radio and opened Twitter, which was considerably more sensational. There were plenty of posts about the "mysterious" death of the "prominent" medium during a "midnight séance" at an "exclusive mansion." One commenter claimed, "It's a dangerous business, contacting the dead and should never be attempted by anyone not thoroughly practiced in the art #failedseance #badmedium #deadmedium." I wondered how one got "practiced in the art" if it was so dangerous. I refrained from going down that rabbit hole in pursuit of further speculation. One hint that Madame Lavalier had mistakenly summoned her killer from the other side of the mirror was enough for me.

I finished breakfast and caught up on the rest of the news in my pajamas. After washing up the dishes, I put on my bathing suit, pulled on a beach dress, and loaded my tote bag with a towel, flip-flops, sunscreen, and a book and headed out.

On Sunday mornings in the off-season, I take Violet and Peony for a long walk along the shoreline or through the woods, but in tourist season they can't come to the beach where I like to swim. I left two very disappointed-looking dogs behind.

Last night's storm had passed as quickly as it had come. Apart from a few small branches scattered across the road, little evidence had been left behind. The sun was rising in a clear sky, and the air was warm. I drove to a reasonably quiet stretch of beach, set up my chair, and swam up and down the shoreline for about half an hour. By the time I emerged from the cool, refreshing water, more people were arriving for their day in the sun and sand. I read for a while and then reluctantly packed up my things and headed home.

Since leaving Rebecca Stanton's house, I hadn't bothered to spend any time thinking about what had happened. Ryan and Estrada were good detectives. They'd sort it all out. I'd offer my help if asked, but that might not be necessary. The circle of suspects was so limited, the killer would be bound to reveal themself before too long.

Not many people are as clever as they think they are.

I arrived at Baker Street at eleven thirty, half an hour before the Emporium was scheduled to open. At Mrs. Hudson's, the breakfast rush was finished and the lunch and afternoon tea crowds had yet to arrive, so I didn't have to wait long to be served. Jocelyn was behind the counter, Miranda waiting on tables. Four women, all with short gray hair, round cheerful faces, practical clothing, and sensible shoes, were drinking iced tea while consulting a psychic fair program book. They leaned back to allow Miranda to place bowls of fragrant sweet potato soup and plates bearing thick sandwiches in front of them.

"As I told you ladies yesterday," one of them said as Miranda dodged purses, program books, and elbows, "I was considering signing up to attend a séance, but eventually I decided it was simply too expensive, and Bart's mad enough at me as it is, what with my using our vacation funds to come to Cape Cod without him. As if he doesn't think twice about renting that horrid cabin for one of his fishing trips. Thank heavens I didn't go. I might have been there last night when it happened. I have an exceptionally sensitive nature." She waved her soup spoon in the air. "The specter might have attacked me instead of Madame Lavalier." She shuddered with delight at the very idea.

"I'm sure you would have been perfectly safe, Jenny," one of her companions said. "From what I heard, it was a spurned lover of hers, now gone to his reward, who took the opportunity to get his revenge when she opened the door to the other side."

"Do you suppose they have police and judges and lawyers and the like on the other side?" The third woman spooned up soup. "If not, then anyone can get away with anything; once they're dead."

That was an interesting question. One I had absolutely no intention of ever thinking about. I left them to their speculation and went to the counter, where Jocelyn handed me, unasked, a takeout cup of tea. I stopped Miranda on her way to greet a table of new arrivals. I jerked my head to indicate the woman delighting in her narrow escape from death at the hands of a visitor from the great beyond.

"Are you okay?" I asked the waitress in a low voice. "After what happened yesterday?"

She gave me a weak smile and ran her fingers through her spiky hair. "Yeah. I'm fine, Gemma. It was all so . . . weird. It was awful, but I didn't see anything, and it had nothing to do with me, right? I told the cops that."

"Why did you attend?"

"Aunt Rebecca told me her friend Bunny set it up, and she suggested I might want to come. Maybe I shouldn't have, but . . . I mean, I don't believe in that sort of stuff but . . ." Her voice trailed off, and she struggled to gather her composure.

"It's okay," I said. "You don't have to tell me anything you don't want to. I just wanted to be sure you were okay."

"I don't mind. I'm having a lot of trouble dealing with my mom's death. My dad and I get on okay, but we've never been all that close. Not like me and Mom. He's trying to take her place, but it's kinda too little too late." She took a deep breath. "I don't know if Aunt Rebecca really thought Mom would appear to us, or if it would somehow help me process her loss. I was pretty skeptical, but . . . well, you heard the dog, didn't you?"

"I heard the sound of a barking dog. I hope you know these people can be manipulative. They would have done their research on the attendees."

"You mean they faked the dog because they knew what happened to my mom?"

"All I'm saying is, don't give them too much credit."

"But something did happen to that woman, Madame Whatever, right?"

"Yes," I admitted. "Something did happen to her. Tell me about Max and Larissa Greenwood."

Her eyes widened. "What do you mean?"

"You seemed to—"

"Miss! Can we have service here, please? We're in a bit of a rush."

"Sorry," Miranda muttered to me. "Gotta go." She straightened her apron and headed for the new arrivals.

Since it was too early to open the shop, I popped into the kitchen to say good morning to Jayne. I found her with her hands sticky with scone dough and a tray of glistening fruit tarts fresh from the oven resting on the counter. Fiona was assembling tea sandwiches.

"Busy morning?" I asked them.

"Very," Jayne said. "We're fully booked for afternoon tea, so I don't have time to chat."

"Always good to hear. Busy, I mean, not no time. I won't be long. Did you give a statement to the police about what happened yesterday?"

"Ryan and Louise came in at seven, as we were opening. I told them what I could, but I got the feeling they'd heard much the same from everyone else last night."

"And what was that?"

"Are you investigating?" Jayne reached for her round cutter and began cutting out the individual scones.

"Most definitely not. Any of those tarts going spare?"

"No."

"Thanks." I helped myself to one. Blueberry—my favorite, made with fresh Cape Cod blueberries Jayne bought directly from a local farmer.

"I don't know why you bother to ask."

Fiona chuckled as she went down the row of sandwiches, adding a thinly sliced piece of white bread to the perfect little rounds of cucumber.

"My mother taught me to be polite at all times." I broke off a piece of my tart and popped it in my mouth. Absolutely delicious, as expected. "As I said, I have no intention of investigating anything or anyone."

"I've heard that before. If you're not investigating, why are you asking?"

"Curious, I guess. I wasn't in the room. I heard much of what was going on, but I didn't see anything. You did."

Jayne put the cutter on the counter. "You have to work while you listen."

"A small price to pay."

"Wash your hands and take over here. Press the cutter firmly into the dough, do not twist it, lift the rounds and put them on that baking sheet over there. Be careful because the sheet's hot."

I ran my hands under the tap while Fiona arranged the cucumber sandwiches on a platter and covered them with cling film before asking, "What's next?"

"Do the salmon, please," Jayne said. "I need to start on some cupcakes."

"I hope you're making coconut cupcakes," I said. "They're my favorite."

"Believe it or not, I don't cook exclusively for you, Gemma Doyle. But yes, if you must know, they're going to be coconut. If you can speed things up a bit there. Just press firmly. You're not cutting out spaceship components."

"I'm trying to maintain a consistency of thickness," I said, offended at having my scone-cutting qualifications questioned.

Fiona chuckled again. "Everyone in town's talking about that medium dying, you know. My mom was on the phone to me before I was even out of the shower, and Jocelyn told me just about everyone who came in for morning coffee was either spreading the news or wanting to hear the news. Can't say I was surprised when the police showed up to interview Jayne."

"Unfortunately," I said, "news spreads, and the fact that the dead woman was supposedly conducting a séance at the time gives it a certain thrill factor."

"I was surprised to hear you two'd been to a séance."

"Strictly research purposes only. I can't swear you to confidentiality, Fiona, as I obviously have no legal authority, but I hope you'll keep what Jayne and I are talking about to yourself. Don't even tell your mother."

"Fear not." She waved a dull knife in the air. "Info between Mom and me goes one way only. I know to keep quiet about what I hear in this place. Both in the kitchen and out."

"Thanks," Jayne and I said.

"I have work to do," Jayne said, "as does Fiona, but I know the only way I'll get rid of you, Gemma, is by telling you what you want to know, so I will. I can't describe what happened all that clearly; it was pitch-dark, and everything happened so fast. Did you hear some of what went on before the uproar began?"

"I did. It sounded as if the so-called medium made contact, so-called, with Miranda's mother and her dog."

"The dog barking was the creepiest thing that happened. Until that guy showed up supposedly wanting revenge from someone. And until it all ended. The whole thing was creepy, and I will never let you talk me into going to anything like that again."

"I've never been to a séance," Fiona said. "Maybe I should try it some time."

"Don't," I said. "As to what I heard, Larissa Greenwood wanted to talk to her grandfather about something she lost. Bunny's manager offered to help her get her career back on track, although I have absolutely no idea how he's going to accomplish that from beyond the grave. Donald was promised a later appointment with Sir Arthur."

"Sir Arthur Conan Doyle?" Fiona said. "Wow."

"No wow about it. That medium was as fake as the diamond I once found in the twelfth night cake."

"What's that?"

"A twelfth night cake? In England, twelfth night is January 6th, Epiphany, the final day of the Christmas season."

"Same day as my birthday," Jayne said. "I didn't know that."

"It is also the date assigned to be the birth date of the Great Detective himself, although I have no idea why that might be. Back to the subject at hand. It's long been the custom in England to bake a special cake on that day. Traditionally, a bean or a pea would be placed inside the cake, and whoever got it in their piece would be king or queen for a day. In more modern times, the pea or bean is often replaced with a prize such as—"

"Gemma, if you're ever going to get out of here," Jayne said, "I need to finish my story. So, may I continue.?"

"Do go ahead." I studied the perfectly cut scones, perfectly arranged on the baking sheet. Fiona swooped in, pulled on oven mitts, and popped the scones into the hot oven. "I promise not to ask any more questions," she said. "Come and help me, Gemma. Lightly butter the bread, then put one scoop of salmon mixture onto each, and top it with another piece of lightly buttered bread."

"I can do that. To continue the conversation, the last thing I heard was some man promising revenge on someone. And then . . ."

"And then . . ." Jayne said. "Sounds like you heard it all. We sat around the table, as instructed, and held the hands of the people sitting next to us. That's important so we don't break the circle."

"More important to ensure attendees don't take a camera or tape recorder out of their pocket, but never mind. Could you see anything?"

"Absolutely nothing. Once you'd left and shut the door, the assistant extinguished the candles. After that, it was so dark in the room that when I closed my eyes, it didn't make much difference. The curtains were so thick we couldn't even see the lightning outside, although the thunder sounded really close. That was scary."

"Did she blow out the candles, pinch them with her fingers, or use some sort of an extinguisher?"

"She had one of those long sticks with a metal cap on the end, to put over the flame. Does it matter?"

"You never know what will matter, until it matters. Madame Lavalier was seated at the head of the table with her back to the fireplace when we came in. Did she move from that position at any time?"

"Not that I saw. She was in the same spot when the lights came back on."

"Counting the dog, I heard voices belonging to a total of four spirits: Miranda's mother, her dog, Bunny's manager, the mysterious angry man. Supposed spirits, I should say. Did I miss any?"

"No."

"Who were you seated beside?"

"Between Donald and Miranda."

"Did they let go of your hands at any time?"

"Donald sniffled a bit and he dropped my hand to blow his nose at one point. Miranda's hand was very clammy. She let go when we heard that dog bark. She yelped and released my hand. That was weird, wasn't it?"

"Weird," Fiona said.

"Likely a recording," I said. "Can you remember the circle? Who was seated where?"

Jayne closed her eyes and thought for a long while before saying, "Not really, but I'll try. I was between Donald and Miranda for sure. Rebecca was on the other side of Miranda, and I think it was Eleanor next to Donald. Or maybe Daniel, sorry."

"The others?"

"I think Bunny was opposite me, but otherwise, I can't place everyone else, sorry."

"Just before the hubbub broke out, Ashleigh said 'she' had broken the circle. Do you know who she might have meant?"

"No."

"Who was seated next to Madame Lavalier?"

"Rebecca, maybe? Yes, I think it was Rebecca on the other side of Miranda from me. On Madame Lavalier's other side . . . I don't know. It's hard to remember, Gemma."

"Do you know if anyone else broke the circle prior to Ashleigh saying someone had?"

"I can't say, Gemma. Really, it was all such a blur. So much was happening, all these ghostly presences coming in and out, the storm outside. People jumped when we heard the thunder getting so close to us. Either Eleanor or Larissa screamed at one point, after a particularly loud peal of thunder. I'm not sure which. I probably lifted a couple of inches out of my chair myself, so likely there was some dropping of hands. Daniel said, 'That was close.' He tried to make it sound like a joke, but I think he was covering up how scared he was."

"When the so-called spirits spoke, or in one case, barked, could you detect any sort of physical manifestation?"

"No. After a while I began to be able to see a little bit, probably from the light leaking in under the door, but nothing more than vague shapes. Madame Lavalier was at the far side of the room, her back to the fireplace, where the light didn't reach. I couldn't even see the outline of her, but that's where the voices were coming from. I have to say, Gemma, they did sound real. The bark, the men's voices."

"Barks can be recorded," I said. "A good performer can alter their voice. Did you sense any communication between the medium and her assistant? Once everyone was seated I mean, and the performance began?"

"No. Nothing."

"You're sure the visiting voices came from the direction of the medium?"

Jayne was quiet for a long time. Her hands moved as she measured ingredients and added them to the electric mixer, but her thoughts were elsewhere. Fiona and I went up and down the rows of sandwiches, working assembly line–style. Eventually Jayne said, "I'm not a hundred percent sure. Maybe something like eighty percent sure? It was quiet, but not totally quiet. People shifted in their chairs, cleared their throats, mumbled under their breath, and the house creaked in the wind. The storm raged outside. Miranda spoke when she thought her mother was in the room, and Bunny did also, to her manager. I think Larissa wanted to speak to her father."

"Grandfather."

"Right. She sounded upset that he didn't come. The medium called on the spirits to show themselves. Everyone made some sort of noise when we heard the thunder."

"The last so-called spirit summoned was a man, a man's voice, anyway. How would you describe that?"

"He sounded mad, like, really angry. I don't know who he was talking to, he didn't say. I thought maybe Madame Lavalier had accidentally summoned an enemy of her own, but I guess she'd know not to do that, don't you think?"

As she hadn't summoned anyone, I didn't speculate.

"Then... total chaos. People yelling and jumping up, someone screaming, something falling over. Ashleigh said the circle had been broken. The assistant—what's her name again?"

"Mary Moffat."

"She tried to get us to rejoin hands, to re-form the circle, but it was too late. I called for you, and you opened the door and turned on the lights, and then we all saw what had happened."

"Did you notice anything in the minutes before this man's voice spoke, Lavalier called out, and everyone started shouting?"

"Ryan asked me that too, and I've been thinking it all over. But nothing. Nothing at all. If someone got up from their seat before the rest of us, I don't know who it was, and I can't say who was the first to break the circle. Maybe several people at once. I didn't see anyone moving behind Madame Lavalier. But someone did, right, Gemma?"

"Someone did."

Chapter Ten

"Is it possible," Ryan said, "the victim was intended to be someone else and the killer got confused in the dark?"

"Anything's possible, but I'd consider it highly unlikely. The medium was seated at the head of the table, her back to the fireplace, in the most prominent position. The hat pin wasn't deployed randomly, but with great precision. No, our killer knew precisely what they were doing. And to whom."

From his perch on the windowsill next to my desk, Moriarty nodded his agreement.

Ryan had dropped into Mrs. Hudson's for a sandwich and take-out coffee around three, and then he came into the Emporium for a quick hello. I'd managed to drag him upstairs to my office under the pretext of convincing him he needed to take a moment to eat his lunch in peace. Moriarty ran on ahead, always eager to hear the latest news and gossip.

Ryan dropped into the visitor's chair, pried the lid off his coffee cup and took a sip, unwrapped a sandwich of roast beef piled high on a Jayne-made baguette, and let out a deep sigh. His eyes were red, the stubble coming in thick on his jaw, his curly hair mussed, and his crisply ironed white shirt no longer crisp nor ironed.

"I don't have to be Sherlock Holmes to conclude you didn't make an arrest last night," I said.

He shook his head. "I'm heading home to grab a quick couple of hours of sleep. Louise and I are scheduled to meet the chief at his house at six for a briefing. Did you catch the news?"

"I heard what little your chief had to say this morning but nothing since. The people at the psychic fair are excited about it, so tearoom gossip and social media tells me. Some people are saying Madame Lavalier accidentally summoned a demon from beyond, and others think it was an old enemy of hers putting in an unexpected appearance. I assume news of the death, at a séance no less, will have people rushing to attend the final day of the fair. Which makes me ask: why do psychics need social media? Shouldn't they already know what's going on?"

Ryan grinned at me. "You're right about increased attendance. We've got officers going around the community center asking if anyone knew Madame Lavalier, and they say the place is packed. It's not the last day, though, just the last day in West London. The whole lot's moving on to Sandwich once they've packed up here."

He hesitated. I said, "What?"

"Aren't you going to ask me if my officers learned anything?"

"Nope. Not getting involved. Last night, I was on the scene, and I attempted to provide what assistance I might be able to. From this point on, you may consider me a simple bystander."

The grin he gave me went a long way toward taking some of the tiredness out of his lovely eyes, the color of the ocean on a sunny day. "Simple is not a word I'd ever use for you, Gemma. But I confess we could use some help—that's if you noticed anything."

"Does Louise know you're asking for my help?"

"Believe it or not, she suggested it in a very casual, round-about way. She told me, by the way, to let you know her date from last night arranged to have a full breakfast delivered to the station this morning."

I nodded toward the sandwich he was taking a big bite out of. "Breakfast for one?"

"I caged a slice of soggy toast."

"He has promise then."

"More than the breakfast did. Eggs, bacon, and toast don't fare well being prepared ahead of time and delivered, but Louise said it was the thought that counted."

"As it so often does."

While we talked, noises steadily drifted up from the shop below. Chimes rang as the door opened and closed. Visitors chatted among themselves or asked Ashleigh and Gale for assistance. The office window was propped open. A steady stream of cars moved down Baker Street, and pedestrians passing below discussed plans for the day. A light breeze caressed the leaves on the big old trees lining the street, and the soft scent of flowers overflowing from the baskets hanging from lamp posts drifted through the window.

"Back to the subject at hand," Ryan said. "This case is unusual, in that the suspects are a select group of people. Just in case you were mistaken about the possibility of someone coming in via the window, I had the area outside the library thoroughly gone over. We found no evidence of any recent disturbance to the plants or the ground beneath the windows. The windows were locked and show no signs of being tampered with. We could find nothing like a trap door under the floorboards, such as you found in the museum in that other case, and there's no direct access from the library to the second floor."

99

"All of which means the killer was in that room the entire time, seated around the table."

"Or, as Louise pointed out to the chief in an attempt to be fair, listening at the door."

I shook my head. "There's only one door to the library and I was outside the entire time. I didn't see—Oh, she means me."

Ryan lifted one eyebrow. "Twelve people in the room. One outside, and we'll consider that one not to be a suspect."

"Thank you."

"One of the twelve died. Leaving eleven people. I will, for now, eliminate Jayne and Donald."

"Ashleigh?"

"She's at the bottom of the list but still on it. Speaking of Ashleigh, she's dressed unusually plainly today."

"Somber's the word. She has what might be the world's largest clothing collection outside of a repertory theater. Or maybe the Princess of Wales on tour. Ashleigh dresses according to her latest whim and her mood. She's pretending yesterday's incident didn't bother her, and she told me she's fine with it. None of our customers would think anything's bothering her, but clearly last night's events upset her more than she's letting on." Her clothes today were suitable for a funeral. Knee-length black wool dress under a matching black jacket, dark stockings, black pumps with half-inch heels, a simple swipe of pale peach blush on her cheeks and light pink lipstick on her mouth, her only jewelry small gold hoops through her ears.

"Those observational skills, Gemma, are why I'm asking you what you might have observed." He put down his sandwich and counted on his fingers. "Other than the aforementioned, we have Bunny Leigh, Max and Larissa Greenwood, Rebecca Stanton herself, Daniel and Eleanor Stanton, Miranda Oberton, and

Mary Moffat. Eight people. One of whom is a cold-blooded killer. To stab a woman in the back of the neck with a hat pin, in a room full of people, and then return to your seat and pretend you didn't have anything to do with it, takes a mighty strong-nerved person indeed."

"Agreed. Because I'm not investigating, just curious, I asked Jayne what she saw last night. You did the same with them all. Anything stand out?"

"Nothing but a lot of chaos. Strange voices, dark room, storm outside. Everyone nervous and jumpy or pretending not to be nervous but still being jumpy. Hands were held and released, but it's all confusion as to who was where when."

"Have you identified the seating pattern? Have you figured out who was next to whom?"

"More or less, although not definitively. There are some contradictions, but I don't read much into that. Witnesses are unreliable, particularly in these sort of circumstances. I'd be more concerned if they all said exactly the same thing." He pulled a scrap of paper out of his pocket and showed me. He'd drawn a circle to represent the table, and a line for the fireplace. Initials represented the names. Madame Lavalier was at the head of the table, back to the fireplace. Going clockwise, he had Rebecca, Miranda, Jayne, Donald, Daniel, Mary Moffat, Max Greenwood, Larissa, Eleanor, Ashleigh, and lastly, Bunny seated on the medium's right. "This seems to be the closest version everyone agrees to. Do you want a copy of it?"

"No, thanks. I'll remember."

"Really? I mean, of course you will."

When Ashleigh arrived at work earlier, I asked her the same questions I'd asked Jayne. Just out of curiously, of course. Like Jayne, she couldn't positively say where most of the group were seated, although she told me she was between Bunny and Eleanor. Eleanor had screamed at the final, and loudest, peal of thunder and let go of her hand in shock, causing Ashleigh to cry out that the circle had been broken.

"Tell me about Mary Moffat," I asked Ryan. "The assistant."

"She's from Chicago but has been living in Las Vegas for a couple of years. She met Madame Lavalier about six months ago. The medium's real name, by the way, is Iris Laval, formerly of Albany, New York. Laval was working as a magician's assistant. According to Moffat, the magician was small potatoes, not very good, and Iris was barely scraping together a living. Moffat herself was making jewelry she tried to sell as protective items and good luck charms."

I chuckled. "I would have thought there'd be a roaring trade in charms in Las Vegas."

He smiled at me. "Only if they work. Anyway, Moffat wasn't doing much better than Iris Laval. They hooked up and started this séance gig. They'd only been doing it a couple of months before coming to West London."

"Why West London?"

"No particular reason, she says. They're following the psychic fair circuit. I got the feeling they weren't doing all that well in Vegas, so they decided to try newer pastures."

"She didn't attempt to convince you they were a legitimate medium and assistant?"

"She's smart enough not to try that. She told us straight out they considered themselves to be an entertainment act. If people want to pay for an evening's entertainment, they're happy to accommodate them. She called it interactive entertainment, actively involving the audience in the performance."

"Twisting of words. They researched people ahead of time and used what they learned to manipulate people's emotions. Did anyone tell you about the barking dog?"

"Donald did and a couple of the others. When I asked Moffat, she admitted it was a recording, but she said they never at any time came straight out and claimed it was Miranda's mother's dog. Miranda leaped to that conclusion all by herself. According to Moffat, dogs are powerful memories from people's childhoods and they help with the," he wiggled his fingers in the air, "entertainment."

"What about the relationship between Laval and Moffat?"

"She claims it was strictly a business partnership. She barely knew Laval, doesn't know anything about her family or private life, and doesn't care. They were sharing a room at the West London Hotel, but that appears to have been only to save money. We checked with the hotel; when Laval made the booking, she requested a room with twin beds. For what that's worth. Moffat claims not to know why anyone would want to kill Iris Laval. She insists she'd never met any of the people at the séance before this weekend, and had not seen any of them speaking to Laval outside of Rebecca Stanton's house. She added that the two of them were not together all the time, so someone might have met Laval when she wasn't there."

"It sounds as though they're busy downstairs, so I should go and help in the shop, but before I do that, let me suggest two lines of inquiry. They may or may not be relevant, but everything in a murder case is relevant until proven otherwise, as you have told me."

"Go ahead."

"Miranda reacted very strongly to seeing Max and Larissa Greenwood on two occasions. First in the tearoom, and then at

Rebecca's house. They, in return, didn't react to her at all. The first time, I might have thought she simply mistook them for someone else, but the second? Did any of them mention that?"

"No. The Greenwoods live in Boston, and they say they hadn't met anyone involved in this prior to last night, other than Mary Moffat, who arranged for them to attend the séance. And they only met her, so to speak, over the phone."

"When did they hear about it? I'm just wondering about the timing."

"They saw a flyer at the yacht club and called the number given. They spoke to Moffat, and she said she had two places available around a table that very night, and so the Greenwoods were given the time and the place. Miranda didn't say anything to me about knowing them prior to finding them in Rebecca's living room, nor did Rebecca. The other thing?"

"Bunny didn't pay for the séance, but she brought not only herself but four guests—Donald, Jayne, Ashleigh, and me. Almost half of the attendees. I find that very interesting indeed. As you said, it's a moneymaking gig for the two women, and they're not so well off they can afford to have their own rooms at a better hotel. Why then would they offer their services to Bunny for free?"

"That also comes as news to me. I asked the Greenwoods what they paid, but I didn't think to ask anyone else. Perhaps Moffat and Laval were trying to get Bunny to invest further in whatever they're planning next?"

"That is a possibility. Moffat paid extra attention to Bunny, to the point of momentarily breaking out of her assigned role as straight-faced assistant to welcome her specifically. You and I know Bunny doesn't have much in the way of money, but I'd be willing to bet a lot of people think anyone who was once famous must have cash to burn. Perhaps they saw her as a source of additional income. I'd suggest whatever was intended to come next, whatever that might be and if there was to be a next, would likely be illegal, but that's irrelevant now. The Greenwoods paid. Find out if Rebecca did also, and if she paid for Miranda, Daniel, and Eleanor."

"I will."

"This might not have anything to do with the woman's death, but out of interest—did your people find any wires or electronic equipment of the sort a fake medium and her assistant would use to create the effects? Moffat and Laval were in the library for quite some time on their own before we were allowed in."

"Laval had a small, high-quality recorder on her. I played it, and yes, it did have the sounds of a dog barking. Also a horse, both neighing and running, and a cat meowing. Did you hear those things?"

"Only the dog. Did either Moffat or Laval come to Rebecca's house earlier in the day?"

"According to Rebecca and Mary Moffat, no. Bunny made the arrangements and conveyed Moffat's instructions to Rebecca. It was Bunny's idea to use the library. She thought the mood would be better than in the dining room. Rebecca's gardening company were working at the house, and she had them move the table and chairs to prepare for it."

He finished his sandwich, rolled up the wrappings, and wiped his fingers on the paper napkin provided. He attempted, and failed, to smother a yawn.

I stood up. "I have a business to run, and you have a more important task to do than chase a killer or killers."

"What's that?"

"Go to bed. You're asleep on your feet."

Chapter Eleven

It might be true I'd decided not to involve myself in the police investigation, trusting Ryan and Louise to do their jobs, but it was also true I didn't exactly have the time to conduct a parallel investigation of my own. I had a shop to run, and it was the busiest time of the year. Sherlock Holmes never had to take time away from his cases, whether sneaking through the opium dens in the foulest parts of London, or taking a train to the "smiling and beautiful" countryside, to earn his living.

However, things do sometimes fall into my deerstalker hat, and such was the case shortly before closing at six. Gale finished work at five-thirty, leaving Ashleigh to help the last few customers. I hadn't been aware the psychic fair was visiting other locations on Cape Cod, so I decided I'd better order still more of the Conan Doyle biography and his own books on spiritualism in case of further interest. I'd finished doing that and was coming downstairs to begin the closing up routine when Bunny Leigh arrived, accompanied by, of all people, Mary Moffat, assistant to the late medium.

"Look who I ran into," Bunny said. Something was off about her voice; it was choked, as though she had to force herself to sound light and friendly. Her smile was off too—also forced, not reaching her eyes.

"Small towns," Mary said with a giggle. "Gotta love 'em. And I do. I lived in Chicago most of my life. I wouldn't have recognized my neighbors if I saw them on the street, much less know all their business. It must be real interesting to live in a town like this one, right, Gemma?"

"In a way."

"Sorry we didn't get a chance to talk last night, but you know how it was. Ashleigh, nice to see you. I love your suit. Very professional."

"Ready, honey?" Bunny asked Ashleigh. She twisted her head, taking her face out of Mary's line of sight, and widened her eyes in a plea.

"Ready for what?" Ashleigh said. "I mean . . . yeah, be right with you. Give me a couple of minutes."

Bunny turned to Mary. "Ashleigh and I have dinner plans so—"

Judging by the look on Ashleigh's face, that came as news to her.

"I love your store," Mary Moffat said to me. "Sherlock Holmes, what fun." She wandered over to the center table and studied the book display. Moriarty leaped off the top of the gaslight shelf, his favorite spot to keep an eye on the comings and goings, sailed across the room, and landed nimbly on the table. Anyone else would have jumped in fright, but Mary just said, "What a nice cat." She held out a hand to his nose. He sniffed it, and then allowed her to scratch under his chin.

"I know you're a specialty store," she said. "And you don't need any advice from me, but you should take advantage of having an international celebrity right here in your little town."

"Who's that?" Ashleigh asked.

"Why your own mother, of course." Mary turned to Bunny, her eyes glowing. "I simply couldn't believe it when I realized that Bunny Leigh herself was visiting the psychic fair. I just had to meet her. I had all her records, and I dressed just like her, and everything. I wanted to be a singer, like Bunny, but I have one small problem. I can't sing." She laughed heartily. "That put a stop to that, although it doesn't seem to be a drawback to a lot of so-called singers today, does it? Then again, no one these days can hold a candle to our Bunny Leigh, can they?"

Bunny shifted uncomfortably. "It was nice chatting with you, Mary, about the old days. But the store's closing now, so we have to be going."

"That's okay," Mary said. "You go ahead and close up, Gemma. Do what you have to do. I'll wait with Bunny. Hey, I've just had the best idea. You don't mind if I join you for dinner, do you, Ashleigh?"

"I—"

"That wouldn't work. Sorry," Bunny said quickly. "We're meeting . . . friends."

"I don't mind." All the time she'd been talking, Mary scratched Moriarty's chin and rubbed his belly. Oblivious to the tension in the room (or maybe willfully adding to it), the big cat closed his eyes and purred happily.

Ashleigh and Bunny threw me matching desperate looks. Why would I not take advantage of the unexpected opportunity? "You can go now, Ashleigh," I said. "I'll finish up." My mind raced, trying to think of something to distract Mary, clearly unwanted as a dinner companion yet oblivious to that fact. "I'd be interested in hearing Mary's ideas about what Bunny can do to help promote the Emporium. I've been wanting her to give me some suggestions, but you know how modest she can be. I lived in England during the height of her fame, so I'm not as well acquainted with her music and her musical influences as I could be. That might be an avenue to explore for the display."

Bunny grabbed Ashleigh by the arm and dragged her daughter to the door. "My bag!" Ashleigh said.

"Get it later," Bunny said.

Mary stared at the closing door and the two figures rushing down the sidewalk. "I didn't realize she was in such a hurry to meet up with those friends. Okay. I'd be happy to help you. I was Bunny's biggest fan when we were young. I absolutely adored her. I still have all the memorabilia I bought. My mom wanted to throw it all in the trash when I moved out of the house, but I told her it would be worth something someday." She looked around my shop. "It's in my storage locker in Chicago, but I have an idea. You can send me and Bunny to sort through the stuff and pick out the best. I bet Bunny only flies business class."

I didn't point out that these days Bunny could barely afford bus fare, as I assumed Mary was suggesting I pay to send her and her idol on the quest for the sort of memorabilia you could buy by the cartload at an antique fair. "I'll think it over. You must have been pleased to have Bunny come to the séance last night."

She clapped her hands in delight. Her eyes shone and, aside from the fine lines around her mouth and eyes, she must have looked very much as she did as a young girl, flipping through teenage fan magazines. "I was beyond thrilled. It was so great. That is, I mean, it was great until Iris died. Madame Lavalier, that is. She was . . . truly talented." Mary put on her sad face.

"Have you always been interested in spiritualism? Must be a fascinating field to explore."

"Oh, yes. It's been the focus of my entire life. There are so many things we don't know about the worlds beyond our own. Unfortunately I'm not a practitioner myself. I wasn't blessed with the gift of moving between the worlds, but I've been lucky to be able to find people such as Iris, I mean, Madame Lavalier, may she rest in peace, who I could work with. You might not believe right now in the validity of our mission, but I'm confident you could be convinced eventually."

"Why do you think I might not believe? I was there, wasn't I, last night?"

"Yes, but, I mean . . ." Her voice trailed off.

Moriarty, bored at her sudden lack of attention, leaped off the table.

"Was Iris okay with you not charging Bunny and her friends for the séance?"

Mary studied my face. "Why are you asking me that?"

"What's next for you? Without Iris, will you be looking for another partner?"

"We weren't partners. I had the honor of being her assistant. People with such a talent live in their own world and are unable to manage the practical matters of running an evening, not to mention an entire business, and the sort of assistance I provide is vital. Such a tragic loss to the spiritual community." She wiped at an invisible tear.

"You and I both know that's not true. You were more than a paid assistant and even more than her partner. You were the brains behind the outfit. And as for a lifetime interest in spiritualism, you didn't take that on until you and Iris hooked up a couple of months ago."

She fixed her eyes on my face. "You've been checking up on me."

I wasn't going to tell her how I knew about her past. Instead I said, "Let's call it returning the favor."

In the brief time I'd been in the company of "Madame Lavalier" I'd caught the unspoken exchanges between her and her "assistant." Mary had been giving her instructions, such as to show me the door. Mary had offered Bunny free admittance to the séance, not only for herself but for her entourage, as a way of seeking approval from her idol and spending time in her company. I considered it highly unlikely her partner-in-deception, Iris, would have agreed to give up almost half a night's revenue for a schoolgirl crush if she had anything to say about it.

I suspected that from the beginning, but when Ryan told me the medium made the hotel bookings, not the apparent assistant, that cinched it.

As for the partnership itself and the whole charade, Mary might have wanted to run the show herself, not bothering to pay someone to play the role of assistant, except Mary couldn't act. Her face was an open book. Her voice was high-pitched, a childish squeak. She wouldn't have been able to project nor to assume deeper men's voices. Iris, Ryan told me, had been a magician's assistant, although not for a very good one. She would have known how to do a sleight of hand and create distractions, whereas Mary made charms and potions.

"So, as I asked, what will you do now? By the way, I have no intention of setting up a Bunny Leigh pilgrimage site in my shop."

"You're good," Mary said. "You almost had me there. The first rule of the scam—tell people you're in the position to give them what they want. If you're looking for a job, let me know. I need a new medium, and your fancy English accent would be a real draw. Think Bunny would be interested? That would be a new angle. We could contact celebrities she knew when she was famous who've since passed on."

"Leave Bunny alone. These days, she wants nothing more than to be a small-town resident and mother to her adult daughter."

"I don't think that's any of your business, but never mind. I've been told you're friendly with the police. Do they have any idea who killed Iris?"

"Do you?"

"No, I don't. The cops asked me about our relationship—of which we didn't have one outside of this gig. I barely knew her, and I told them that. I figure one of the people last night was a nut job and did her in before she could summon their worst enemy from the other side of the mirror." She wiggled her fingers in the air and made the sort of scary noises adults make when playing with small children. Moriarty took his attention away from something under the nonfiction bookshelf, gave her a sneering look, and shook his head. Beneath the shelf, that something rustled.

"Anyone who forks out good money for a *séance*," more wiggling fingers and scary sounds, "isn't entirely stable, now are they?"

"It doesn't bother you?" I asked. "Taking money from grieving people?"

"Why should it? Does it bother you taking money from people who want to read about a fake detective? Like I told the cops, we were selling entertainment, same as you."

I could have disagreed with her—quite strongly. Playing with people's emotions, preying on their grief, offering false comfort and hope, is a dangerous, not to mention cruel, business indeed. But I let it go and kept my voice calm. "You were on the alert last night. You had to be. That was your role. Did you see anything unexpected? Anyone acting, for lack of a better word, suspicious?"

"The cops asked me all that, and I said no. I never knew who—or rather, what—Iris was going to conjure up."

"That's obviously not true. You did the preliminary research on the suspects." During which she realized I wouldn't fall for their tricks. "You then instructed her as to what buttons to push." Such as the barking dog. "In case the police didn't ask you, I'm asking you: Did anything in your research indicate if any of the people in the library last night knew Iris from other occasions?"

"No."

Mary and Iris wouldn't have dug too deeply into us. For one thing, they didn't have enough time—Jayne and my attendance at the séance was only decided late in the afternoon, and the others not much earlier. Max and Larissa were last-minute attendees. I doubted Mary and Iris had the computer skills to search deeper for anything that wasn't common knowledge. Noticeably, they hadn't known anything about Larissa's late grandfather's lost . . . whatever. Max would have given his last name when he arranged to attend and sent payment, and that name would have been different from Larissa's grandfather's.

Something dark crossed Mary's face. She hesitated, and then she took a deep breath. "Okay, I'll tell you something for nothing. Yeah, we might have done some research. That's all part of giving the client what they want, right?"

"If you say so."

"Bunny told me earlier she's been lost since the death of her agent. It was easy enough to look him up, and Iris is . . . was . . . good at voices. Same with Rebecca's sister. But that last visitor?

That was Iris all the way. I mean, sometimes, she'd think up things out of the blue and give it a try. If no one reacted, then she'd drop it and move on. But this time, it seemed different. I don't know who she was contacting. We hadn't talked about anyone like that. I mean, no one wants to hear that someone's coming to get revenge on them from beyond the grave, do they? What we do is all about offering comfort and hope."

No one wants to pay good money to hear something like that, I didn't say.

Mary Moffat shuddered as though an unexpected cold wind had blown in from the Arctic, right through the door to my office. She wrapped her arms around herself. "That last voice? I've no idea where it came from."

Chapter Twelve

A s my final task of the day, I always clean Moriarty's litter box and lay out sufficient food and water to see him through the night.

He crouched on the floor behind my desk as I topped up the water dish. I can never quite tell if he's mad at me for leaving him alone or glad to see the back of me.

Probably the latter.

"Now remember," I said, "I'm leaving my livelihood in your capable paws. Be on guard."

I was answered with an enormous yawn.

"If it's not too much trouble."

I usually walk to work and today had been no exception. The heat and humidity of the day was breaking, and I enjoyed the soft summer air. The shops were closing, but people streamed into restaurants and bars. The expanse of the open Atlantic Ocean spread out before me.

At the bottom of Baker Street, where it meets Harbor Road, the parking lot in front of Andy's restaurant was packed, and people milled outside waiting for tables. The outdoor seating area on the pier was almost full, and waitstaff hurried about, taking orders and delivering food and drinks.

I had nothing planned for tonight and was in no hurry to be anywhere, so I walked slowly, watching the bustle all around me, deep in thought. I'd suggested a couple of lines of inquiry in the death of Iris Laval for Ryan to pursue. He might, or might not, tell me what he uncovered. He didn't always. Some things were confidential, and he tried to not cross that line. Other things, of course, were available to anyone who knew where to look and how to look for it.

When I let myself into the house, I got the usual over-the-top greeting from my dogs. I responded with an equal amount of enthusiasm. I've never had a pet before. We didn't have dogs or cats when I was a child due to my mother's allergies and my parents' work schedules. When I moved out of the family home, I lived in university accommodations or in small, crowded flats with roommates. During my, thankfully brief, marriage, we worked all hours of the day and often through the night getting our bookshop near Trafalgar Square up and running. That is to say, I worked all hours; he had other things on his mind, and for once my observational skills failed me. A matter of refusing to see, no doubt. But eventually I could remain blind no longer, and the marriage ended. I sold my share in the shop to the lying, cheating cad and accepted Great-uncle Arthur's offer to move to America and buy a half-share in the bookshop he'd opened on a whim because he, lifelong Sherlockian that he is, fancied the address. He might have had a brilliant idea for a shop, and he might have liked the address (221 Baker Street was not for sale), but my uncle doesn't exactly have a head for business. As soon as the shop was set up to his liking, stocked with all of his favorite things, he got bored with it. But he was unable to sell it, and thus he made the offer to me to come and run it for him. In the meantime, he found a tiny, starving black kitten in the alley one rainy winter night and brought it in for a sip of milk and a warm. He named the cat Moriarty, and Moriarty settled in permanently. I sometimes wondered if the wretched beast would like me better if his name was Midnight or anything other than that of a Sherlockian villain.

I left England without giving a lot of thought as to if I really wanted to move to America, if running a bookstore was what I wanted for the rest of my life, or even if I wanted to share a house with a man in his eighties. But it all worked out very well indeed, and I was happy with my life here in West London.

My pets were now an important part of that life. One day, in a typical Uncle Arthur whim, he decided I needed a companion when he was away (without asking my opinion on the matter), and he walked in the door with an adorable cocker spaniel puppy tucked under his arm. He named her Violet, after the four Violets in the Canon. A few years later, Peony was abandoned when his owner died, and I took pity on the lost, frightened, confused little guy, and he joined our household.

Over-the-top greetings over, I let the dogs into the enclosed yard for a romp and a sniff around and then served up their dinner. Uncle Arthur's the cook in our house, and when he goes away, he leaves the freezer well stocked with precooked meals for me. I heated a serving of lasagna in the microwave, tossed together a quick salad, and settled at the kitchen table with my dinner and my laptop and got to work.

It's amazing what you can find out about people these days with nothing but a minor amount of computer knowledge. I first searched for Larissa and Max Greenwood.

Almost instantly, I found what I was looking for. Six months ago, they'd been involved in a fatal car crash that resulted in the death of the driver of the other car. The other driver's name was Amy Oberton, returning from a dog show with her purebred Shih Tzu, Frederick McKenzie Daylight. Freddy, as he was affectionately known, had won the silver ribbon in his category.

Max Greenwood had been charged with careless driving causing death.

I leaned back with a sigh. Rebecca's sister was named Amy; Miranda's surname was Oberton. Amy Oberton had to be Miranda's late mother. That would explain why Miranda had such a powerful reaction upon seeing the Greenwoods. It might also explain why they, in turn, didn't recognize her or Rebecca.

I read on. The case never went to court, and charges had been dropped due to lack of evidence.

Ryan would know all this—he might have been aware of it when I told him to find out if a connection existed between Miranda Oberton and the Greenwoods. I'd love to know more about why the case had been dropped. Was it really a lack of evidence, or some political underhandedness? Max Greenwood was, I determined on further reading, a wealthy man, highly connected in the New England real estate world. His wife was well known for her charity work and political fundraising.

I searched further, and one other item of interest caught my eye.

A couple of weeks before the accident that killed Miranda's mother, the Greenwoods hosted a major fundraising effort for the cancer society. A gossip website featured numerous pictures of the Boston glitterati gathered at their home for the event. It was around Christmas time; the house overflowed with elaborate yet tastefully arranged decorations. A bushy eight-foot-tall fir tree, draped and illuminated in shades of white and red, filled the living room while huge logs blazed in an open fireplace. Black-and-white-clad waiters passed drinks and canapés to guests wearing black tie or sleek gowns. More than a few diamonds sparkled in the firelight. Max was in a tuxedo, and Larissa wore a wide-skirted taffeta dress. Smiles were on their faces, but when I looked closer at the pictures, I could see the strain in their eyes and the stiffness of those smiles.

The party, I read, was in honor of their son, Maxwell Jr., who died the previous year of cancer. He'd been nineteen years old.

A dead son. A grieving family.

Had the Greenwoods come to the psychic fair and then to the séance in an attempt to get in touch with Max Jr? I would have assumed that was the case, but why was Larissa asking about her grandfather? Might she believe they were together in the afterlife? But that still wouldn't explain why she hadn't asked about Max Jr. I thought back to what I'd heard that night. Larissa seemed to be wanting her grandfather to tell her where something was. It made little sense, in light of what I knew about their loss, but the séance hadn't finished before it ended so abruptly.

I dug a bit deeper into Larissa's background. Born Larissa Franzen, of a respectable (according to appearances) upper-middle-class family in New Orleans, she'd studied psychology at Tulane before going into private practice in that city. She and Max met at university and married shortly after graduation. They'd had three children: Tina, Maxwell Jr., and Laura, who was now eighteen. The family moved to Boston ten years ago to expand Max's real estate company. The only item of interest to me was that Larissa's paternal grandfather, one Oliver Franzen, was rumored to have had criminal underworld connections throughout Louisiana. Oliver died thirty years ago. Larissa's mother's father was still alive.

Was it possible Larissa believed her grandfather, Oliver, had hidden some sort of treasure and was trying to contact him to find out where it was?

Seemed far-fetched to me, particularly after all these years, but then again, attending a séance in the first place seemed far-fetched to me.

I considered that the mention of a grandfather might have been a cover for their actual purpose in attending: to contact their son. Was it intended to be a test of the medium? To see who (what?) she'd attempt to reach?

I put aside thoughts of long-hidden gangster loot and wondered if it might have been nothing more than coincidence that the Greenwoods attended a séance at the home of Amy Oberton's sister.

It might be. Coincidences do happen. Although not as often as some writers of fiction want us to believe. The psychic fair was a big deal: it had been advertised all over New England.

If the Greenwoods wanted to reach their son . . .

Yes, that was possible. But still, the grandfather reference made no sense.

I went on to search for information on the other attendees at the séance whom I didn't know anything about: Daniel and Eleanor Stanton. Again, I had no difficulty. They lived in Los Angeles, and their major web presence was advertising for their line of men's wear. It didn't take me long to find out the business wasn't doing well and never had. They had no large customer accounts, the products weren't stocked at big, or even small but fashionable, stores. Mainly, they had a mail-order outfit fronted by a website featuring professionally shot photographs of moderately handsome men wearing their clothes. As a person with a retail business, I know very well online ordering is increasingly the done thing these days. But I would have thought clothes needed to be bought in person. After all, one has to try things on.

The business was small potatoes. Extremely small potatoes, I would have thought, for Ron Stanton's son. Then again, if Daniel wanted to go his own way in life, good for him. The website for their company talked a great deal about the importance of working with locally sourced materials and employing local people. Plenty of pictures of handsome men, with beautiful women as accessories, posing in sunlit fields, in front of pristine cityscapes, or dramatic ocean backgrounds. All wearing sleek clothes, of course. The About Us page had a picture of Eleanor and Daniel, arms wrapped around each other, beaming at the camera. The brief bio mentioned Daniel's fashion credentials (which seemed mighty sparce to me for a man approaching forty, but I assumed he was self-taught). Of Eleanor, it only said she was "thrilled to be working with my incredibly talented husband to turn our dream into a reality."

I dug further into Daniel's past, and discovered he'd originally intended to be a chef. He spent a year in Europe at a prominent cooking school. Or rather, from what I could tell, he spent a year in Europe not going to the prominent cooking school in which he'd enrolled. I could find no evidence that he'd ever worked as a professional chef. Daniel, I was beginning to believe, was what in England we call a layabout.

I became aware I was being observed, and I lifted my head from the computer to see four liquid brown eyes staring at me.

I also became aware my lasagna had gone cold and the only light in the kitchen was coming from my computer screen. "How time flies." I shut the lid to the laptop and stood up. "I guess you two are ready for a walk."

At the magic word, the dogs yipped and ran to the mud-room door. I got down their leashes, and we set out.

Chapter Thirteen

When I went into the tearoom for my tea and a blueberry muffin Monday morning before opening the Emporium, Fiona informed me that the murder, and its possible supernatural connections, was still the number one topic of conversation among the breakfast and take-out coffee crowd. The psychic fair had closed its doors yesterday afternoon. Attendance, she reported, had been so heavy the police were called to help direct traffic in and out of the parking lot of the community center.

"They've gone to Sandwich," Ashleigh told me when she came in. "At first I was worried Bunny would follow them, hoping to find someone else who could get her in touch with that manager of hers."

"She didn't go?"

"No. Mary called Bunny to suggest they go together, but Bunny made an excuse. She adores meeting her fans, but sometimes the price of fame can be high. Or so she says."

"Because of stalkers and the like?"

"Yes." Ashleigh lowered her voice and leaned toward me, although the store was empty of customers. Today, she wore one of the outfits she has on regular rotation: middle-aged gardening enthusiast with limited vision. I was pleased the mourning attire had been dispensed with. "I might have helped, just a teeny bit, with that. Despite her concern about running into Mary, I feared she'd still go. I said to her, 'Would a genuine medium be shilling at a small-town fair? Wouldn't a real medium, with a good reputation, be able to count on customers coming to her?'"

"Maybe you should have just told her that real mediums don't exist and she should forget about re-creating her career with the help of a deceased manager."

Her face twisted in thought. "Should I have done that? I mean, she's sort of got her hopes up on rebuilding her career. I thought she'd given up on it, but every once in a while, it comes bouncing back."

"I don't know, Ashleigh. I don't know much of anything about being a pop star, but I do know most of those stars burn out very fast and are never heard of again."

"I don't know much about how to be a daughter," Ashleigh said.

I put my hand on her arm and said, "You'll find a way."

The chimes over the door tinkled, and a couple came in. They were, they informed us, looking for *The Wanderings of a Spiritualist* by Sir Arthur Conan Doyle, which, fortunately, I still had in stock.

We had a busy and satisfying day. Turns out that attendees of psychic fairs are also big readers of gaslight mysteries: stories set around the time of Sherlock Holmes, which is often called the gaslight era, named for the fuel that powered the lights that illuminated the homes and streets of London and New York when Victoria and Edward occupied the throne. We also sold a lot of Holmes-pastiche novels and story collections as well as merchandise to people accompanying the spiritualism and gaslight lovers.

"A good day," I reported to Jayne when we were enjoying our tea in the window alcove later that afternoon.

"In here too. Andy says he's turning people away by the busload."

"Is that good?" I studied the sandwich offerings. Measly they were, and no cucumber, my favorite. I selected an egg pinwheel.

"Yes, it's good. It means the restaurant's full every night. Sorry, I don't have any scones to offer you. They all got eaten. Which is also good. Speaking of which, I need to get more made for tomorrow." She swallowed her tea in one long gulp and stood up, leaving me to finish my tea and eat my egg sandwich alone.

Ashleigh finished work at five, and I stayed until closing at six. That done, I popped my head into the tearoom kitchen and asked Jayne if she needed a hand.

"Thanks, but no. Jocelyn's agreed to put in some overtime, so we won't be much longer."

"My mom's got the kids tonight," Jocelyn said as she watched the mixer whirling butter and sugar together. "My husband's out of town for a few days. He's helping a buddy who runs a charter fishing boat out of Provincetown. I could have had a nice quiet night at home watching TV with my feet up and a take-out dinner on my lap, but my dad always said summer in Cape Cod is for making money. We can relax over the winter."

"See you both tomorrow, then," I said.

I trotted down Baker Street, thinking a night in front of the TV and a take-out pizza didn't sound too bad. I was debating whether or not to treat myself to an after-work cone from the ice-cream stand on the boardwalk when my phone rang.

Ryan.

"Hi," I said. "I've left work and am heading home. Dare I hope you're calling to say the case has been brought to a successful conclusion and you can take me to dinner tonight? I just happen to be free."

He chuckled. I could tell by the tiredness accompanying that chuckle that he was not calling for any such reason. "Sadly, no. You'd think with the limited number of suspects such as we have, it would be easy to identify the culprit. No such luck. Every one of them claims to have seen nothing and heard nothing until the commotion started."

"They, other than the person responsible, are likely telling the truth. Jayne says much the same. It was dark, a storm was going on outside, everyone was nervous and on edge to begin with."

"We're trying to find a connection between Iris Laval and the people who attended the séance, but other than Mary Moffat, we're not having any luck on that score."

"Give it time," I said.

"The more time that passes, the harder it is to make a case. The Greenwoods are still in town, but I don't know for how much longer, and I can't keep them here. Same with Daniel and Eleanor Stanton."

I kept my voice low as I walked, but everyone I passed was enjoying the seaside evening and paid me not the slightest bit of attention. "I assume you know Max Greenwood was driving the car that killed Rebecca's sister, who was also Miranda's mother?"

"I do. Seeing as Max was not the victim in the séance killing, I don't know that it matters. But the coincidence has my spidey senses tingling, so . . . we will see."

"Any forensic evidence yet?"

"Nothing worthwhile. Everyone told us where they'd been sitting, and their prints were on the table in front of them and the chair in which they sat, as you'd expect, but other than Rebecca's, nowhere else in the room. Mary Moffat's and Laval's prints are on everything, but Moffat told us they'd arranged the furniture themselves to get it the way they wanted it. Plus prints of random people, which are likely the gardeners who helped move the dining room table and chairs earlier in the day. I'm having those checked to eliminate them. That's about it."

"As I would have expected. The whole thing was set up like a stage set."

"Of interest, a portion of the mantle above the fireplace is so clean, it was obviously wiped down. Not even Rebecca's prints there."

"Interesting. What do you take from that?"

"Laval was seated in the chair closest to the fireplace, with her back to it. The killer had to walk behind her chair. Did this person accidentally touch something they shouldn't and quickly gave it a swipe? Possible."

"What about what I found in the vase?" I asked. "The cloth and the bit of plastic?"

"That plastic is what was used to protect the bearer from the end of the hat pin, as you guessed."

"I—"

"Sorry. You never guess. I should know better by now. A standard cleaning cloth, available anywhere and everywhere. Rebecca Stanton has no idea what her housekeeper uses to clean, and when the housekeeper was asked, she said she buys them by the case and can't tell if any are missing or not. It's clean and so highly textured, we'll never get usable prints off it."

"It was well chosen, then. I assume you showed it to the witnesses and asked if they'd seen that specific item before."

"No one had. Or so they say."

I turned left into Blue Water Place, my street. It was still early enough the sun was up in the western sky, but shadows of the large old oaks and red maples lining the road were long. One of my neighbors passed me, walking an ancient golden lab. The equally ancient gentleman said, "Evening, Gemma."

"Evening . . . uh . . ." I never did get his name.

A kid flew past on her bike, peddling hard, black hair and blue ribbons streaming behind her.

"The presence of the cloth means malice aforethought," I said into the phone. "Obviously it was brought to cover the hands so as not to leave fingerprints and to wipe surfaces after."

"I'd say carrying a hat pin indicates malice aforethought."

"Good point."

"I've had officers asking around at the psychic fair if anyone stocks anything like that hat pin. Some booths sell antique jewelry, including ornate broaches with mighty vicious ends, and men's tiepins, but no one claims to recognize that particular pin. We're searching for the source, but although it's attractive, it's not particularly valuable—the silver is real but the pearl isn't—so it'll be hard to find a record of its sale, if there ever was one."

I reached my house and turned into the driveway. My neighbor, Mrs. Ramsbatten, was comfortably settled in the shade of her front porch, her book open on her lap and something cold in a glass on the table next to her. She gave me a smile and a wave, and I indicated the phone I was holding.

Great-uncle Arthur and I own a saltbox house, built in 1756. A saltbox is a traditional Cape Cod design of two and a half stories, the upper level situated at the front of the house. It's a big place for two people, but we love the history of it and enjoy all the modernizations that have been done. Uncle Arthur's suite is on the upper level, including a small balcony on which he can sit and gaze longingly at the sea spreading to the horizon from the base of Blue Water Place. Seaman since he was a boy, once master and commander of one of His Majesty's great battleships, Great-uncle Arthur doesn't stare longingly for long before he answers the ocean's call.

I let myself into the mudroom at the back of the house to be greeted by two wildly enthusiastic dogs.

"Sounds like you're home," Ryan said.

"I am. I wonder what it's like to always be happy to see someone. I love you, Ryan, very, very much, but even I don't go into a frenzy of joy whenever you appear."

"You don't?"

I smiled to myself. "Not always."

"Time to let you go. Louise is waving a piece of paper at me, which I hope means she's come up with something. Before I do . . ." His voice trailed off. I crouched down, keeping the phone to my ear, and gave Violet and Peony enthusiastic greetings in return. I waited for Ryan to say it.

"We could use some help, Gemma. This was an intensely personal murder, not a spontaneous act of anger or sudden mad impulse. It was planned ahead of time. I can find absolutely nothing to connect Iris Laval to any of these people, other than Mary Moffat. We can find no one who noticed any animosity between them, although that might just be that cursed custom of never speaking ill of the dead. I know you dismissed the idea, but I have to consider that Laval might have been killed by mistake. If you happen to be talking to any of the interested parties . . ."

"I'll let you know what I learn. Bye."

"Bye. Oh, in reply to your earlier comment, allow me to say I love you equally much. And next time I see you, I expect hugs and scratches and cuddles and frenzies of joy."

"I'll even toss you a dog biscuit."

He laughed and hung up.

* * *

I always prefer to catch people unawares. Obviously that means sometimes I don't catch them at all, but on this occasion, I decided to risk it. I fed Violet and Peony, changed out of my work clothes, and had a quick shower. I cut the dogs' postprandial walk short, and once that was over and they were back in the house, I got out my car and drove to Harbor Road intending to pay a call on Rebecca Stanton.

The sun was lowering behind the trees, and the shadows were even longer now. The sky over the ocean was dark, and on the water, boats were heading for shore. The streetlights were coming on and the pier by Andy's restaurant was a blaze of white light. To the south, the lighthouse flashed its nightly rhythm.

In Britain, when the authorities say someone is "helping the police with their inquiries" they mean being questioned as a suspect. In my case, I hoped I genuinely was helping the police with their inquiries by asking questions Ryan and Estrada could not ask, did not think of, or getting answers they would not. People tend to be wary of the police. Some with good reason; many because they're simply nervous at being involved in something as serious as a murder. Often, they don't want to bother the detectives with what they think is an unimportant detail. And said detail turns out to be the key to the entire case.

Whereas, no one ever seems to worry about bothering me, nor are they wary of me. After all, what am I but a five foot eight, thirtysomething English bookshop owner with a pretentious accent, out-of-control curly hair, and not particularly good dress sense?

No cars were parked outside Rebecca's, but the garage doors were shut and lights shone from inside the house.

I rang the bell and put on my friendliest smile as the sound of the chimes echoed through the house. It wasn't long before I heard the tap of heels and the door opened.

"Gemma." Rebecca returned my smile. "This is a surprise. What can I do for you?"

"I was passing," I said. "That made me think about what happened the other night. I'm sorry I didn't call and check up on you earlier. I hope you're okay. It must have been quite upsetting."

"Upsetting for everyone, but thank you for asking. Please, come in. I've finished dinner and am about to watch a movie, but it can wait. Would you like something to drink? I'm having coffee, but—"

"A cup of tea would be nice," I said.

"Then you're in luck. I had lunch at Mrs. Hudson's last week, and I bought a packet of the deluxe Earl Grey. Do you like Earl Grey?"

No, I thought. "Perfect," I said.

I was familiar with Rebecca's kitchen from the time Jayne and I catered the fundraising tea. It was an enormous space, all steel and glass and marble. Top-of-the-line appliances, black-and-white check ceramic flooring, red leather-topped stools pulled up to the island. On my previous visit, the kitchen had been clean to the point of looking as though no one ever used it. Tonight, dishes were piled in the sink, a wine bottle peeked out of the overflowing trash can, and used take-out containers were scattered around the top of the island. Rebecca began opening and closing cupboard doors, searching for the tea. Clearly, she wasn't accustomed to doing much in her own kitchen. "Good. Here it is." She flourished the package. "Milk? Sugar?"

"A splash of milk, please."

She plugged in the kettle and began rummaging for a cup. I didn't particularly want tea, but I hoped the act of gathering things together to make it would help her relax and put her in the mood for a nice long chat.

"Sorry about the dreadful mess," she said. "You know what it's like, having guests, I mean."

The kitchen was disorganized, but I wouldn't call it a dreadful mess. Mine often doesn't look much better. "Are Daniel and Eleanor still staying with you?"

"Yes, they are." She opened the fridge door to reveal the usual rows of condiments, a carton of cream and one of milk, and a couple of bags of limp vegetables, along with a collection of white wine bottles and cans of beer. Rebecca, I knew, wasn't much of a drinker. Daniel and Eleanor were clearly making themselves comfortable.

Rebecca grabbed the milk jug and shut the door.

"Have the police finished with the library?" I asked.

"They have. And I'm glad of it. I spent what was left of Saturday night at a friend's house, and I was only allowed back here late the next evening."

"Did your house guests go to this friend also?"

"No. She doesn't have enough space for us all." Rebecca laughed without humor. "Fortunately, Miranda was able to retire to her room above the garage. It's a separate building, so the police said they had no interest in it, but Daniel and Eleanor couldn't stay in the house. It's not easy finding last-minute accommodation at a hotel in West London at this time of year, in the middle of the night, and at a hotel Daniel considers suitable. But we managed. Shall we go through?"

She'd brewed the tea in a cup, not a pot, and had barely dipped the bag into the hot water before adding an excessive amount of milk. It resembled used dishwasher.

One of my chores as a proud Englishwoman is to teach Americans to make a decent cuppa. In that, other than at Mrs. Hudson's itself, I have failed miserably.

Didn't matter. I didn't intend to drink the stuff anyway. I thanked Rebecca and accepted the cup. We went into the living room and settled down.

My impression of Rebecca has always been of a practical, levelheaded woman. I was interested in why she'd held the séance, but I wasn't sure how to come right out and ask. Instead, I began by engaging in casual chitchat. I can engage in casual chitchat. If I have to. I try not to make a habit of it. "Are Daniel and Eleanor planning to stay with you for long?"

"I certainly hope not. Sorry, did I say that out loud?"

I grinned. "Yeah, you did."

She picked up her coffee cup and held it in her perfectly manicured hands. "It's no secret my stepson and I don't get on, although I do try, Gemma. His mother died several years before I met his father, so it's not that I broke up their marriage. More that Daniel and his father didn't get on and he transferred that resentment to me. In all fairness, I tried to be neutral in their disputes, but I did generally agree with Ron, so Daniel has no reason to be overly fond of me."

"Any particular reason father and son didn't get on, as you put it? If you don't mind my asking?" Yes, that was an intensely personal question to ask of someone I had nothing more than a nodding aquantance with, but Rebecca had opened the door to a discussion about her family relationships, and once the door was thrown open, I had no qualms about walking through it.

I never mind asking intensely personal questions, but I have recently been made aware (thank you, Jayne) people don't always appreciate my interest.

"I don't mind," Rebecca said. "Daniel is Ron's only child. Men have expectations of their sons. Wealthy, self-made men in particular expect sons to follow in their footsteps. Daniel wanted to do his own thing. I agree with that, in general terms. Young people need to find their way in life, and parents shouldn't expect anything different. But, Daniel . . . Let's just say Daniel took going his own way to extremes. He failed to realize the most important thing of all about being independent."

"Which is?"

"You have to pay for it and be willing to take responsibility for it. Daniel didn't agree. Doesn't agree. He expected his father to continue being the bank of Dad well into his thirties. At first, Ron offered him financial help. Daniel got a lackluster degree in art history, but he didn't want to continue with that to get the higher degree he'd need to secure a position at an art museum or a teaching job. Instead he decided to go to culinary school in Italy. Ron paid for it, although it cost a great deal more than if he'd been educated in America. Ron and I married around the time Daniel returned from Italy. Ron found out Daniel hadn't finished the course, although he neglected to tell his dad. Instead of studying and working, he spent a full year enjoying the bohemian lifestyle in various cities around the Mediterranean, using the funds Ron thought were going to his education and work experience. When Ron confronted Daniel, he said the school had nothing to teach him. He then decided to go into fashion and moved to Los Angeles on a whim. He flitted between a couple of short internships—unpaid of course—at fashion houses before deciding he'd learned all he needed to know. He then asked his dad for more money to pursue his idea of having his own men's leisure-wear company. Setting up a business, with little background and virtually no experience, as you probably know, Gemma, is a hugely expensive proposition. Not to mention, doomed to fail. At last, Ron said no, wisely in my opinion. Daniel never had a lick of business sense; he couldn't stick out one of the best culinary schools in Europe; he couldn't be bothered to put in the time to learn the ropes from the ground up at a clothing business." Rebecca's eyes filled with tears, and she looked out the window. The drapes were open, and the outside lights illuminated the expansive lawn running down to the sea and the edges of the thick grove of trees lining the property to the south. In the far distance, a cruise ship lit up the dark sky. "Daniel accused me of influencing his father against him. Of wanting to keep Ron's money to myself. Of hoping his father would die soon so I could have it all." She dug in her pocket for a tissue. "Ron was a good deal older than me, but we were happy together. The situation with Daniel was never easy. For years, despite his better instincts, Ron continued giving him money. He always hoped the boy would finally find something he could stick with. But every venture was yet another failure. Finally, Ron put his foot down. He told Daniel he'd help him settle back in Massachusetts and get an entry-level job in his company. Otherwise, if he wanted to stay in California, he'd have to manage on his own. I wasn't party to that conversation, Gemma, but

Daniel said things that upset his father very much. I've no doubt Ron said things in return, things which could not be unsaid. They never, to the best of my knowledge, spoke again. Ron died less than six months later, very suddenly. He'd changed his will after that last argument, leaving everything to me. Not a penny to his only son. Daniel didn't come to the funeral." She dabbed at her eyes. "It was all so sad, and so unnecessary."

"But he's here now, visiting you?"

"He emailed me a couple of months ago, suggesting we let bygones be bygones. I was pleased to make contact, for Ron's sake. Then, a couple of weeks ago, he said he and his wife would be coming to the East Coast on a business trip, and they'd like to pay me a visit. I said they were very welcome, and they were. Initially. But now I fear he's only extended the olive branch because he needs money. He and Eleanor run the clothing business and, from what I can see, it's struggling. To put it mildly. Nevertheless, they have plenty of grand ideas for expanding across California. All they need, of course, is financing. I've seen no evidence of this business trip that supposedly brought them east, so I suspect the entire purpose of the visit was to come here. To ask me for money."

"Are you going to give him what he wants?"

"I don't know, Gemma. Ron didn't trust his son's business sense, and Ron was highly astute. On the other hand, Daniel now has Eleanor, and I like her. She's rather vague about her work history, but she does have some good ideas about things such as advertising and establishing an internet presence for their company."

"How long have they been married?"

"A little over a year. I didn't even know Daniel had married until that email. Do you know what an influencer is?"

"Someone whom large numbers of people follow on social media because they supposedly like or admire that person, so they buy things that person buys. A rather nebulous status."

"Eleanor claims to be an influencer in the world of contemporary West Coast fashion."

I nodded but didn't say anything. I'd come across nothing of the sort when I checked up on the couple, but a good many people want to be thought of as "influencers," even though their social media reach doesn't extend much beyond their mum and her bridge club.

"How's your tea?" Rebecca asked.

"My tea? It's fine."

"You're not drinking it. Is it too strong?"

"It is most definitely not too strong. It's late. I sometimes have trouble sleeping if I have tea near bedtime."

She picked up her coffee cup again. "Not me. Caffeine addict, day or night."

"Have you decided if you're going to help Daniel with this project?"

"That, Gemma, is my dilemma. If they'd asked me for a couple of thousand, I would give it to them, and happily, as a way of trying to repair bridges with my only stepchild. But they want me to finance an entire year of operation and expansion. Not only is that far beyond my means . . . I know I'm more than well off compared to most people, but my funds are not unlimited, and I am only in my fifties, with the intention of living a good deal longer."

"Glad to hear it," I said.

She gave me a smile. "Ron would tell me the amount Daniel's asking for means he doesn't plan to invest anything of his own, or even stick his neck out and ask for a bank loan. On the other hand, Daniel didn't inherit anything from his father. His mother would have wanted him to get something."

"Is that Daniel talking or you?" I asked.

She blinked. "An astute observation, Gemma. At one time, Daniel would have come right out and said it. This time, he managed to plant the idea in my head so I thought it was mine."

I'd come here tonight intending to ask Rebecca what she knew about the people who'd been at the séance, and thus if she could think of a reason one of them would kill Iris Laval. Instead, she seemed to need to talk about her family. I was fine with that. Everyone needs a sounding board sometimes, to help them come to the decision they've already made but don't yet know they've made.

"How does Daniel get on with Miranda? Any resentment on his part that she might inherit from you?"

"At first, Daniel was borderline hostile to her, but Eleanor, having more common sense, has gone some way to being friendly. When Daniel realized that not only is my niece living above the garage in the former servant's quarters, she's working for barely more than minimum wage as a waitress, he decided he could be friendly too. There's a big age difference between them, so I wouldn't expect them to become genuine pals or anything. Poor Miranda's still in mourning for her mother. It's been hard for her. As an aside, immediately after Ron's death, I rewrote my own will, giving Daniel a substantial part of the estate, along with bequests for Miranda and my other nieces and nephews. But, as I said, I intend to live a good, long life."

"Are you aware of the details of your sister's death?"

"Why do you ask that?"

"The driver of the other car was charged, but charges were dropped. Or so I heard."

"Yes. I know. Miranda's father was angry about that, but the police said they didn't have enough evidence to proceed."

I thought back to Saturday night. Max had introduced me to himself and Larissa without mentioning a surname, and it's entirely possible they did the same with Rebecca. Thus, she might have been unaware that Max Greenwood had, carelessly or not, killed her sister. Plenty of men named Max in the world. Miranda saw the couple earlier in the tearoom, but she might not have wanted to talk about it with her aunt, or she didn't get the opportunity.

I studied Rebecca's face as I asked the next question. "How did Larissa and her husband—what's his name again?—arrange to come on Saturday? Are they friends of yours?"

"He's called Max, I think. I'd never met either of them before they knocked on my door, and I scarcely spoke to them after that. They seemed very much on edge, which I thought was natural enough, considering why we were all gathered here. Bunny told me earlier a couple of additional people had been invited to make up the optimum numbers. I didn't mind. It wasn't intended to be a private affair."

I debated whether or not to tell Rebecca about Max's involvement in her sister's death, but I decided to hold my tongue. For now. If the information seemed pertinent, then I would reconsider.

The silence stretched out. Through the glass doors leading into the garden I could hear the soft murmur of the sea as waves crashed against the rocks. The house was set far back from the road, so the sounds of the night's traffic didn't reach us.

Rebecca stifled a yawn, and I remembered why I'd come. "Were you acquainted with Iris Laval before Saturday?" I asked.

"No. The police asked me, and I could honestly say I'd never seen the woman until I opened the door to her and her assistant that evening. Bunny set everything up. Dear Bunny. So like her to put B before A and then need help getting to C. She called me in a total panic, saying she'd arranged a gathering and then realized she didn't have any place to hold it." Rebecca smiled at the memory. "She didn't want to pay for a meeting room in a hotel, and she has no room in her small apartment to fit everyone around a table. Never mind that she doesn't have much in the way of a table. Naturally, I said of course they could come here."

Rebecca put down her empty cup and looked directly into my face. "I find you easy to talk to, Gemma, although I'm not entirely sure why. Maybe that soft English accent makes me believe I'm a character in a historical novel, taking tea in a grand manor house after a tour of the gardens. Or perhaps you have a kind face."

I smiled kindly at her. No one's ever said that to me before. Maybe people confide in me because they think I'm, unlike most people, prepared to listen to them. Often they confide in me because they think I know already. And then I know what I didn't know before, because they told me.

"I had no hesitation in offering my home for a séance because the minute Bunny mentioned it, I had this crazy, wild idea."

"To ask Ron for his advice on what to do about Daniel's request."

"Exactly! You don't think it's totally crazy do you? I mean, you came too, right?"

Rebecca had decided what to do about Daniel's request for money, although she hadn't known it yet. She was going to turn him down flat. She knew what her late husband would have done—indeed, what he'd done before—but she wanted to hear him say it. No doubt if it had come to Rebecca's turn to ask a question of the medium, Madame Lavalier would have replied in a deep, rolling male voice, "You know what I think of that idea." Then Rebecca would have been comfortable doing what she'd previously decided to do.

It would have been interesting to hear Daniel's reaction.

But the question hadn't been asked, and it hadn't been answered. Had Daniel killed Madame Lavalier to stop her from pretending to contact his father?

I couldn't see it. The medium's response would have been so vague Daniel could argue that Ron Stanton had said whatever Daniel wanted Rebecca to believe the ghostly presence had said. Unless Daniel himself was a true believer, although I hadn't been given the impression he was.

"How did Daniel come to be at the séance?" I asked. "Do you suppose he also wanted to contact someone?"

"In the cold light of day, or rather, of a warm evening sitting here with you, I know how ridiculous it all was. Daniel is many things, but he's not a total fool. When I told him and Eleanor about it, he scoffed at the very idea and said no thanks, he had better things to do with his evening. But Eleanor overrode his objections. She was enthusiastic immediately. She told me she's been to séances before, and on more than one occasion, she spoke to her late grandmother. Before agreeing to marry Daniel, or so she said, she asked her grandmother, and that lady told her to go ahead." Rebecca's face crunched up in thought. "I'm not entirely sure if Eleanor was joking or not. Anyway, she talked Daniel into attending, and he begrudgingly agreed. Even without what happened that night, things are getting awkward here, Gemma. If they don't indicate they're leaving soon, I'm considering telling them I'm going to

Boston for an extended visit with Amy's husband. Do you think they'll get the hint?"

"Probably not. Speak of the devil." At that moment, the front door opened and footsteps and voices sounded in the hall.

Rebecca gave me a rueful look and put her fingers to her lips. I gave her a wink and did the same in return. *Our secret.*

"There's a car in the driveway. Do you have company, Rebecca?" Daniel and Eleanor came into the living room. "Oh. Hi."

"Hello," I said.

"Did you have a nice dinner?" Rebecca asked politely.

"Yes, we did. Thanks for the recommendation," Eleanor replied, equally politely.

"Nothing special," Daniel said. "More expensive than we were expecting."

"Cape Cod isn't cheap," I said.

"No place is, not these days," Daniel muttered. "I'm getting myself a beer." He headed for the kitchen without asking if anyone wanted anything.

Eleanor gave me an embarrassed smile before kicking off her shoes, dropping herself onto the couch, and curling her legs underneath her.

"Is this your first visit to Cape Cod?" I asked.

"Yes. And I'm loving it. Everything's so beautiful. And this gorgeous house. Rebecca's been so dreadfully kind to let us enjoy it."

"She should." Daniel returned, carrying a bottle of beer. "It's my father's house."

"Did you grow up here?" I asked him innocently.

"We lived in Boston when my mother was alive. He only moved here permanently when he met . . . her."

Rebecca shifted uncomfortably. Daniel was in a combative mood tonight. Not a good way to win Rebecca to his side and get the money he needed, but perhaps he realized he'd already lost.

"It's too bad what happened the other night," Eleanor said, helpfully bringing up what I wanted to talk about. "You didn't know the dead woman well, did you?"

"I'd never met her before," I said. "Do you go to a lot of séances?"

She waved her right arm at me, and the rings on her fingers caught the light. "Oh, yes. I totally believe in it. Those who have passed have so much knowledge to extend to us, if only we'd open our minds to listen. But then . . ." Darkness crept into her eyes, the smile faded, and she ducked her head. "I don't know what happened. It . . . shouldn't have been like that. Maybe the storm brought out forces that . . . should never have been summoned."

Daniel laughed. "What utter nonsense."

"Don't mock what you don't believe," Eleanor snapped. She looked genuinely angry.

"I'm not mocking anything. I'm saying, just because the cops haven't caught whoever killed that woman, doesn't mean someone crept out from their grave to do it. My money's on that assistant; she was a mighty creepy one, bowing and scraping like the butler in one of your stupid TV shows. I don't know why the police keep badgering us about it."

"They're not badgering anyone," Rebecca said. "They're simply asking questions. As is their job."

"Whatever. I told the both of you having a séance was a stupid idea. But would either of you listen? No. You never do. Either of you. I'm going to watch some TV for a while."

He left without wishing us a good night.

"Never mind him," Eleanor said with a dismissive wave of her ring-encrusted fingers. "He's just grumpy because I ordered a more expensive bottle of wine than he wanted. We're on holiday, I told him. We should be able to kick back and enjoy ourselves." She snuck a peek at Rebecca, who made no reply. "We're so lucky to be able to stay here, in this lovely house, and not have to fork out for a hotel, so we can afford a nice bottle of wine now and again." She swung her bare feet to the floor. The nails were painted a deep purple. "The police finally packed up their things and gave us the house back. I mean, gave Rebecca the house back. Let me show you the library with the lights on, Gemma. The chandelier was covered the other night. It's fabulous. One of a kind, made by this really famous guy. Dale Ch . . . Ch . . ."

"Chihuly," Rebecca said.

"I saw it on a previous occasion," I said. "I agree it's a stunning piece."

"I love that whole room. The library, I mean. It's exactly like something you'd see in a real European castle. You're English, right, Gemma? I adore your accent. Did you have a library like that in your house?"

We had, but I didn't want to feed into the stereotype of all English people living in castles and being related to the king, although my mother's side of the family is minor aristocracy. Minor and dirt-poor to boot.

"The fireplace is super cool," Eleanor said. "Maybe we can come for a visit again over the winter when we can have a real blazing fire. We don't get to do that in Southern California. I particularly love that solid old mantlepiece and the way it feels beneath my fingers. The wood is so strong, yet warm and soft. You can almost feel the ancient forest vibes coming up through it." She clapped her hands in delight. "I can't wait to see firelight reflected on it."

Pointedly, Rebecca pretended not to hear Eleanor's suggestion of another visit. "It's getting late, Gemma. I'm sure you need to be on your way." She stood up.

I took the hint and also stood.

Eleanor waved to me from the couch. "Nighty night."

Rebecca walked me to the door. "I'm sorry about Daniel. Sometimes he's not very polite."

"You mean he's a jerk. No need for you to apologize."

"I'm surprised he didn't present me with the bill for dinner. As for Eleanor, she seems wired tonight. She's not usually so chatty."

I laughed. "At least one of them had a good evening."

Chapter Fourteen

A s long as I had my investigator's hat on . . .
The police say most cases need to be solved quickly, or
they're never solved. People leave town, overlooked (but vital)
evidence is disturbed, memories fade. Other matters take
priority.

The Greenwoods would soon be leaving West London, if
they hadn't already. I didn't have phone numbers for them, and
I didn't know where they were staying.

Ryan would have that information, but it fell under those
pesky details about which he took confidentiality seriously.

The one thing I did know about them was that they'd docked
their boat at the Cape Cod Yacht Club, which just happens to be
not far at all. It was shortly after nine, not too late to try and
hunt them down.

I drove north on Harbor Road, and shortly before leaving
the boundaries of West London, I arrived at the entrance to the
club. I'd been here before, once with Jayne to meet with the
events coordinator to make arrangements for her wedding reception, and earlier in pursuit of a "case." The most recent visit
resulted in a successful meeting at which Jayne and I left confident the club was the perfect place to host her important day. At

the conclusion of the earlier incident, if it had been up to Louise Estrada, I'd have been arrested for stealing a boat, kidnapping the pilot, and imitating a police officer. Fortunately, calmer heads prevailed and, considering I had successfully apprehended the guilty party, my minor indiscretions were overlooked. It was after nine o'clock, but it was July, and the place was busy. I parked among a collection of expensive vehicles, both flashy and subdued, climbed the steps, and strolled into the building as though I belonged here. I could hear a band playing in one of the banquet rooms and the sounds of people having a good time. A wedding, most likely, judging by the dresses and shoes worn by a group of women I passed on my way in, already digging in their tiny, bejeweled evening bags for cigarettes and lighters.

The lobby bar was full, as was the spacious veranda on the far side of a wall of glass looking out over the sea. I approached the young man, nicely dressed in a white shirt and a blue blazer displaying the club's logo, standing behind the reception desk with a broad smile on his handsome face.

"Good evening." I raised my voice an octave and increased the strength of my accent. "So sorry to bother you. I'm looking for a guest here, but. . ." I gave an embarrassed giggle. "I seem to have lost her phone number."

He flashed a row of blindingly white teeth at me. "How do you think I can be of help, Madam?"

"Her name's Larissa Greenwood. She and her husband Max have docked their boat here. I mean, that's what she told me, anyway." I fluttered my eyelashes and giggled once more. "They're from Boston. Their boat's from Boston. They're not. I mean, they are now, but not originally."

"I can't give out personal information on our members or guests. I'm sure you understand."

I pouted prettily, or at least I hoped it was a pretty pout. "Of course, of course." I leaned over the desk. Instinctively, he leaned toward me. "Could you check and see if their boat's still docked here? I can't remember if Larissa told me they were leaving today or tomorrow, and I'd love to catch up with her, if possible."

He gave me a wink. "That should be okay." He turned to the computer next to him and clicked keys. Unfortunately, I couldn't see the monitor, not without clambering over the reception desk and peering over his shoulder. He might think that a mite odd. Then again, the English do have a reputation of being eccentric.

If necessary, I could break into the business office, no doubt closed at this time of night, and hack into the computer, but I hoped it wouldn't come to that.

"*The Louisiana Lady*, registered to Maxwell Greenwood, is here. Berth 207. Booked in until tomorrow."

I clapped my hands in delight. "Thank you so much. I'll pop out and have a quick peek. I might catch them having drinkies on the boat deck."

"You can't go there, Madam."

"I can't?" I said, as if I didn't know.

"The gates to the berths are locked. Members and guests only."

"It'll be okay. I'm a guest of Mr. and Mrs. Greenwood."

"Sorry. No." He sounded like he meant it, which was just as well since I didn't expect to find the couple on their boat at this time of night.

"I understand. Can you phone them and let them know I'm here?"

He hesitated. I smiled and stood my ground.

"I suppose I can do that." He reached for the desk phone and, keeping his eyes on the computer screen, punched buttons. I followed the movement of his fingers and mentally recorded the number. He didn't bother to let it ring more than twice before hanging up. "Sorry, no answer." He looked past me. "Yes, sir, Mr. McNamara, how can I help you?"

"Evening, Reggie. I can't find the sign-up sheet for the children's regatta. Do you know what happened to it?"

"Thank you for your time," I trilled as I walked away. I had the Greenwoods' phone number, but I decided to have a quick glance in the bar and restaurant before calling them.

"Good evening," the young woman behind the hostess stand said to me. "Are you meeting someone?"

Noticeably, she didn't ask if I wanted a table for myself.

"Yes, I am. Do you mind if I have a quick peek? I'm so dreadfully late—car problems—I'm afraid my friends might have given up on me." I gave another embarrassed giggle. I didn't bother waiting for her reply and stepped through the doors onto the veranda.

Most of the tables were taken. The people were generally older, gray hair and glasses, plenty of jewelry and pastel colors, and what passes among the yachting set as nautical attire. Candlelight reflected off silver cutlery and crystal glasses, and black-clad waitstaff hurried past with laden plates or empty dishes. Candles in hurricane vases sat on every table, sparkling in the night. Combined with the tiny white lights wrapped around the wide white veranda pillars, they gave the place a fairy-tale atmosphere.

Fortune, as teenage Bunny's fortune teller had said, favors the brave, and my luck was in tonight. I spotted my quarry almost immediately. Max and Larissa were seated at a table for four against the railing. Golf club–quality grass and immaculate flower beds extended down the gentle slope to paths lining the water. Yellow light glowed from tall lampposts. A locked gate led to rows of piers at which boats of all sizes and types were tied up, bobbing gently in the protected waters of the harbor, thrusting tall masts and furled sails into the night sky.

Larissa sipped from a small coffee cup while Max scraped up the last of his dessert.

"Hi," I said.

They both looked up. They smiled. "Good evening," Max said. "Gemma, right? You were at Rebecca Stanton's the other night."

"Are you a member here?" Larissa asked me.

Uninvited, I sat down. I didn't answer her question either.

They exchanged glances and then turned back to me with stiffening smiles. I can usually count on the general politeness of strangers to give me the opening I need to stick my nose into what might be considered other peoples' business.

"Terrible what happened at Rebecca's, wasn't it?" I said.

"Horrible," Larissa said.

"It was." Max pushed his plate aside. "Ready to go, dear?"

"What?" Larissa blinked in confusion. "You haven't had your brandy."

"Don't feel like it after all."

"Brandy, sir." The waiter placed a glass bowl big enough to float a bouquet of roses onto the table. It contained a generous amount of amber liquid. "And a Drambuie for the lady." A smaller glass was put in front of Larissa. He turned to me. "Can I get you anything, Madam?"

"A cappuccino would be nice, thanks."

Once he'd left, I said to my companions, "Good service here."

"It's a wonderful spot," Larissa said. "Our dinner was excellent. Do you come here often?"

"Not as often as I might like. Busy with my business interests, you know how it is."

"We do," Larissa said. "We don't often get a nice break such as this one. It has been nice, hasn't it, dear? Despite . . . everything." Her smile faded, and a darkness moved in behind her eyes.

Max took a hefty slug of his brandy. Larissa sipped at her own drink. I decided to get straight to the point. If they didn't want to talk to me, so be it. "What brought you to the séance the other night?"

"Mild curiosity," Max snapped.

Larissa stretched a hand across the table. "It's all right, dear. Gemma was there too, although, as I recall, she was asked to leave." She studied my face. "Too skeptical perhaps?"

"Or one too many for the table, but your choice of words is correct. Skeptical barely covers it. I'm not convinced, one way or another, about the existence of the supernatural, but I do believe plenty of people are ready to take advantage of other people's grief."

"You think Madame Lavalier was such a person?" Larissa said.

"I do."

"Do you think that's why she died?"

"The woman had a heart attack," Max said. "Small-town cops are making something out of nothing. Gives them something to do, makes them seem important. I'm sorry, Gemma,

151

but my wife and I do not want to talk about it." He drained his glass.

"One cappuccino." The waiter placed a foam-topped, wide-brimmed cup in front of me. A small biscuit rested on the saucer beneath it. "Can I get you another brandy, sir?"

"No!" Max said. "Nothing more. We'll have the bill, please."

"Pardon my husband," Larissa said. "We've recently had a great loss, and sometimes . . ."

"I'm sorry." I pushed my cup aside. Out of nowhere, I felt bad. These people were still grieving the death of their son, and I'd allowed my own curiously to intrude.

"Can't say I was at all sorry to see her go," Max said. "The woman got what was coming to her, whether someone did her in or not." He stood up. "Settle the bill, Larissa. I'll meet you at the car."

As she watched him walk away, her eyes filled with tears.

"I am sorry. I shouldn't have intruded," I said.

"It's fine. Max and I told the police we'd never seen Madame Lavalier before. That was true, but . . ."

"But not the whole story?"

"No. We'd never met her, but we knew of her. Max told the police we attended the silly séance out of mild curiosity. Once he'd done that, I couldn't very well tell them differently, could I?"

"Are you saying you know things you should have told the police but didn't?"

"I fear I am. We shouldn't have gone, but Max wanted to, and I went along with it. After what happened at the séance, we decided to leave first thing Sunday morning, but there was a problem with the boat engine and we couldn't get it seen to until this afternoon. I told Max we need to tell the police what we know, and he said he will if they ask again. But they haven't called on us."

"You know that's not an excuse. They won't like it if they find out you're withholding information."

"I know."

"If you know something, even if it doesn't seem important to you, it might help them find whoever did kill her."

"I know that too." She sighed deeply and straightened her shoulders. She'd come to a decision. "The topic is very painful for us, and we had the classic excuse—we don't know what happened and we don't want to get involved. I'll tell Max I'm going to talk to the police. He can come with me or not."

"I think that's for the best," I said.

"She was a fraud, but you suspected that, didn't you?"

"Seeing as how I don't believe in mediums or contacting the deceased, I knew that, yes."

"Our family suffered a recent loss. Our youngest daughter, Laura, has had the hardest time of all of us dealing with it. She's a sensitive girl, always has been." Larissa smiled softly. "Comes from being the youngest in the family, probably. A school friend of Laura's got in touch with this medium, Madame Lavalier. Laura and her friend went to a séance without telling us anything about it. She went several times and came home increasingly distraught after each session, although she still didn't tell us where she'd been. I put her state of mind down to her trying, and failing, to process her grief. She'd been accepted at Columbia in the fall, but she simply stopped going to school and didn't graduate. Max said to give her time. Laura has a small amount of money, left to her by her grandmother to assist with her education. Quite by accident, Max discovered that money's rapidly depleting. We thought at first she'd been spending it on drugs.

She wasn't eating, going days without showering. Our older daughter, Tina, eventually broke her sister's confidence and told us Laura had been seeing a medium. This Madame Lavalier. We confronted her about it."

"A bad business."

"Far from comforting her, the sessions disturbed Laura even more. According to the medium, our son is unhappy where he is. He wanted Laura to keep making contact to help him feel better about his situation." Larissa sobbed gently. The well-mannered patrons at nearby tables pretended to be paying us no attention.

"That's not nice," I said, which was possibly the greatest understatement of my life.

"We finally managed to persuade Laura to stop seeing this *person* and to return to her therapist. I'm pleased to say, it seems to be going well. She's working hard to get caught up on her high school qualifications."

"Was Mary Moffat serving as the medium's assistant at those sessions?"

Larissa blinked. "I don't know who else, if anyone, was involved. We only knew the one name: Madame Lavalier."

"Did you follow Iris Laval, aka Madame Lavalier, here to West London?"

"Strangely enough, no, we didn't. All this with Laura happened over the spring. Max wanted to go to the police at the time, but I discouraged him. Laura would have had to press charges, perhaps testify that she'd been tricked. It would have embarrassed her and set her progress back. She hadn't even spent a great deal of money, not in the scheme of things. I hoped we'd all emerge the wiser for the experience and get past it. We did seem to be getting past it. What happened with Laura, I mean.

We'll never get past losing our son. Max and I decided to go on a little holiday, and we took the boat out for the first time in a long while. And what did we see the first day of our visit to West London but a flyer advertising the ridiculous psychic fair and none other than the so-called noted spiritualist Madame Lavalier." Larissa let out a long sigh. "I wanted to simply turn around and leave, go someplace else. But Max . . . For all Max is a level-headed businessman, he can get some crazy ideas in his head. Without me knowing it, when I was at the spa, he called the number on the flyer and arranged for us to attend one of her fake séances."

"Why?"

"Why attend? He planned to confront her during the séance. He persuaded me to pretend I wanted to speak to my grandfather about some money he'd hidden before his death. Which, incidentally, is something Max made up. Neither of my grandfathers had stashed away any secret treasure, as far as I know. When the medium pretended to have contacted the spirt of this grandfather I never had, Max's plan was that he would leap to his feet, denounce her in front of everyone, and thus ruin her reputation. Obviously that didn't happen."

"You're being very frank with me, Larissa, so I'll be frank with you on two points. You do realize what you've told me will give the police reason to believe you or your husband might have killed the woman?"

She dipped her head, but I could tell the idea didn't come as a surprise to her.

"They might conclude that's why Max didn't tell the police about your history with her."

"I realize they could make that assumption, but we had no intention of killing her! All we wanted was to reveal her for the charlatan she was. A great many other people likely also had reason to want revenge on her."

"That's why the police need all of this information. So they can put the puzzle together and get the full picture. You've withheld an important piece of the puzzle."

"I told you, Gemma. I'll talk to them."

"The other item: I assume you recognize the name Oberton."

Her eyes narrowed, and she studied my face. "You seem very well informed. Someone told me you own a bookstore. Is that true?"

"It is. You should visit before you leave town. The Sherlock Holmes Bookshop and Emporium. 222 Baker Street. Don't go to 221 by mistake. The owner of the establishment located at that address gets highly annoyed when she's mistaken for us."

"I'll keep that in mind." Larissa put her napkin on the table and folded it neatly. She picked up her purse. "My husband's waiting for me." She stood up and looked down at me. "Tragedy upon tragedy. It has not been an easy year for our family. Yes, I know the name. Not long after our son died, my husband and I were in a car accident. We were unharmed, although our car was written off. The other driver did not survive. It was late at night, a country road. Her headlights were on high when she came around a corner, and they disoriented Max. He swerved over the line and . . . Why do you ask about that?"

"We can never escape our past, try as we might. It would be better if you don't go to Mrs. Hudson's Tea Room again."

"I think I understand what you're saying. I thought the young waitress there, the one who also came to the séance, looked familiar, but I couldn't put my finger on it. I never met Mrs. Oberton, of course, but I've seen pictures of her. Her daughter—I assume that's who that young woman is—looks much like her. Rebecca Stanton, who hosted us that night, who is she?"

"Amy Oberton's sister."

She took a breath. "I'll be going now. No more questions, please."

I watched her walk away. My cappuccino had gone cold, but I nibbled on the little biscuit—absolutely melt-in-the-mouth.

The police weren't the only ones who would think Max Greenwood, maybe Larissa also, might have wanted revenge on Iris Laval. The question would then be: how far would they go to get that revenge?

That remained to be seen.

As for Miranda's mother, Larissa was surprised I knew about the car crash, and she said she recognized something about Miranda.

Had Max?

Did it matter?

Perhaps not. But it was all part of the puzzle.

I left the Cape Cod Yacht Club with plenty to think about.

Chapter Fifteen

When I got home, I let Violet and Peony out, made myself a cup of tea, called for the dogs to come in, took a seat in the den, and continued thinking.

There could be no doubt Iris Laval had been killed by one of the people who'd gathered in Rebecca Stanton's library on Saturday night for a supposed séance.

I considered it highly unlikely the medium had been killed by mistake and that someone else had been the intended target, but the possibility had to be considered. Someone who planned to commit murder, if they weren't experienced in such matters, would be very much on edge. Mistakes did happen.

As for Iris herself, Max, and perhaps even Larissa, might indeed have come to the séance intending to expose the medium, but was it possible that the sight of her getting ready to fleece other unsuspecting people pushed one of them over the edge. And so they killed her?

Possible. But, again, unlikely. That hat pin had to have been brought into the room with the specific intention of using it.

Eleanor Stanton claimed to have been to many séances and to be a believer in their legitimacy, but her husband, Daniel, was skeptical about the whole thing. Despite his skepticism, had he accompanied her on other occasions?

Might they have attended previous séances with Iris Laval and, like the Greenwoods, be out for revenge because they believed they'd been cheated? They told Ryan they'd never met the medium before, but people don't always tell the police the truth, particularly if they're covering up a crime.

I hadn't thought to ask Rebecca specifically when the couple announced their intention to visit. Was it before or after the psychic fair dates were publicized?

I reached for my phone. Violet woke with a start, leaped to her feet, and barked. Only then did I realize the time. It had gone two. Perhaps too late to be calling anyone. The timing of the visit likely didn't matter. Had Eleanor and Daniel, like the Greenwoods, accidentally stumbled on the person they were after?

I settled back against the cushions and listened to the silence of the night. Violet watched me. Next to her, Peony whined in his sleep. I wondered what he was dreaming about.

Rebecca and her niece Miranda might have had reason to kill Max Greenwood. They knew Max caused the accident that killed Rebecca's sister and Miranda's mother, although the Greenwoods didn't recognize them in return.

Except Max and Larissa hadn't died, which brought me back to wondering if there'd been a mistake.

If I accepted, and I did, that my friends hadn't committed the murder, the only other possibility was Mary Moffat, the so-called assistant. She told me she and Iris hadn't been working together for long, but was that true? Maybe they had a long and sordid history of committing fraud together.

But surely, if Mary did want to get rid of her inconvenient partner, she had plenty of better opportunities to do so without drawing so much attention to herself.

Violet scratched lightly at my leg. As long as I was awake, she seemed to be saying, I might as well offer her a treat.

I reached down and gave her a scratch between the ears. She wiggled happily at the attention.

I jerked upright. *Drawing attention was the entire point.*

The mysterious death of Iris Laval, aka Madame Lavalier, noted medium, at a séance no less, had attracted a lot of attention. Attendance at the psychic fair had increased to the point the police had to be called to help with crowd control.

Did Mary Moffat plan to take advantage of the extra attention to find another medium to work with? Maybe she'd assume that role herself, helped by her newfound fame. She might even be able to claim that the ghost of Madame Lavalier was her new spiritual partner.

The fair had moved on to another town. Had Mary gone with them? I opened my iPad and searched for information about the psychic fair.

* * *

"How's Bunny?" I asked Ashleigh when she arrived for work on Tuesday morning.

My assistant gave me a sideways glance. "Fine. Why are you asking?"

"No reason. Okay, maybe I have a reason. Is Mary Moffat still hanging around bothering her?"

"No, and I'm glad of it. Mary went to Sandwich with the fair. She asked Bunny to come with her, having some notion of them setting up a booth and selling Bunny memorabilia. Bunny told her what tokens she kept from her youth and her career are not for sale. Mary said okay, and then she started again on her idea of them gathering together an exhibit for us to display here, at the store. Bunny eventually hung up on her."

"A difficult situation."

"For sure. Everyone thinks it would be so great to be famous, but it's not really. Don't tell her I said this, Gemma, but all this attention from her fans only reminds Bunny that she's getting old and she's past it. Some people even come right out and tell her they expected her to look younger. I suppose the fame thing's manageable if you have a house with a big gate and security guards and bodyguards when you go out and the like, but Bunny, my mom, doesn't have any of that. Not anymore."

"She has you," I said.

She smiled at me. "I hope that's enough." Ashleigh looked as though she were about to set out for a cruise on her own yacht this morning in white trousers, white T-shirt, and blue blazer decorated with miles of gold trim. Blue-and-white espadrilles were on her feet and a jaunty captain's cap perched on her head. "After Bunny hung up on her, Mary sent a bunch of texts, mostly saying she was just throwing ideas out there, and if Bunny didn't like them, what would she suggest they do together? Bunny didn't reply, and last night she got a text saying Mary was going to Sandwich for a few days, in case Bunny changed her mind and wanted to come after all."

"Do you know if Gale has anything on today?"

"Why would I know that? She's not due to come into work."

"I'm wondering if she mentioned anything. I need to go out this afternoon for several hours. I'll ask her if she can fill in at the last minute."

I ran upstairs, closely followed by Moriarty. I'm sure he didn't deliberately intend to slip between my feet at the top of the stairs, causing me to trip, so I only saved myself by grabbing the banister with both hands before I plunged the full seventeen steps to my doom.

When my heart stopped pounding and my breathing returned to normal, I called Ryan. I've learned it's not a good idea to call him in the middle of the night when I've had a sudden idea for a direction his inquiries should take, so I'd forced myself to wait until this morning.

"You might want to interview the Greenwoods again," I said after we'd exchanged pleasantries.

"For once, I'm ahead of you, Gemma. Mrs. Greenwood called the station first thing this morning and made an appointment to come in. I'm expecting them any minute. Shall I assume you're responsible for that?"

"I just happened to run into them last night having dinner at the yacht club."

"Because you're a member there. Not."

"Coincidences do happen, but it helps if one arranges them. Yes, we had a chat. Mostly Larissa and I chatted. They didn't lie to you, but they might have not been telling you everything they know, and I told her that was never wise."

"However it came about, thanks. What have you got on today?"

"Nothing special." I crossed my fingers behind my back. Moriarty growled at me.

"Try and keep it that way," Ryan said. That he didn't leave me with a more affectionate sign-off meant someone was listening.

"Love you," I said to the empty air.

Moriarty thought I was speaking to him. He narrowed his eyes and hissed in response.

My next call was to Jayne. "Feel like taking a few hours off today? We can play tourist. Maybe go for a nice drive, see the scenery."

"Why would I want to do that?"

"You've been working so hard. I thought you'd enjoy the break."

"You mean you're doing something you shouldn't and you need someone to act as your wingwoman."

"If you want to put it like that."

"I hate to imagine what trouble you'd get into without me. As it happens, I got a lot of baking done yesterday and today's Tuesday, which is usually our slowest day of the week. I should be able to manage a couple of hours this afternoon."

"Excellent. Be at my house at one."

* * *

Gale was able to come in with little notice, and I left the Emporium at noon. The dogs were overjoyed to see me home in the middle of the day, but their joy was short-lived when I told them I wasn't here to play. I went into the guest room and rummaged through dressers and closets in search of what I needed. I spent a good deal more time in front of the mirror than normal until I was satisfied with my appearance.

Precisely at one o'clock, the dogs set up a chorus of barks, informing me Jayne had arrived.

I opened the mudroom door. "Come on in."

She paused with one foot in the air. She stared at me open-mouthed. She cocked her head to one side, and then to the other. She put her foot down. "I've met your mother, so I know you're not her. Have I fallen through a warp in the space time continuum or something? And what on earth is that on your head?"

"As you may have suspected, I have a destination in mind for our little outing, and I'd prefer not to be recognized."

"It's uncanny," Jayne said. "You look like you, Gemma, although a good twenty years older."

"Glad to hear it." I'd applied makeup to deepen the circles under my eyes, rubbed in a touch of putty to create lines around my mouth and wrinkles on my neck, and added more makeup to accent them. I'd topped the whole thing off with a wig in an unappealing shade of reddish brown straight from a bottle of drugstore hair dye. I tied some padding around my rear end and then pulled on a pair of slightly baggy Bermuda shorts and an ill-fitting pink golf shirt. The entire effect was topped off with gold hoops through my ears and a tiny fake diamond necklace on a chain. I also wore a plain gold band on the third finger of my left hand.

"Come into the guest room," I said. "I've laid out some things for you to wear."

Jayne looked down at herself. "What's wrong with this?" She wore her usual work clothes of black yoga pants, loose-fitting sleeveless T-shirt, and well-worn trainers. Her blond hair was pulled up behind her head in a bouncy ponytail. Her blue eyes sparked with good humor and youth.

That would never do.

She gave her head a shake and followed me into the house. I'd laid out an arrangement of clothes on the bed for Jayne to try on. Not clothes from my regular wardrobe, but things I kept in case they might be needed one day. "Try that skirt and jacket first."

She put her hands on her hips. "Not until you tell me what's going on. I don't like to be rude, Gemma." Her expression indicated she didn't mind at all. "But I am, in case you haven't noticed, quite a bit thinner than you, not to mention shorter. Your clothes won't fit me."

"Which, considering you bake for a living and I do not, proves once and for all that life is not fair. Don't worry about things not fitting properly. I have some padded undergarments that will do the trick." I held up a one-piece bra and pants set stuffed with additional layers of fabric.

"I am not wearing padded undergarments, Gemma."

"No one will recognize you. Which is rather the point of the exercise. Try them on, please, and I'll explain."

"Oh, for heaven's sake," she grumbled.

"We're going to Sandwich in search of a medium."

"I'm not going to another séance," Jayne said as she struggled into the clothes.

"Nor am I. I want to find out what Mary Moffat's up to, that's all. Meaning, I want you to find out what she's up to. My original plan was to present myself, in disguise, as someone needing a consultation. But I was signaled out at the séance, no doubt at her instigation, and then she and I had a nice long chat the other day in the Emporium. We talked one-on-one, so I'm not sure any disguise I can throw together in a hurry will fool her for long if we talk. Considering she's a fraud and a confidence trickster, she'll be on her guard."

"She met me at the séance."

"Yes, but you didn't converse with her at any time, and you were only one of the numbers. Plus, you didn't stay long. You were allowed to leave ahead of the rest of them."

165

I stepped back and studied my handiwork. "Yes, that will do. Your lack of height will be an advantage here. You were wearing heels at Rebecca's, so with those flats, you'll be a couple of inches shorter than you appeared then. Now, into the bathroom."

"Are you going to make me look like my mother?"

"You should be so lucky."

When I was finished, she studied herself in the mirror for a long time. "This is genuinely creepy, Gemma. It's me but . . . not me. Where on earth did you learn to do this? You never told me you had a background in theater."

"I have many and varied interests, of which doing makeup for theatrical productions is not one. My sister taught me."

"Pippa?"

"Like many young girls, and more than a few boys, I went through a rebellious phase. My parents moved me to a new school, and I was immediately, shall we say, not a favored student there. During the first term break, the headmistress invited my parents to drop by for a chat when school resumed. Pippa, who was home for a short visit from Oxford, where she was completing her doctorate in Russian literature—"

"Hold on a minute. Pippa has a PhD in Russian literature? In Russian?"

"Or course. One can't truly appreciate the nuances of the classics in translation. My own Russian, I am forced to admit, is poor. Little more than a handful of basic words I picked up from her."

"By which I assume you could walk into the Kremlin and convince them you belong. Never mind that. What about your school?"

"Pippa intercepted the letter. She decided the less contact my parents had with the headmistress the better. She would have gone in our mother's place herself, but she had an appointment that could not be missed, so she taught me how to present myself as my own parent. I've learned a few tricks from my sister over the years."

"And this headmistress fell for it?"

"At the time. Pippa either didn't think things through to their logical conclusion—which I don't believe for one minute—or she was having fun at my expense. Considering neither the headmistress nor my parents are idiots, when they eventually did meet, the game was, as they say, up."

"What happened then?"

"That's best forgotten. Fortunately, in the interval, I'd decided to buckle down to my studies, and I was doing reasonably well, so I was sternly reprimanded but not expelled. Shall we go?"

* * *

Two middle-aged, middle-class women, hoping to add some spice to their lives by attending a psychic fair, left my house.

Jayne wore a dress in swirls of orange and brown that came to slightly below her knees, topped by a tattered jean jacket (circa 1990). A jaunty orange scarf was tied around her neck and sturdy, flat sandals were on her feet. Her lovely blond hair was tucked under a wig formed into a chin-length bob dyed blond with numerous gray streaks. I'd done my best with the makeup to roughen her skin, and to take some of the natural color out of her lips and cheeks, and replace it with pale powder and blush.

"I feel absolutely ridiculous," she said.

"We'll take your car in case anyone sees us arriving. The Miata won't suit the image I want to project."

"Plenty of middle-aged women like sports cars," Jayne said.

"True, but Mary might have seen my car outside Rebecca's house."

"Does Ryan know about this?" she said as she backed out of the driveway onto Blue Water Place.

"We're not doing anything illegal, Jayne."

"Meaning, no, he does not. What are you hoping to prove, Gemma?"

"Mary Moffat's the only genuine suspect we have, unless other people have a history with Iris Laval we don't know about. I'm struggling to come up with a reason anyone else would have not only killed the woman but planned it ahead of time. The latter, I believe, is the most pertinent point. Why bring a concealed weapon to a gathering if you don't plan to use it?"

"I suppose I can buy that. How's this going to work?"

I would have outlined my plan, but that would mean I had a plan. I did not.

The day was clear and the sun bright, and traffic was light getting out of West London and continued to be so all the way down Route 6 to the town of Sandwich. I'd looked up the location of the fair and used the sat-nav on my phone to direct Jayne to the recreation center where the event was being held.

The parking lot was almost full. I had no way of knowing if that was normal for this place at this time of day, or if the psychic fair had attracted similar crowds as in West London.

Only one way to find out.

Jayne circled the lot until she found a place to park, and we got out of the car. She tugged awkwardly at the uncomfortable skirt and then reached for her hair.

"Don't touch that wig," I warned. "It might fall off."

Her hand jerked back.

We went into the hall. The entrance fee was a shocking ten dollars each, twice as much as in West London.

"Your shout," Jayne said, using an English expression she'd no doubt picked up during our visit to London. Meaning, I was expected to pay.

I did so.

The hall was crowded with booths and the aisles full of people checking everything out. Vendors beckoned browsers to investigate their wares; the air was full of the scent of incense sticks, fruity candles, and too many people gathered in an indoor space on a hot day. Jayne and I mingled with the browsers.

While Jayne pretended to admire a display of crystals, I said, "I'm looking forward to having my palm read," in a plummy Boston accent. "There seem to be several choices." I waved the program book we'd been handed when we (meaning I) paid in the direction of the booth owner. "Can you make any recommendations as to who might be best?"

She wore a swirling-multicolored dress. Her black hair, liberally streaked with gray, was tied into a long braid tossed over one shoulder. Silver rings adorned every finger, and rows of bracelets ran up her arms. "Everyone here's fully vetted and qualified." I didn't ask vetted and pronounced qualified by whom. "Personally, I've found Mrs. Varga to be excellent. She's recently arrived from Hungary and is a genuine Roma who had to flee her homeland to escape persecution. Her grandmother was renowned far and wide for her intelligence and insights into the human condition." She pointed, bangles clattering, vaguely to our right.

"Thanks," I said. "I'll talk to her. June, have you found any information about a séance yet? June?"

"What?" Jayne said. "Oh. Me. You're talking to me. I'm going to ask around, uh, Emma."

"You might not have much luck with that," A bearded and bespeckled man selling tarot cards called to us. "Finding a séance, I mean. The medium associated with this show tragically passed away a few days ago. I don't know that anyone's taken her place yet. Have you heard anything about that, Dottie?"

"There's been some interest, but I haven't heard anything specific. It's kinda a blow to the show, if you know what I mean," Dottie said. "A genuine medium is a powerful draw. If you take two bags of those crystals, honey, I can throw in one of the hanging arrangements at a twenty-five percent discount."

"I'll think about it," Jayne said. "We just got here, and I want to check everything out before I decide."

"Deal won't last much longer. I'm expecting a busy day."

We wandered off, making a show of scrupulously studying everything. "What now, Gemma?" Jayne whispered.

"I'm going to have my palm read. You keep asking about séances and try to get a bite. I'm hoping someone will contact Mary Moffat to say they have a mark. I mean, an interested client."

"What do I do then?"

"Meet with her and ask about having a séance, of course. See what she says in reply. Text me if you have any luck."

Jayne gave me The Look. Then she shrugged, shook her head, and set off on her journey. She wasn't able to restrain herself from giving her wig a solid tug.

I found Mrs. Varga with no trouble. Her booth was a rather rickety-looking structure constructed of tent poles. She'd strung scarves and pashminas from the frame, supposedly to give her clients some privacy. She was in her late fifties. Hair dyed a shocking shade of black, vampiric makeup, a slash of bloodred lipstick across her thin lips. She had no other customers, and I was soon seated on a small stool in the makeshift tent, having my palm read. I was pleased to hear I had a substantial amount of money coming my way, and my husband would soon recover from his recent indiscretion and come back to me. Apparently one of my children would be accepted into the college of her choice after all. Oh, and my own business would prosper and grow.

I clapped my hands in delight and thanked her profusely.

I hadn't had to say much to get all that information either. Just emit a sigh in the right place, a twisting of the ring on my left hand accompanied by a deep swallow, and a muffled sob at the mention of my twenty-five-year marriage. I also commented on how competitive Ivy League colleges are these days and how it can be hard to make a small business grow.

"Thank you so much," I said to Mrs. Varga, whose Hungarian accent was as fake as my Boston one. "I'm here with a friend, and I'll be sure and bring her over."

"Yes, yes. You do!"

I didn't even begrudge the money I'd paid. It had been as entertaining as any movie.

It was excessively warm in the hall, and I was considering going in search something cold to drink when my phone buzzed to tell me I had an incoming text.

Jayne: *Success! I'm meeting Mary in the refreshment area in ten minutes.*

Me: *Do not pay any money or commit to anything. If she offers you a séance, string her along and ask for the medium's qualifications (sic). I want to know if she's playing the medium or the assistant. Text me when you're finished.*

Jayne: *Bond, Jayne Bond, signing out.*

I put my phone away and continued browsing, showing an interest in everything. I wondered how many of the attendees were true believers and how many were simply out for a fun day to see what it was about. As I turned a corner between yet another crystal vendor and a booth offering spiritual healing (whatever that might be), none other than Mary Moffat herself cut in front of me. "Excuse me," I said. "So sorry." I needn't have bothered going to all the trouble of wearing a disguise. So intent was she on her mission, she didn't spare me a glance, and she paid no attention to anyone or anything else around her either. She almost shoved a couple of elderly ladies walking with the assistance of canes out of her way.

A woman on a mission. Very good indeed.

I decided to check out the bookseller while waiting for Jayne to complete her own mission and was heading in that direction when I stopped short at the sound of an angry voice.

"Not you again. Are you following me?" a man demanded.

"Not at all," said a very familiar voice. "I came to see if you took my recommendation and got in some of the books I was telling you about."

Donald Morris gestured toward the display racks. A somewhat garish collection of sci-fi and fantasy novels along with books on interpreting dreams, controlling astral travel, and reading tarot cards. "I don't see any."

"Books don't appear on shelves just because I want them to, you know," the other man said. "I have to put in orders, wait for delivery, and unpack the stock."

"I suggested you go to the Sherlock Holmes—"

"Bookstore in West London. Yeah, I heard you. More than once. I don't buy retail."

"There's a Sherlock Holmes bookstore in West London?" A third man said. "Where's West London?"

Donald turned to the new arrival with a smile. The bookseller groaned and threw up his hands. "Not more than forty minutes from here," Donald said. "Charming little town on the top of the peninsula between the ocean and Nantucket Sound, not far from Chatham. The shop is at 222 Baker Street—clever, isn't it?—and they stock anything and everything to do with the Great Detective and his esteemed creator. Are you a follower of Sir Arthur Conan Doyle?"

"I wouldn't say I'm a follower, but I always enjoy Holmes books and TV shows. My wife and I are visiting from Oregon. She's having her cards read." He lowered his voice. "I'm killing time. Just having a look around. What does Conan Doyle have to do with this stuff?"

"Sir Arthur intensely believed in spiritualism and spent much of his life in the study and promotion of acceptance of the phenomenon." Donald settled comfortably into lecture mode. "He participated in many séances, joined the search for fairies, took part in so-called spirit photography. A great many people of his time, particularly during and following the devastation of the Great War, were desperate to find meaning beyond death. Even when it could be proven he'd been the victim of a hoax, he didn't waver in his insistence on their validity. *The History of Spiritualism* is perhaps the definitive book by Sir Arthur on his beliefs." Donald led the man away from the bookseller's booth. The vendor watched them go. *If looks could kill.*

I followed, blending with the crowds swirling around us but keeping close enough to hear Donald discussing his idol and his best-known creation as well as singing the praises of my shop. Donald's enthusiasm can get carried to extremes sometimes, and he fails to notice that not everyone is as keen as he is. But this chap seemed genuinely interested, and they chatted for a few minutes until the man checked his watch and said he had to meet his wife. He promised to pay a visit to West London.

"Excellent scones at Mrs. Hudson's Tea Room, adjacent to the bookstore," Donald said. "If you want the full afternoon tea experience, you need to make a reservation."

"Thanks. My wife would love that." The man from Oregon walked away, leaving Donald looking highly pleased with himself.

I slipped up to him. "Pardon me. I couldn't help but over-hear. You were talking about Sherlock Holmes?"

"Yes!" Donald beamed at me. "Are you also interested in him, or in Sir Arthur, perhaps? Many Americans are not aware that Sir Arthur Conan Doyle was a prominent member of the early twentieth century spiritualism community and that he—"

"Got it, thanks," I said in my own voice.

He eyes narrowed. He leaned forward and peered into my face. "Gemma?"

"The one and only."

"What . . . I mean . . . what happened to you?"

"I'd tell you I had a ghostly encounter that aged me twenty years overnight, but that's not actually true, so I won't."

"You're undercover." His eyes widened in delight. He touched his finger to his lips and gave me a broad wink. "Your secret is safe with me, my dear."

"Glad to hear it. If we run into each other again, you don't know me."

Another wink.

My phone buzzed with a text.

Jayne: *Finished*

That was quick.

Me: *Meet me by the front doors*

"You're here with Jayne," Donald said. "Shall I ignore her too?"
"Yes, please."
He gave me another conspiratorial wink and a nod and walked away.

Jayne and I toured the parking lot while she filled me in on her meeting with Mary Moffat. "I did what you suggested and told people I was interested in organizing a séance for a group of friends. Several of them told me about Madame Lavalier's death, saying they didn't know what was happening now. Finally, I met someone who said her assistant might be able to put me in touch with a medium. She called Mary. Mary, obviously, wasn't far, and she came right away."

"First, did she recognize you?"
"No. I'm pretty sure she didn't."
"Did she offer you a séance?"
"No, she didn't. She told me that due to the sudden death of her employer, she's searching for someone of, and I quote, power, to whom she can offer her assistance. Can I take off this wig and jacket now? I'm hot."

"Not yet. She might come out any minute, and I don't want to rumble us in case we have to go back and talk to her again."

"Rumble?"

"I'm trying out my American gangster expressions. Is that right?"

"I have absolutely no idea, Gemma. Not being an American gangster, or any other type of gangster. Anyway, Mary was very forthright. She gave me her card and asked for my contact information. I gave her my mom's number."

"Your mom?"

"I couldn't very well give her mine, now could I? Not if I don't want to be 'rumbled' if she calls. She didn't ask me for any money, and she didn't offer to arrange anything specific. She said she enjoys helping people get in contact, one last time, with their dearly departed—her words, not mine—and hoped to be able to do so when the circumstances are again favorable."

"She didn't suggest she could act as the medium?"

Jayne shook her head. Her hair didn't move. "I asked her if she'd consider leading the session herself, but she said no. She said it's the great tragedy of her life that she hasn't been gifted with the ability."

Which was probably right. If by ability she meant the ability to put on different voices and accents and to manipulate the space around her without appearing to be doing so.

Mary Moffat needed a new junior partner.

"Okay," I said. "I've got enough. Let's go home."

"Thank goodness. I hope you're not too disappointed I didn't learn anything."

"Disappointed? Not in the least. Learning a negative can be as important as a positive."

"Huh?"

"We learned it's highly unlikely Mary Moffat murdered Iris Laval. For her, it would have been killing the goose that lays the golden egg. Moffat needed Laval to keep them in business. Laval's death brought a lot of attention to their nasty little operation, but that attention is useless without a medium to continue the work. It's unlikely you're the only one coming to this thing searching for someone to lead a séance. Yet the best Moffat can do is get your phone number and say she'll be in touch. I'd love to see Moffat banged up for fraud, but that's not our purview. Hopefully Ryan can talk the Greenwoods into helping him build a case."

"What do the Greenwoods have to do with anything like that?"

"I'll fill you in later. Let's go."

"Is that Donald over there? Walking across the parking lot with his head down, so determined not to look in our direction he doesn't see the pole looming directly in front of him?"

"That would be our Donald." I let out a long, piercing whistle strong enough to make him look up in shock. And thus, he saw the obstacle in front of his nose.

I pulled off my wig. "This thing's hot, and it itches. Let's go home."

Chapter Sixteen

When we got back to West London, Jayne let me off in the alley behind Baker Street.

"You're sure you don't want to go home and, uh, return to normal before going in?" she asked.

"I'd rather not take the time. I asked Gale to work until five and it's almost that now. I keep some spare clothes here, in case of emergencies, and I can change quickly."

"Okay. For anyone else, an emergency is coffee spilled on a white blouse. For you, it means the sudden need to assume an impenetrable disguise."

"Are you going straight home?"

She chuckled. "I will admit I considered going into the Blue Water Café and demanding to speak to the chef, but I decided probably better not to give Andy the fright of his life."

"Thanks for this," I said.

She threw me a huge smile. "Any time, Gemma. You make my life interesting."

I used my key to let myself into the Emporium through the back way. A small queue waited at the counter to be served while Ashleigh rang up a satisfyingly large stack of books. Gale was helping customers at the children's and YA shelf.

"Good afternoon," I said in my own voice.

Gale froze in the act of taking *Jewel of the Thames* by Angela Misri off the shelf. Her mouth dropped open. "What the—"

"Carry on." I headed for the stairs. "I'll be down to take over from you momentarily, Gale."

As I climbed the stairs, I heard Gale say to Ashleigh, "Is that—"

"I've learned," Ashleigh said, "not to ask too many questions. Gemma comes, Gemma goes. Gemma does strange things."

Moriarty streaked past me, but this time I was on guard, and I nimbly avoided him lying in wait on the landing.

I gave my hair a good brushing, scrubbed off the excess makeup, and changed into black leggings, a loose T-shirt under a cotton jacket, and ballet flats. I slipped the fake wedding ring into a desk drawer and went downstairs.

Time to go to work.

As I'd said to Jayne, I believed we'd proved a negative— Mary had not killed Iris Laval. Unfortunately, our little outing had taken me no further forward in proving a positive—who had killed the medium.

When Ryan admitted he'd like my help, I knew he meant providing ideas and suggestions. He wouldn't approve of me taking action in an investigation, so on the grounds that what he didn't know would never hurt him, I hadn't yet called to tell him about our expedition. I would, however, bring it up at some point. The police depend on concrete evidence and provable fact. My understanding of character or observation of minor details would be of no use to them in court, but my impressions of Mary's behavior and motives might be of help in determining where, and upon whom, he should focus his attention.

I thanked Gale for coming in on short notice. She peeked at me out of the corner of her eye and only said, "Any time you need me."

She went upstairs for her purse and when she slipped out, still watching me, she held the door for Larissa Greenwood.

"Welcome," I said.

"Thank you." Larissa looked around. "What a lovely store you have, Gemma. I haven't come to buy, I'm sorry to say. I'm meeting Max in a few minutes, but I wanted to take the opportunity to come in and thank you."

"Thank me for what?"

"Max and I went to the police station this morning. We had a long talk with Detectives Ashburton and Estrada. They were not happy to hear we hadn't told them of our prior knowledge of Iris Laval, but they thanked us for eventually doing the right thing. I'm glad we did."

The door behind her opened, and two teenage girls came in.

"Why don't we step out of the way?" I suggested. I led the way to the reading nook and invited Larissa to take a seat in the comfortable wingback chair. I sat on the window ledge beneath the big bay window facing Baker Street.

She perched on the edge of the chair and shifted nervously. Moriarty appeared out of nowhere, as he's sometimes inclined to do, and leaped onto her lap. Larissa started, and then she broke into a small smile. "What a lovely cat. What's his name?"

"Moriarty."

He graciously allowed Larissa to stroke his back and scratch under his chin as she talked. "Detective Estrada said that seeing as how Madame Lavalier—Iris Laval, that is—has died, they obviously can't go after her for embezzlement. However, they can refer the case to Boston, and the police there can attempt to

find out who assisted her in setting up and conducting the supposed séances. Max asked her not to do that. He doesn't want
our daughter upset any further, but it was pointed out that if
Laura was a victim of fraud, she's unlikely to be the only one. To
be completely honest, Gemma, Max doesn't much care what
happened to anyone else, he only wants to put an end to this. I
managed to convince him, for the time being anyway, to let the
authorities do what they have to do."

Moriarty purred and stretched his neck as high as it would
go, allowing Larissa to scratch his throat. He loves that. Not that
I know from personal experience: on the few occasions I've tried
to stroke him, I've had to go in search of bandages.

"Have you told your daughter what happened here? To Iris
Laval?"

"No. Max insists we say nothing, but I'm not convinced that
would be best. Laura will eventually find out, certainly if the
police investigation grows. I suspect we'll have an uncomfortable sail to Boston. After we left the police, I asked Max if we
should go to Rebecca Stanton. Tell her who we are, and extend
our condolences and apologies for the death of her sister. Max
said no. He wants to just slip quietly out of town."

"I think that's probably wise."

She gave Moriarty a concluding pat and indicated he could
get down. He snuggled in further. She said, "Off you go now,
you beautiful boy."

He didn't get the hint, and after further failed encouragement, Larissa finally had to pick him up and plop him on the
floor. He walked away, tail swishing behind him, without a backward glance, letting us know such had been his intent all along.

"We're leaving in the morning," Larissa said. "It's unlikely
we'll be back, so I wanted to thank you in person."

"I hope it all works out. For you and your daughter."

* * *

Ryan called shortly before closing to invite himself to my place for dinner. He'd pick up take-out Indian food on the way.

He arrived, fragrant bags in hand, shaking rainwater off. Behind him, cars splashed through puddles quickly forming on the street.

I took the food from him and said, "It's raining. I checked the weather forecast earlier, and it said nothing about rain."

"As reliable as ever," he said as he came into the house to be greeted by the two dogs.

I dished up heaping plates of rice, chicken korma, lamb curry, saag paneer, and crispy papadums, and we dug in. As we ate, we talked about nothing in particular: the news of the day, updates on our families and mutual friends.

Once our plates were scraped clean and the leftovers stacked in the fridge, we snuggled together on the couch, listening to the rain falling outside, and argued over what movie to choose, watched over by Violet and Peony. I'd decided to tell Ryan, while he was in a relaxed frame of mind, the bare-bones details of my expedition to Sandwich, concluding that I didn't believe Mary Moffat had killed her golden goose.

"Sounds reasonable," he said. "But she's not out of the woods yet. Her history in Vegas isn't entirely on the up and up, and it would appear she and the so-called Madame Lavalier were involved in some nasty stuff in Boston. I will say no more about that except that you seem to know as much as I do, if not more. As you so often do."

It hadn't been confirmed to me that Mary had acted as the assistant to Laval when she'd fleeced young Laura Greenwood.

Now it had been. I didn't say so.

He flicked idly through the movie offerings on the streaming service. "As for who else might have been responsible for the killing, we're not getting far, Gemma. We don't need a motive to prove a case, but it certainly helps build the foundations of one, and I've got nothin'. Other than Moffat, who I'm not ruling out despite your conclusion, none of these people seem to have even met the woman before that night. The Greenwoods had reason to wish her harm, but I have no evidence indicating they did so."

"That doesn't mean someone hadn't met her previously. It just means the guilty party hasn't told you about it."

"Precisely. I've heard this movie is good. The guys at the station say it's nonstop action."

"I have no need for nonstop action, fictional or otherwise, in my life. What about that one? The lead actor plays such great romantic roles."

"Nothing with spontaneous acts of equestrianism," he said.

"Nothing with explosions and flying bodies," I said.

"I believe we're at an impasse then."

I plucked the control out of his hands and switched the screen off. "Whatever will we do with the rest of the evening?"

He grinned at me and took my face between his hands. "Maybe some nonstop action?"

Chapter Seventeen

Wednesday afternoon, precisely at 3:40, I turned to Ashleigh and opened my mouth.

"Partners' meeting. Back in thirty. Got it."

"Like Pavlov's dog," I said.

"The question is, which of us is Pavlov and which is the dog?" she replied.

I pondered that as I went into the tearoom. The espresso machine hissed and emitted steam as Fiona prepared a latte for a take-out customer. The restaurant was clearing out at the end of the day, but a few guests still lingered over the last of their tea and pastries. The table for six in the center of the room was occupied by a group of women. Laptop computers and notepads were open in front of them, next to the fine china teacups and matching plates. The two three-tiered silver stands in the center of the table had been cleaned off, napkins were crumpled and discarded, and side plates were dusted with crumbs.

"Gemma." Rebecca Stanton called me over with a wave and a smile. "Another beautiful tea. Do you know everyone? Ladies, I'm sure you all know Gemma Doyle."

We exchanged greetings. The women were all of an age—midfifties to late seventies—and a type—well groomed, tastefully dressed. I recognized most of them, prominent figures around town, active in one charitable committee or another.

"We're meeting to put together plans for the Christmas house tour," Rebecca explained. "This year, the proceeds will go to the hospital foundation." Her eyes lit up. "I've just had the most brilliant idea. How about—"

"Here comes Jayne now," I said. "Nice chatting with you, ladies." I escaped to the safety of our window alcove before it could be suggested that Jayne and I help with the fundraising.

As I fled, I heard one woman say, "Gemma Doyle. Isn't she Arthur Doyle's niece? They live in one of the best-preserved salt-boxes in West London, perhaps . . ."

"What's the matter?" Jayne said as she took her seat opposite me.

"Why do you ask?"

"You're not the only one who can read faces, Gemma. You look like you've swallowed a lemon seed."

"I fear I've leapt out of the frying pan and landed directly in the fire. In trying to avoid being roped into catering—at cost, of course—the Christmas house tour, I suspect I'm about to be roped into hosting a display house. I'd better warn Uncle Arthur what's coming."

"Yup." Jocelyn put a plate of sandwiches and pastries in front of us. "I know that Sandra Picard. Once she has an idea in her head, nothing can shake it. I noticed her writing *Call Arthur D—house on BWP* onto her action items list as I passed."

I groaned. "Doomed."

"Her very long and very detailed action items list. What do you want for tea?"

"English breakfast will do today, thanks. Is Miranda not working today?"

"It's her day off," Jayne said. "I'll have the English breakfast too, thanks. Mom called me a few minutes ago. She's made an appointment for us at the bridal store for next Wednesday morning. If you don't show up, Gemma, you're out of the wedding party."

"Is that intended to be a threat?"

"Most amusing."

The chimes over the door tinkled. Jayne turned to tell the new arrivals the tearoom would be closing shortly, but she stopped when she recognized Daniel and Eleanor Stanton.

Daniel, in particular, did not look happy.

Eleanor hesitated in the doorway, but Daniel spotted his quarry and headed directly for Rebecca's table.

"Hope I'm not interrupting anything," he said, interrupting Mrs. Picard midsentence. She gave him a piercing look of lofty disapproval, which he ignored.

Rebecca slowly turned in her chair and looked up. "You are interrupting us, as it happens, Daniel. We're having a business meeting."

"I want to know why you instructed your maid to pack our suitcases first thing tomorrow morning."

"I would have assumed that would be obvious," Rebecca said. "I told you I'm going to Boston tomorrow in order to pay a visit to my brother-in-law. As I also told you, I don't like having people in the house when I'm not there."

Daniel's arms hung at his sides. His fists tightened. I got to my feet. He wore bright-yellow, slim-fitting trousers with a blue-and-yellow checked shirt under a loose-fitting blue jacket. The clothes were likely from his own line, but the outfit was far too cheerful for his mood and better suited, I thought, for having drinks at a beach resort than for wearing in town.

The occupants of the other tables turned in alarm, alerted by the tone of his voice that something was not right.

"Miranda's going to be there," Eleanor said. She wore fashionably shredded white jeans under a pink light summer jacket. Her long, glossy hair tumbled in a smooth, dark river down her back. Pink trainers matching the jacket were on her feet. At some point earlier in the day, she'd stepped in a patch of mud; dried residue clung to the side of her right shoe. Last night's rain had been brief but heavy, and the streets were still wet when the dogs and I ventured out this morning. Eleanor didn't stand with Daniel but lingered uneasily in the doorway.

"Miranda's not living in the house, now is she?" Rebecca said.

"You can't kick me out of my father's house," Daniel said.

The women at Rebecca's table exchanged glances. A tall, large-bosomed, helmet-haired lady rose to her feet. "This is neither the time nor the place, young man."

"I'm not talking to you," he snarled.

Her eyes opened wide and color rushed into her plump, heavily rouged cheeks. "I—"

Rebecca turned away from Daniel, picked up her teacup, and took a delicate sip. Her hands didn't waver in the least. "Any further matters to discuss, ladies?"

"I'm talking to you, Rebecca," Daniel said. "It wasn't my idea to confront you in public, but you've been hiding from us all day. Good thing Eleanor remembered you told her about your little tea party."

"Hardly a party," the helmet-haired woman said. "We're conducting important business here."

"It's fine, Nancy," Rebecca said. "This gentleman has stated his case, more than once, and I've said all I have to say on the matter. Please don't wait until tomorrow to leave, Daniel. I'd prefer you be gone before I get home this evening."

His face tightened. A vein pulsed in his forehead. "You haven't heard the last of this, Rebecca. I'll get what's mine, one way or the other."

I glanced at Eleanor. The slightest of smiles touched the edges of her mouth. She caught me looking, and the expression died.

"I'm sure you'll try," Rebecca said. "Unfortunately for you, my late husband chose not to mention you in his will, and there can be no doubt about that."

Jocelyn had come out of the kitchen, the teapot containing Jayne's and my tea in her hands. Fiona stood behind the counter, watching. She'd taken her phone out in case she needed to summon help

All conversation had stopped at the other tables.

"Jocelyn, dear," Rebecca said, "would it be possible to have a splash more hot water in my teapot?"

Jocelyn's hands were full. Fiona said, "I can get it for you, Mrs. Stanton. Would you ladies like anything else?"

"No, thank you," they chorused.

Daniel didn't move. Fiona ducked her head as she reached around him to get the teapot—a lovely contemporary Royal Doulton Crown Derby design in cream and gold.

"Let's go, honey," Eleanor said. "You don't have to stand there and be insulted by your father's *second* wife."

In his rage, Daniel swatted the teapot out of Fiona's hand. It flew across the room and crashed against the wall, shattering into a thousand pieces, spilling damp tea leaves. Fiona stepped back with a sharp intake of breath. The ladies around the table gasped and shoved back their chairs. One pulled out her phone and snapped a picture of Daniel's furious face. Jocelyn carefully put down the teapot she was holding.

"Oops," Eleanor said. Her eyes twinkled. She was, I thought, enjoying this.

I ran across the room and took a firm grip on Daniel's arm. He whirled around to face me and tried to shake me off. I held on. "Jayne will send you the bill for that teapot, and be warned, it is an original, not a knockoff, so the charge will not be insubstantial. Now, I'd like you to leave, please. Fiona, call 911 if this *gentleman* is still on the premises in twenty seconds."

"Got it, Gemma," she called.

At last, Eleanor did something. "Come on, honey. You've said your piece. Let the lawyers sort it out."

"I have another stop to make following this meeting," Rebecca said. "I'll be home at seven. Please vacate my house before I get there."

Daniel gave me one last formidable (in his opinion anyway) stare. I let go of his arm, but I didn't allow myself to relax. He turned and walked away.

"It's after four o'clock already," Eleanor said. "We'll never get a hotel room in Cape Cod tonight. We'll leave tomorrow instead, okay, Rebecca?"

Rebecca said nothing. The chimes over the door tinkled merrily as Daniel stormed out.

"Great," Eleanor said. "Thanks so much. Uh, sorry about that. I mean, Daniel shouldn't have spoken to you that way in front of your friends. Must be really embarrassing, like. When he gets angry, he says things he doesn't really mean. I've learned to ignore it."

"You are not helping," I said.

"Oh, right. Sorry. I'm leaving now." She followed her husband. "Are you okay to drive home on your own, Daniel?" she asked in a loud voice. "If we're leaving tomorrow, I'd like to go back to that dress shop now."

"Do whatever you want," he snapped as the door shut behind them. "You always do."

The women hastily gathered up their things and scurried for the exit. Sandra squeezed Rebecca's shoulder lightly as she passed and said, "I'll get the list of action items sent out first thing tomorrow. It's going to be a wonderful house tour. I can feel it already. Gemma, do you know where Arthur is these days? Can he receive emails?"

"No," I said. "He's completely incommunicado. Sorry."

"I'll try anyway," she said. "Perhaps I'll have more luck than you."

"I'm serious about sending him that bill, Jayne," I said when they'd left. "Find out how much a replacement is going to cost, will you?"

Fiona ran into the back for a broom. Jayne flipped the sign on the door to Closed while Jocelyn presented the occupants of the other tables with their bills and apologized for the disturbance. "What a thoroughly nasty man," a woman said.

I pulled out the chair next to Rebecca and sat down. "Are you okay?"

She gave me a weak smile. "Nothing like having your prejudices confirmed. I know now, if I didn't before, why Ron didn't trust his son with money. In the absence of children of my own, I've left most of Ron's estate to be split between my late sister's children, including Miranda, and Daniel himself. I think an appointment with my lawyer to rewrite the will is overdue."

"Maybe hanging around Gemma has given me a suspicious mind," Jayne said, "but does Daniel know he's mentioned in your will? For now, anyway?"

"I haven't told him, no."

"Perhaps best not to do that," Jayne said.

Rebecca unhooked her purse from the back of her chair. "I'm sorry about the commotion. I'll pay for the teapot. You'll never get the money out of Daniel."

"That's not necessary," Jayne and I said at the same time.

"Nevertheless, I'd like to." She rummaged in her purse and took out her wallet.

We turned at the sound of rapping on the glass of the door. A man and woman stood there, peering in. The man held up his watch and pointed.

"I'll get it." I stood up, hurried to the door, and opened it a crack. "I'm very sorry, sir, madam, but we had an emergency, and we had to close a few minutes early today. I do hope you'll come back tomorrow."

Rebecca squeezed past me. "Thank you again, Gemma." She gave the couple a broad smile. "They do a marvelous afternoon tea here. Truly a highlight of West London."

"We'll keep that in mind," the woman said.

"We open at seven for breakfast, both take-out and table service," I said as I watched Rebecca make her way down Baker Street.

"Thanks. While we're here, can you tell us how to get to the Ocean Breeze Motel? The GPS on my phone has us going around in circles."

"All those seafaring names do get confusing sometimes." I directed them as best I could.

When I went back inside, Jocelyn was getting out the vacuum cleaner while Fiona cleared the center table. "What are you going to do with this?" She pointed to a hundred-dollar bill resting beneath the used cup at what had been Rebecca's place.

"Oh for heaven's sake," I said. "I don't want her money, and that's far too much."

"Not really," Jayne said. "A replacement will set me back more than two hundred bucks."

"That much?"

"Fine English china, Gemma. It's not cheap, as you yourself said. I brought out our best things for Rebecca and her party."

"Rebecca can clearly afford it, but she didn't break the teapot, and she shouldn't be paying for someone else's temper tantrum. Her stepson is not five years old. Did they leave you a tip?" I asked Fiona.

"Yes, one that's more than generous."

"In that case." I folded the bill. "I'll return this to Rebecca later. It'll give me an excuse to pop around and check on her. She tried to appear not at all concerned by the altercation, but it had to have been upsetting. I don't trust Daniel to leave without making more of a fuss. She said she'll be home at seven. Jayne, what are you planning to do now?"

"Now? Work. I have prep to get done for tomorrow."

"Will you be finished shortly before seven? Seeing as how I didn't bring my car today, I'll need a ride to Rebecca's house."

Chapter Eighteen

Jayne's car swung into the driveway of the Stanton home at ten past seven. Rebecca said she'd be home at seven, and from what I knew of the woman, she was punctual. I considered phoning ahead but decided not to. She'd refuse the return of the money and insist she could handle Daniel by herself.

Rebecca might be more than a match for Daniel in terms of self-possession and strength of will, but he was a much younger man and an angry one to boot. I didn't like the idea of he and his wife spending another night under Rebecca's roof.

Jayne pulled up in front of the steps. The garage doors were closed. A compact car, which had all the signs of being a rental, was parked outside. A light shone in the window above the garage, and the lamps over the front door of the house were on, although the sun was still up.

"What are we going to do if she's not home?" Jayne asked.

"We can't wait all night. If I were Rebecca, I'd spend the night at a friend's rather than risk running into Daniel. Then again, if I were Rebecca, I'd call the cops on him if he won't leave."

"It's gotta be hard on her," Jayne said. "I get the feeling she loved her late husband very much, and she'd like to have a positive relationship with his son."

"By all accounts, Ron Stanton didn't get on with his son either, but I hear what you're saying."

We heard a car coming up the driveway behind us and got out to face it.

"Good timing," Jayne said.

A silver Lexus pulled up next to us, the window lowered, and Rebecca peered out. "Gemma, Jayne. I didn't expect to see you two here so soon. Not that you're not welcome, of course. Let me put the car away, and I'll be right with you."

She pressed the remote control attached to the window visor. One of the garage doors rose soundlessly, and Rebecca drove in. The door shut behind her, and she appeared a moment later through the door at the side of the garage.

Above her head, lights flicked off and then on again, a curtain moved, and Miranda gave her aunt a wave. Rebecca returned the gesture. The curtains dropped back into place.

"Come in," Rebecca said to us. "It's been a long, tiring day, and I need to sit back and put my feet up." She indicated the car parked in the driveway. "I see my unwelcome guests are still here. I do not want to have to change the locks, but I will if I have to."

"You can have Daniel removed by the police," I said.

"I know, I know. I truly do not want to do that to Ron's son, but I'll do what I have to do. Why he thinks badgering me is going to convince me to give in and give him what he wants, I have no idea. Anyway, let's talk of nicer things, shall we? The plans for the Christmas house tour are coming on well. Thank you so much, Gemma, for agreeing to be part of it."

"What?"

"Sandra Picard called me a few moments ago. She spoke to your uncle, and he said you'd be delighted to put your house on the tour."

I opened my mouth. I closed it again.

Jayne laughed, and I glared at her. She settled her face into a deep frown, but she couldn't stop her eyes from twinkling.

"The tour works best when we have a comfortable mix of ultra-stylish, midcentury modern, and historical homes for people to visit." We climbed the steps, and Rebecca put her key in the lock. Before we went inside, we heard another car coming down the driveway.

It was a taxi. Eleanor jumped out, dragging several bags from the women's wear shop on Baker Street with her. The taxi drove away, and she skipped happily across the driveway. She was wearing the same outfit she'd had on earlier at the tearoom. At some point in the afternoon, she'd found the time to tie her hair back into a high ponytail, touch up her makeup, and clean off her shoes. "Hi there. I've had a super successful shopping expedition."

"How nice," Rebecca said dryly. "Did Daniel not join you?"

"He's never been one for helping me shop."

"You can't stay here any longer, Eleanor." Rebecca unlocked the door and led the way into the house. "I'm completely serious about you leaving tomorrow."

"Yeah, well, that's up to Daniel, isn't it? Nothing to do with me. I know you and he don't get on, but there's no need for you to be so actively hostile to him. I mean, he and his dad had their disagreements, but what father and son don't?"

Rebecca threw her keys into the wide blue-and-green glass bowl on the small table by the door. "You believe what you want,

Eleanor. Gemma, Jayne, you know the way to the living room. I'm getting myself a glass of wine. Would you like something?"

Jayne glanced at me.

"Just water, please," I said. "We won't stay long."

"Wine would be great, thanks," Eleanor said, although she'd pointedly not been offered any.

Rebecca headed for the kitchen, and Jayne and I went to the living room. The air-conditioning had been turned off, and tonight the temperature in the house was pleasant, not the near-Arctic winds of the night of the séance. Eleanor tagged along behind Jayne and me, like the unwelcome guest she was. Her voice took on an unpleasant whining tone. "Our car's outside. I wonder where Daniel got to. He's probably hiding in our room, not wanting another confrontation with Rebecca. I don't know why she has it in for Daniel the way she does. My dad could be a real jerk sometimes, but we always made up eventually, although I have to admit, I never saw much of my dad when I was growing up. He and my mom weren't married; they didn't even live together. It's so sad Daniel and his father never got the chance to make up. They would have, right? I mean, it's not like Rebecca can't afford to cut Daniel in on a fair share of his dad's estate."

I turned to her. "Eleanor, this line of conversation is totally inappropriate. We're guests in Rebecca's home, and she's our friend. We're not taking sides, because this is none of our business, but if we were to take sides, as her friends, we'd be firmly on hers."

"Gemma's right," Jayne said. "And, frankly, it's not any of your business either. The relationship between Daniel and his father was up to them to deal with."

Eleanor lifted her hands. "Geez. I'm just saying, that's all." She dropped onto the couch and swung her legs up.

"I'll help Rebecca with the drinks," I said. "Jayne, give me a hand."

"Sure."

We found Rebecca in the kitchen. She was not getting drinks but rather leaning against a stool at the island, trying to control her breathing. She lifted her head and gave us a tight smile when we came in. "Houseguests can be exhausting. Never more than when they don't want to leave."

"Jayne and I aren't here for a social visit." I took the hundred-dollar bill out of my bag and put it on the island next to her. "First, we're returning this, but mostly we came because we wanted to check up on you. I suggest you stay with me tonight and get Daniel and Eleanor out of the house tomorrow."

"I'll be fine, Gemma. I'm not Daniel's favorite person at the moment, but he's not going to attack me while I'm asleep in my bed."

"I agree that's unlikely, but things aren't comfortable for you here, and you don't deserve that in your own house."

"I'll ask Miranda to come in tonight. I have another guest room she can use." She took a bottle of wine out of the fridge and held it up to us in question.

"No thanks," I said. "If you're sure you're okay, we'll be on our way."

She poured herself a generous glass. "Thank you, Gemma. Jayne. I'm perfectly fine. I have no desire to return to the living room and try to make light, friendly conversation with Eleanor. Fortunately, it's a lovely night. I'm going to take this outside and enjoy the view and then watch TV from my bed for a while. I love the ocean at this time of the evening. Everything settling down for the night. Birds returning to nest. Boats coming into harbor." She sighed, and her expression indicated she was far away, enjoying pleasant memories. "Ron and I so loved sitting out together, sipping our drinks, watching the day end."

"Call me if you need anything," I said.

"Me too," Jayne said. "Please."

"I will. Thank you both." Rebecca walked with us to the door, and we wished her a good night.

"I'd like a quick word with Miranda before we leave," I said to Jayne once the door had closed behind us.

"You think Rebecca won't ask her to move into the main house for the night?"

"I'm positive she won't. Rebecca doesn't like to show what she thinks of as weakness."

"Do you believe Daniel's a danger to her?"

"Not physically. I don't expect he'll be emotionally abusive either, not tonight anyway, but simply having him here is stressful for Rebecca."

"Why do you suppose Daniel's still hanging around? He's not exactly endearing himself to her, is he?"

"Stubborn, I suspect. Some people don't know when to give up a lost cause. Despite all her protestations that this is between her husband and his stepmother, I suspect Eleanor's subtly egging him on. Thus, she's adding to the toxic mix by threatening his image of his manly self-confidence. Miranda's likely aware of the situation, but I'd like to be sure before we leave."

A set of steps ran discreetly up the side of the garage. Lights were on inside the apartment, and a light bulb burned above the door. Jayne and I climbed the steps. The door opened before I had the chance to knock.

"Hi." Miranda had settled in for the night in a pair of pink summer pajamas illustrated with drawings of mischievous black cats. "Everything okay?"

"Not entirely," I said. "Rebecca would like Daniel and Eleanor to leave, but he's being difficult."

"To say the least," Jayne added.

"He's a jerk," Miranda said. "He tries to act all nice and friendly, but he can't keep it up for long. The pretense slips, and he says something backhanded and nasty. He wants money from Aunt Rebecca, but he has nothing in the way of family friendship to offer in return. She'd probably give him what he wants if she trusted him to behave like an adult, but she doesn't."

"She told them to leave tomorrow," Jayne said. "We're worried he's not going to."

"I'll keep an eye out," Miranda said. "It's what my mom would have wanted, after all. The sisters were very close."

"Have you run into the Greenwoods again?" I asked.

She shook her head.

"They're also leaving town tomorrow, or so I've been told."

"Glad to hear it."

I admired Miranda for not trying to confront them. Seeing Max here in West London, where she'd come to try to recover as best she could from her mother's death, had been a considerable shock. It would have been easy for her to seek out those she considered responsible, to shout accusations and attach blame. Easy but entirely self-defeating, and she would have ultimately walked away feeling considerably worse.

"I'll see you at work tomorrow, then," Jayne said.

"Bright and early."

Jayne and I turned to go. I'd put my foot on the second step when a piercing scream broke the silence of the lingering dusk, immediately followed by another, even louder and more urgent. The voice was that of Rebecca Stanton.

I flew down the stairs, conscious of Jayne and Miranda right behind me.

Chapter Nineteen

The scream was loud and clear, not muffled as though it had passed through walls and closed windows, and it sounded as if it had come from behind the house. I dashed across the driveway and hit the flagstone path curling around the right side of the house. I knew my way; when Jayne and I catered the theater fundraiser, that was the route guests used to get to the party being held in the back garden.

"Help!" Rebecca yelled. "Someone help me!"

Outdoor lights had automatically come on as daylight began to fade. Small white bulbs hung from the trees surrounding the expansive entertaining area. The light above the back door showed an entire outdoor kitchen, better equipped than the kitchen at my house.

The good-sized rectangular swimming pool, about 16 feet by 40 feet, lay between us and the dining area. An eerie blue glow illuminated the pool from below. Water washed against the sides as two people floundered in the depths.

Rebecca's colorful skirt flowed around her, dancing cheerfully on the churned-up water. She treaded water, cradling a man in her arms, his head back, staring up into the darkening sky.

I kicked off my shoes as I ran toward them. Unsure of the depth of the pool, even at what appeared to be the deep end, I didn't want to dive, so I jumped in feetfirst. I went straight down. Chlorinated water filled my mouth and nose, and I kicked hard against the bottom, propelling myself back to the surface. When my head cleared, I could hear Jayne yelling into her phone that we needed an ambulance.

I reached Rebecca with one stroke. She stared at me through wide, panicked eyes. Daniel Stanton did not move. I put my right arm around his upper chest, and Rebecca and I pulled his limp form to the shallow end, where I guided him onto the pool steps.

Miranda jumped into the water. She crouched down and helped steady him while I began CPR. Rebecca sobbed softly next to me. Jayne, struggling to keep her voice calm, told the 911 operator what was happening.

Another scream. Startled, I looked up to see Eleanor Stanton standing at the edge of the pool. She lifted her index finger, pointed it directly at Rebecca, and yelled, "What have you done?"

"Jayne, take Eleanor inside." I returned to my task and kept working, although Daniel failed to respond.

"I'm not going anywhere," shouted Eleanor. "She killed him. She killed him." She jumped onto the pool steps and tried to grab Daniel. I shoved her hard, and she fell backward into the water. We were at the shallow end, but she went right under. She emerged, her long hair streaming behind her like seaweed, sputtering and spitting, but managing to continue screaming accusations.

"Stop it. Stop it!" Miranda let go of Daniel, grabbed Eleanor by the shoulders, and gave her a good shake. Rebecca clambered out of the pool, gasping and coughing.

I heard sirens tearing up the driveway.

"We're around the back," Jayne said into the phone. "Tell them to follow the path."

And then people were crouching at the edge of the pool, and a low, calm voice said to me, "Pass him to us, please." I floated Daniel's unresponsive body toward them, and uniformed arms reached for him and lifted him out. Jayne helped me out of the water. She looked into my eyes and said, "Are you okay, Gemma?"

I nodded. "Okay."

Two medics crouched over Daniel, their equipment bags on the ground beside them. He was fully dressed, still wearing the colorful clothes he'd had on at the tearoom earlier, including his shoes.

Eleanor broke free of Miranda, climbed out of the pool, and lunged at Rebecca, her nails reaching for the older woman's face. "He can't swim. You know he can't swim. You did this. You killed him."

Miranda stepped between them, and I grabbed Eleanor and wrenched her arm back with enough strength to pull her off balance. "Enough of that. You don't know what happened here."

"I do. I do. She killed him."

"You're crazy," Miranda said.

"Will you people get out of the way?" one of the medics shouted. "He's not dead until we say he is."

"What's going on here?" Two uniformed officers arrived at a run.

"Arrest her!" Eleanor yelled. "That woman. She killed my husband."

"First, move aside," Officer Stella Johnson said. "The medics need space to work."

I tentatively relaxed my hold on Eleanor, and she pulled herself free with a huff, keeping her head averted. I put my arm around Rebecca's shoulder and led her shaking body toward the patio table. She hadn't said a word in the face of Eleanor's accusations. No cushions were on the wrought-iron chairs, but I decided that didn't matter, and I helped settle Rebecca. Miranda dropped to her knees next to her aunt, and the two women wrapped their arms around each other.

It had been a hot day, but night was settling in and the temperature was dropping quickly. Rebecca, Miranda, and Eleanor were soaked. I looked down at the puddle spreading around my own feet.

"Gemma, what happened here?" Officer Johnson asked me.

The medics were working on Daniel. One had taking over CPR from me, while the other prepared defibrillator pads. He placed them on Daniel's unmoving chest and shouted, "Clear." The first medic rummaged in her bags and took out a needle and a small bottle of liquid. She began to prepare the injection.

"Gemma?" Johnson repeated.

"I don't know what happened. I heard Rebecca, Mrs. Stanton, calling for help. Jayne and I had been in the kitchen with her only a few minutes earlier. We'd left the house but hadn't yet stepped into our car."

"I can tell you what happened." Eleanor shoved me to one side. "She killed him." She pointed at Rebecca, sitting on the chair with her head in her hands. Her previously perfectly arranged hair hung in sodden strands around her face, pale from shock, her wet skirt spread around her. Rebecca did not react.

Miranda gave Eleanor a poisonous look and said, "Don't listen to her, Officer. She doesn't know what she's talking about."

"You are?" Johnson asked.

"Eleanor Stanton. That's my husband, Daniel."

"Yes, I remember. We met the previous time the police were called to this house. Let's wait to hear what the medics have to say. Your husband might not be dead."

I glanced behind me. The two medics were still working on an unresponsive Daniel.

"If not," Eleanor spat, "it's no thanks to her."

"The detectives have been contacted," Johnson said. "Because a serious incident happened here less than a week ago, they'll want to be notified. Until they arrive, I'd like everyone to go into the house, please. We'll wait for the detectives in there."

"I need to be with my husband," Eleanor said.

"Please," Johnson said. "We'll let you know if . . . when something happens."

The officer who'd come with Johnson opened the doors leading into the house. No one moved.

"My aunt's freezing," Miranda said. "She needs to get out of these wet clothes."

Johnson hesitated, unsure if she should allow the potential witnesses to go their own way.

"Let's clear this scene." Louise Estrada came around the corner. Johnson relaxed fractionally, relieved command had been taken out of her hands.

"Detective Ashburton is wrapping something up and will be here shortly. I want every one of you in the house. Now. Anyone who needs to get out of wet clothes can do so. If you have something to change into, that is."

"I can find wraps or sweaters or something for Gemma in my aunt's closets," Miranda said.

"That'll do." Estrada glanced at the medics, and I followed her gaze. One of them was on the phone, turned away from us, keeping his voice low. Noticeably, they were not rushing Daniel into the ambulance.

Estrada caught my eye and gave me a sharp nod. "Let's move, people. Johnson, I want you in the house. Officer Singh, keep an eye on the property. No one's to come into this area unless they're with us."

"Got it, Detective," he said.

*　*　*

"Déjà vu all over again," Jayne whispered to me when I settled myself on the couch next to her with a sigh.

More officers had soon arrived, and Stella Johnson accompanied first Rebecca, and then Miranda and Eleanor while they changed into dry clothes. By the time Miranda returned with a lurid pink tracksuit for me, my clothes were already beginning to dry in the warm night air. Thank heavens the air-conditioning hadn't been turned up as high as it had the other night or icicles would be forming in my hair.

Jayne had been allowed to go into the kitchen to make tea and coffee for everyone.

Estrada went back outside to check out the scene, and eventually I heard the ambulance leaving.

Rebecca allowed Miranda to help her change, but the older woman had not said a single word all this time. Eleanor, once again, tried to tell the police Rebecca was responsible for whatever happened to Daniel, but Johnson snapped at her to wait until she was questioned.

Eventually, Estrada came in, accompanied by Ryan.

I wiggled my eyebrows in greeting, and he tried not to moan too loudly.

Eleanor stood up. "What's happening? Where's my husband? You have to let me see him."

He stepped toward her, his blue eyes fixed on her face. I could tell by the kindness in those eyes the news he had to give was not good. "I'm very sorry, Mrs. Stanton, but your husband didn't make it. He was pronounced dead at the scene."

She dropped into the chair behind her.

"In light of the incident which occurred here last week," Estrada said. "We'll be regarding this death as suspicious unless we determine otherwise."

"Mrs. Stanton. I mean, Eleanor Stanton," Ryan said, "my officers tell me you made an accusation."

Eleanor recovered quickly and jumped to her feet once again. "You're darn right I made an accusation. She killed him." She pointed a finger toward Rebecca. Rebecca didn't react. She was wrapped into herself under a thick blanket, saying nothing. "They had an argument earlier today, in public, in front of a bunch of her fancy ladies-who-lunch friends. She was embarrassed, humiliated. She wanted revenge, and she got it."

I stood up. "I was there, Detective. I witnessed this so-called argument. I and several others, including Jayne here, can testify that the argument came from one direction only and that was not Rebecca Stanton's. In addition, both Jayne and I were with Rebecca this evening, only minutes before she discovered Daniel in the pool."

"She killed him before you two got here, you fool," Eleanor snapped. "She's using you as her useful idiot."

"Rebecca arrived here after Jayne and I did," I pointed out.

Ryan lifted one hand. "Enough. We'll speak to you all individually. Ms. Doyle, you first."

"Yup," Jayne said. "*Déjà vu.*"

* * *

"Can you two not keep yourselves away from crime scenes?" Estrada said to me when we were comfortably settled in the dining room. That is, I was comfortably settled, in my borrowed clothes, with a cup of hot tea in front of me. Estrada paced, and Ryan looked out the window. The table and chairs had earlier been returned to their places.

"Believe me," I said, "it is a not a habit I engage in willingly."

Ryan turned from the window. "First things first. Gemma, do you have reason to believe the death of Daniel Stanton is related to that of Iris Laval?"

"I don't see how it can not be. Saying that, I have absolutely not the slightest idea of how they can be connected. It might not have been the same person, but my belief in the possibility of coincidence simply doesn't stretch that far."

"Which is a roundabout English way of saying, yes," Estrada said. "Tell us about this so-called argument you overheard earlier in your restaurant."

I did so, and then I went on to explain about returning the hundred dollars and wanting to check on Rebecca. "Jayne and I were still in our car when Rebecca drove up at ten past seven. I'm positive of the time, as I'd deliberately timed our arrival. We came briefly into the house, but we didn't stay long. Before leaving, I wanted to have a word with Miranda, so we went to her room. The one over the garage. We hadn't been gone more than ten minutes, at the most, when we heard Rebecca screaming for help and ran to see what was going on. She was in the pool, in the deep end, treading water and trying to hold Daniel's head up."

"You're sure she was holding him up?" Estrada asked. "Not down?"

I hesitated.

"Or attempting to appear as though she was trying to save him?" Ryan said. "A person can drown in far less than ten minutes."

I said nothing. I didn't for one minute believe that Rebecca, always so calm and controlled, showed Jayne and me to the door, went back inside, saw Daniel passing the pool, ran outside, pushed him in, jumped in after him, and then held his head underwater. I didn't believe it. But I had no way of proving it.

Chapter Twenty

B y the time Jayne and I were allowed to leave, night had fallen. The blue and red lights of emergency vehicles lit up the Stanton driveway, and powerful lights had been brought in to illuminate the pool area and its surroundings. Men and women dusted at the edges of the pool and poked through the shrubbery.

Ryan and Estrada spoke to Eleanor for a long time, and then they allowed her to pack a few things. They arranged for an officer to take her to the hospital to see Daniel and then to check her into a hotel. Jayne offered to accompany Eleanor to the hospital so she wouldn't be alone, but my friend was rebuffed quite rudely, presumably because we'd told Eleanor earlier we were on Rebecca's side.

Rebecca was interviewed next. She didn't return to the living room, but I heard the soft step of her bare feet as she went down the hallway toward the bedrooms.

"Thank you for your time, Ms. Doyle and Ms. Wilson," Estrada said. "We won't need you any more tonight."

"I don't mind staying," I said. "Someone should be with Rebecca."

"It's okay, Gemma," Miranda said helpfully. "I'm here. I'll spend the night in the house."

Estrada smirked.

"That's good then," I said. "Let's go, Jayne. Call us if you need anything, Miranda."

"Officer Johnson, see these ladies to their car. And make sure they actually leave the premises, will you." Estrada walked away.

"So sorry," I said, once the detective had gone. "I need to use the loo first. Won't be long. Be right back." I ran out of the room before Officer Johnson could gather her wits. What woman's going to stop another woman from using the restroom?

The small powder room (such a cute American expression) off the hallway was conveniently located next to the dining room, the door of which had not fully closed behind Detective Estrada.

I took my time locating my desired destination and politely ensuring no one was inside.

"If I didn't know better," I heard Estrada say, "I'd think Gemma Doyle is either cursed or blessed, depending on how she sees things. Why is she always to be found at the scene?"

"Do you expect an answer to that, Louise?" Ryan said.

"No. I'd like to take Mrs. Rebecca Stanton to the station, question her further there."

"On what grounds?" A floorboard creaked as Ryan paced.

"In any case, we consider it suspicious when two people have an altercation and one of them ends up dead only a few hours later."

"From what I heard, it didn't sound like much of an altercation."

"Not an out-and-out bar brawl, no, but Mrs. Stanton has a position in this community. She was humiliated, insulted in front of other prominent people. No one, not even Gemma

Doyle, wanted to come right out and say it, but it's pretty obvious Daniel was overstaying his welcome, and the situation between him and Rebecca was becoming more than merely strained. I think it entirely possible she saw her stepson standing by the pool and went outside with the intention of confronting him. Did he insult her again, and she decided she'd had enough and shoved him into the pool?"

"The timing of what you're speculating happened would be mighty tight."

"What timing we know is only according to Doyle."

"Even you have been known to admit Gemma has an eye for detail," he said.

"Reluctantly admit, yes. Okay, I'll agree Doyle's right about the time. How about this: Is it possible Mrs. Stanton killed Daniel earlier, and then she made a big show of discovering him in the pool and calling for help when she knew witnesses were still on the property?"

"By that reckoning, he could have been killed earlier by someone we're not aware of, and Mrs. Stanton was the one who found him. It's also possible the guy fell into the pool by accident. His wife says he couldn't swim. Let's wait for the autopsy. If we're lucky, it might show how long he'd been in the water and if he'd had help either getting in or staying under."

"Gemma! What are you doing?" Stella Johnson stood at the end of the hallway, her hands on her equipment belt, glaring at me. She looked as though she wanted to use that gun. "If the detectives know you're eavesdropping, it'll be on me."

The door to the dining room slammed shut.

Chapter
Twenty-One

"Big excitement at Rebecca Stanton's house once again, Gemma," Fiona said the following morning when she handed me a cup of tea and a muffin.

"So it would seem."

"The cops were here soon as we opened. They wanted to talk to Jocelyn and me about what happened yesterday between Mrs. Stanton and that guy."

"What did you tell them?"

"He was rude and angry and broke things, and you threw him out on his ear. What else was there to tell?"

"That's about it."

"They were interested in the exact timing. I could help with that because I remembered people came to the door after Mrs. Stanton's group left, and you told them we'd closed early. So, it was a couple of minutes before four, right?"

I was aware of people in line behind me, ears flapping, so I just said, "Thanks."

I slipped into the kitchen, passing Jocelyn, coming out with a tray of muffins and breakfast biscuits approximately the size of dinner plates, warm and aromatic straight from the ovens.

"Everything okay?" I asked Jayne.

She sighed and wiped at a wayward lock of hair escaping her hairnet. "As well as it can be. Miranda called to ask if she could have the day off. What could I say but yes, even though it looks as though weekend traffic is already building. I called Lorraine, and she can come in to give me a hand in here for lunchtime so Fiona can wait tables."

"Is Lorraine's wrist okay enough for her to work?"

"She can't carry heavy trays or stacks of dishes, but she says she's fine to do simple stuff, like make sandwiches and slice vegetables."

"I can do that too, so let me know if Lorraine seems to be struggling, and I'll come over if we're not too busy in the Emporium."

"Thanks. Oh, by the way, my mom called a short while ago. She didn't understand why someone was trying to interest her in attending a séance. Then she finally realized this person thought she was me."

"Excellent! We have a hit. Mary Moffat found herself a medium, then."

"So it would appear. Unfortunately, I forgot to tell Mom to string her along, so Mom hung up on her. Shall I call Mary back?"

"Let me think about it. The death of Daniel Stanton throws this business in an entirely new direction."

"Did you come to any conclusions last night?"

"I did not. I haven't spoken to Ryan yet either. Maybe we'll get lucky and he'll have wrapped it all up in a nice bow by now."

"You wish," Jayne said. "Don't forget we're due at Mom's at seven tonight."

"I didn't forget," I said, although I had. "Shall I pick you up?"

"Sure. I'm hoping to get off work on time this afternoon and have a short nap before going to Mom's."

I unlocked the sliding door joining the Emporium to the tearoom and left it open. Since it was close to nine thirty, I unlocked the front door also. Ready for another day of business.

"Good morning, Moriarty," I called.

The big cat did not rush to greet me. Then again, he never did.

I used the computer behind the sales desk to check on the status of books I'd ordered and greeted the handful of early customers who wandered in from the tearoom, take-out cups in hand.

The front door opened, and I looked up to welcome the newest arrivals. My smile died.

Irene Talbot, crack reporter with the *West London Star*. Normally, I'd be happy to see her, but I recognized that journalistic gleam in her eye, and I didn't care for the way she made a determined beeline for me.

"I do not," I said loftily, "have a statement for the press."

Two young women were posing for a selfie next to the life-size cutout of Benedict Cumberbatch and Martin Freeman as Holmes and Doctor Watson, signed by none other than Cumberbatch himself. The word "press" tore their attention away from their own image.

"Sure you do, Gemma," Irene said. "You were a witness to last night's tragic drowning, or so my sources at the police station say."

The selfie-taking women abandoned Sherlock and his friend and colleague and edged toward us.

"I've missed you, Irene," I said. "Not. I'm surprised you haven't been around before this."

"I was out of town visiting my mom and stepdad in Arizona, and I couldn't get away. The guy who subbed for me didn't come and speak to you, did he? He was useless, nothing much more than a stenographer for the cops."

"You simply cannot get good help these days," I said without a trace of sympathy.

"Whatever. I got home on Tuesday and have been trying to catch up on the earlier murder. When, what do you know, there's been another."

"Murder," I said to the two women now edging ever closer. "We sell a range of mystery novels here. As well as Sherlock Holmes pastiche, I have a wide selection of historical mysteries set in his era. May I show you some?"

They exchanged glances and shrugged. "No thanks. We don't, like, read books."

"How unfortunate. For you. In that case, don't let me keep you."

"We saw that poster, like, and thought it would be a hoot to get a picture. Then we saw it's signed by, like, Benedict himself?"

"No," I said. "I signed it for him. Like."

Their faces fell.

"Have a nice day," I said.

They left my shop in somewhat of a hurry.

"I don't know how you stay in business, Gemma, with an attitude like that," Irene said.

"They weren't going to buy anyway, and I don't want them telling all their friends I'm wrapped up in a murder investigation. Which I am not, so please don't go around saying I am."

"But you were there? In both instances?"

"Maybe. Maybe not."

"You know I'll get it all out of Jayne."

"Not today. She has a waitress off sick and is overwhelmed."

"Miranda Oberton. Rebecca Stanton's niece. Yeah, I know about that. I paid a call at Rebecca's before coming here. I was, if you must know, chased off the property. Politely, as is Rebecca's way, but firmly nonetheless."

"She didn't release the hounds, then? Glad to hear it. Now, if you don't mind—"

"I never mind. I know I'll never get anything out of you that you don't want to give me, so instead I'll give you something. The buzz on the internet says the ghost that killed Madame Lavalier hasn't left and is still hanging around Rebecca's for unknown reasons, and he . . . she . . . it? Whatever. Has struck again. I hear traffic out of Sandwich is heavy this morning, and it's coming this way at rapid speed."

Irene gave me a wink, and left.

* * *

The shop was busy for the rest of the morning, and once again, the books on Sir Arthur Conan Doyle and his interest in spiritualism sold well. I overheard more than one customer saying that the psychic fair in Sandwich had proved uneventful, so they'd returned, hoping to capture the "energy" in West London.

Ashleigh arrived for her regular shift at one o'clock, and I was considering escaping upstairs to call Ryan and ask if he had any updates to share when Bunny Leigh rushed in, grinning from ear to ear, her eyes bright with excitement. She clapped her hands together and bounced on her toes. "The most exciting thing has happened."

"Oh dear," Ashleigh mumbled before saying, "What's that, Mom?"

"You remember Mary, don't you, sweetie?"

"Mary? You don't mean Mary Moffat? The woman you told to get lost and never to bother you again?"

"Yes, yes." Bunny waved away that triviality. "Never mind that now. She called me last night, and guess what?"

"I don't want to know," Ashleigh said.

"She's found a medium who will be absolutely perfect for getting you in touch with your former manager," I said. "What's his name again?"

"Rupert."

"Right. Rupert. Either this medium can contact him or Mary has suddenly discovered she herself is gifted in that regard and will lead the séance. At a special discounted rate only for you."

"Yes. And no," Bunny said. "Madame Lavalier was obviously not on form the night she died. The imminent arrival of her own death would have interfered with her abilities, and thus Rupert prematurely departed."

"For the second time," Ashleigh mumbled.

I didn't laugh. Something Bunny said had caught my attention. "Mary called you last night? Is she back in West London?"

"I don't know exactly where she is, but she's been lucky enough to get in touch with Mrs. Rosechild, who's incredibly famous. She's famous among people who are interested in that sort of thing, anyway. Mrs. Rosechild lives in New York City. She heard about Madame Lavalier's tragic passing and is hurrying to Cape Cod to continue her valuable work. Isn't that marvelous? Mary wants me to set up another séance. She suggested that since Rebecca Stanton's home was so perfect last time, we should do it there again. I tried calling Rebecca before coming here, but her niece answered and said she wasn't coming to the phone. She, the niece, was pretty rude. I told her it was important, but she hung up on me."

"Have you heard the local news today?" I asked.

"I try to avoid the news whenever I can," Bunny said. "It's never anything good, is it? Do you think I should drive over to Rebecca's and speak to her in person?"

"I think that would be a very bad idea indeed. Why don't you let me handle the arrangements?" Ashleigh threw me a confused look, but I carried on. "I'll talk to Mary and see what day she's thinking of doing this."

Bunny clapped her hands once again. "That would be so great, Gemma, thanks. Ashleigh, you'll come of course. And Donnie. I'll see who else I can round up." She headed for the door. Then she stopped and turned around. "Uh, if Mary has a different medium, she might want to be paid. Can you find out what it'll cost, Gemma? Tell Mary it would be nice if we can agree to the same arrangement as before."

And then she was gone.

"What Bunny means is she can't afford to pay for the services of this incredibly famous medium," Ashleigh said. "Never mind that, for now. Why on earth did you encourage her, Gemma?"

"I have my reasons. I thought Bunny realized Mary Moffat's nothing more than your average celebrity stalker trying to get close to her former idol. Why the sudden change?"

"My mother is perfectly capable of holding two ideas in her head at the same time, Gemma. Stalker/conduit to the other side. Her career is finished, and she needs to move on to ever be happy again and this dead manager can help her revive it. Are you going to talk to Rebecca? I doubt after what happened last time, she'll want another séance in her house, but you never know."

"You don't listen to the news either, I take it."

"Sure I do. Sometimes. Why?"

"You'll find out before too much longer. I have to make a phone call. Be right back."

I ran upstairs to my office and shut the door. I dropped into the chair behind my desk and called Ryan.

He answered almost immediately. I could tell by the tinny sound of his voice and the steady background noise he was in the car using Bluetooth. "Gemma, I'm with Louise, and we're on our way to the hospital morgue for the autopsy on Daniel Stanton."

"I have something you'll want to know."

"Go ahead."

"First, I told you Mary Moffat had gone to Sandwich following the psychic fair trying to find someone else to play the medium in her little scam."

"You did," he said.

"She's back. Or coming back. It would appear she's found a new medium and she's trying to set up another séance at, of all places, Rebecca Stanton's home. I've also been told the psychic community is abuzz about Daniel's death, claiming the ghost that killed Iris Laval killed him too."

"We care about this why?" Estrada said. "I'm not setting out on a ghost hunt."

"For one thing, we wouldn't know where to start chasing ghosts," Ryan said, "but I think I follow you, Gemma."

"*Cui bono?*" I said.

"Who benefits?" Estrada said.

"Precisely. Mary Moffat is benefiting. First, she has an excessive devotion to Bunny Leigh, and she's managed to wiggle her way back into Bunny's life by inviting her to yet another séance. Second, she's back on the map in the psychic world. I'd originally dismissed Mary as a suspect in the death of Iris Laval, believing it would have been a case of killing the golden egg–laying goose. But what if, for the sake of speculation, Laval was intending to move on without Moffat, and Moffat figured she could find someone else to do the job. Which, it would now appear, is exactly what happened."

"We're looking, Gemma," Ryan said, "but so far we can find nothing at all that connects Daniel Stanton with either Iris Laval or Mary Moffat. Do you think it's possible he saw something that first night?"

"It's possible. It's also possible Moffat's trying to create a haunted house, for lack of a better word, in West London. My sources tell me people are leaving the psychic fair in Sandwich and hurrying back to West London in light of the news about the latest death. Is Moffat trying to set herself up as the authority on paranormal goings-on in this area?"

No one spoke for a while. I heard the sounds of traffic passing, the steady buzz of the car engine, static on the line. Finally, Estrada said, "It's a heck of a reason for murder."

"I've known less," Ryan said. "Okay, Gemma, thanks. We've had a pretty deep dive into Moffat's background, but I'll have someone go over it all again. We're going into the autopsy in a few minutes, and after that I'll try and locate Moffat and have a chat with her about her whereabouts yesterday evening."

"Even if she was in town," Estrada said, "why would she be creeping around the Stanton house?"

"That is the question, isn't it?" I said. "Scouting it out maybe, wanting to try something more spectacular for her next trick? Think about the property, Detective. You remember from last time. It covers a substantial amount of ground. The pool area isn't visible from the road or even from the driveway, and the property's accessible from that stretch of heavily wooded land to the south, running along the cliffs. The fence isn't well maintained, and Rebecca told us hikers walk along the cliff on occasion and she makes no attempt to keep them out. Anyone could have accessed Rebecca's property simply by walking in. Leave their car a few streets over, or take a short stroll from town, slip into the woods, and approach the house that way. They wouldn't be seen from the road because of the trees, and they could easily climb through or over a break in the fence. Did this person slip out of the woods, see Daniel standing by the pool, and give him a shove? Apparently he couldn't swim, but you should ask the pathologist if he suffered a blow to the head before falling in."

"Never would have thought of checking on that," Estrada said. But I could tell her heart wasn't truly into delivering the retort.

Chapter
Twenty-Two

And that was that. I was happy to wash my hands of the whole affair. Mary Moffat murdered Iris Laval and then Daniel Stanton for her own twisted reasons. I had provided the reasoning and could comfortably leave it to the police to uncover the evidence that would put her away.

I was in a good mood when I picked up Jayne to go to her mother's house for dinner and to discuss wedding plans. Andy's mom, Trish, would be joining us.

Andy's three older sisters all had big splashy weddings, Andy told us. His mum had gotten weddings out of her system, so she wasn't likely to exert much control over his.

This turned out to be the case, to Jayne (and her own mum's) obvious relief. Before we got down to discussing the wedding, Leslie Wilson and Trish Whitehall had plenty of questions about what we knew regarding the goings-on at Rebecca Stanton's house, which Jayne and I did our best to avoid over predinner drinks. We enjoyed a delicious meal of grilled salmon and salads on the deck and then pushed our empty plates to one side and switched the topic to color schemes, flowers, and guest lists. Andy and Jayne both grew up in West London, so they (and their mothers) knew a lot of people who'd expect invitations.

"You can invite Pippa and Grant, if you like, Gemma," Jayne said.

"No," I said. It wasn't that I didn't like my older sister (I did, sometimes) or her partner, who'd been a friend of mine before they met, but where Pippa went, trouble followed. And by trouble I mean the sort you read about in the international papers or see on network news, not just the *West London Star* and the local Twitter feed. "I'm hoping to get to London after the wedding to visit them and my parents," I added.

The soft warm night had settled around us by the time we finished the business of the evening and were preparing to leave.

"It's going to be a marvelous wedding," Trish said as she gave Jayne an enormous hug. "I cannot wait to see your dress. You are going to be the most amazingly beautiful bride."

"That she will be," Leslie said with a fond smile.

"Tell me, Jayne dear," Trish said, "unless it's none of my business or you want to keep it secret, are you going to change your name to Whitehall or keep Wilson?"

"What's that saying, Mom," Jayne asked, "about changing the name but keeping the initial, which is supposedly bad luck?"

"Something like that," Leslie said.

"I haven't decided," Jayne said. "But I'm leaning toward taking Whitehall. Wilson isn't exactly an unusual name."

"Whatever you like's fine with me, dear," Trish said. "Andy's father, being more of a traditionalist, might have other ideas, but you needn't worry about him. I'll set him straight." She laughed at the thought.

"I like Andy's mum," I said to Jayne as we drove through the nighttime streets.

"I do too. He gets on with both his parents really well."

"Mind if I ring Ryan?"

"Go ahead."

As we'd been digging into our dessert of fresh local raspberries with ice cream, I'd received a text from Ryan, asking me to call when I had a chance. *Nothing important*, he added.

I made the call now.

"What's up?" he said.

"I'm just returning your call. I'm with Jayne in the car, heading home. We had dinner at Leslie's and did some wedding planning."

A touch of fear crept into his voice. "Nothing I need to get involved with, I hope."

"Your job, Detective," Jayne said, "in light of the fact that Andy doesn't have any brothers, is to make sure the groom shows up at the right place at the right time."

"And suitably dressed," I added.

"I can probably manage that," Ryan said with a chuckle.

"You wanted to talk to me?" I asked.

"Couple of things I thought you'd be interested in. One, the autopsy confirmed much of what we suspected. Stanton drowned in chlorinated swimming pool water. No signs of a blow to the head or anywhere else, and no defensive wounds on his body. His blood alcohol count was extremely high. It's entirely possible, the doc said, he passed out at the side of the pool and simply fell in."

"Thanks for letting me know," I said.

"As for your idea about Mary Moffat, she has an alibi for yesterday evening."

"What? Surely not? How reliable is this alibi?"

"About as solid a one as you can get. She was stopped by the Sandwich police at six thirty. Given a ticket for speeding in town."

"You mean her car was stopped. Perhaps someone else was driving it?"

"The woman behind the wheel matched the driver's license she produced. And her name's the one on the ticket."

"Might it have been someone else pretending to be Moffat? The police don't look that closely at the driver of a stopped car, do they?"

"The moon might be made of green cheese, Gemma, but it's unlikely. Louise sent the officer who'd issued the ticket a picture of Moffat, and he identified her."

I watched my carefully considered reasoning fly out the window. "You're sure of the time?"

"The time stamp on the ticket is six thirty. It's, at the absolute minimum, thirty-five or forty minutes from Sandwich to here. Moffat was not killing Daniel Stanton, or anyone else, around seven o'clock last night."

"How accurate is the time of death? She might have done it earlier and been returning to Sandwich, not leaving?"

"We know Stanton was alive at four o'clock, because you and a good number of other people can place him at the tearoom. Between four and six fifteen, Moffat was at the fair, helping a friend staff his booth. The friend confirms the time."

"Don't you think the timing's suspicious? She was seen by the police and this friend at exactly the right time to have a much-needed alibi? Maybe she arranged someone else to do it."

"That's something we'll look into, but I think it's a long shot."

"Okay. Thanks, Ryan. What's next?"

"Digging, digging, and more digging. I've got some calls into Los Angeles, where Daniel lived, which I want to follow up on. To be frank, Gemma, if it wasn't for the earlier death at which Daniel Stanton was present, we wouldn't be putting much time into his case. It appears, so far, to have been an accident."

"Rebecca?"

"Rebecca Stanton's not entirely in the clear, but the woman has no history of violence, no police record of any sort, and when we spoke to her teatime companions from yesterday, they said she was more annoyed by him than angry."

"Thanks for this," I said.

"Talk to you later. Bye, Jayne."

"Bye," she said as I disconnected.

I pulled up in front of Jayne's building.

"What do you take from all that?" she asked me.

"I have to admit, it's entirely possible Daniel's death was an accident. He was angry at Rebecca, still nursing a heck of a lot of anger at his late father, drinking out of that anger, which is never good, and thus likely not paying a sufficient amount of attention to his surroundings. He could have tripped on the rim of the pool, or even his own feet, and gone over the edge. As for Mary Moffat, if you're invited to a séance, say no."

"I have no intention of ever going to one of those things again." Jayne put her hand on the door but hesitated before opening it.

"Something wrong?" I asked.

"Not wrong, no. I'm just wondering . . ."

"Wondering what, Jayne?"

She took a deep sigh and thought for a few seconds before speaking. "About what Trish asked me earlier. I've been debating whether I want to take Andy's name. Wilson's not exactly rare and unusual, and my mom's not going to care about the continuing of the family name. But, I don't know. It seems like a big step. If we have kids I'll want them to have Andy's name. He's never said so, but I know he'd like that. It would be weird having a different last name than my own children. Right?"

"Wilson-Whitehall has a nice ring to it, don't you think? I hope I never fall in love with a man named Conan. Conan-Doyle or Doyle-Conan would be too much for me to live with."

She smiled.

"Where did this come from? You've not getting any pressure from Andy, are you?"

"Goodness, no. We haven't even talked about it."

"You've got months to decide, and you know all Andy wants is to be with you."

"I worry sometimes, more than I should maybe, about being a wife." She made quotation marks in the air with her fingers. "I love Andy so much, but I value my independence. Me, Jayne Wilson. Not Mrs. Andy Whitehall."

"From what I know of the both of you, neither of you are going to allow yourselves to be submerged into the identity of the other. You're each independent people, and together you'll be one exceptionally strong pair. Jayne and Andy. Andy and Jayne."

She leaned over and gave me a huge hug, the angle awkward in the car seats. "You're the best, Gemma."

"I try."

She opened the door and jumped out of the car. "See you tomorrow. And don't forget, we're going to the bridal store next week to try to find me the perfect dress. I can't wait."

She skipped up the walkway, and I smiled to see her go. When she was safely inside the building, I threw the car into gear and drove away.

Silly Jayne. As though she had any reason to worry about losing her individual identity once she became Andy's wife.

A thought burst into my head, and I was so startled I almost crashed into the car in front of me that had stopped at a red light.

Chapter
Twenty-Three

Dogs are dogs, and no matter how impatient their owner might be to get on with the concerns of life, they have to be walked before settling down for the night.

When I got home, I snapped their leashes on them and we headed off. Violet and Peony trotted happily down the tree-lined streets, moving in and out of the soft glow thrown by the streetlamps. Lights shone from behind curtains, and I caught the occasional glimpse of a flickering blue light that indicated someone was watching telly.

Full of impatience, mind churning, questions tumbling all over each other, I tried holding both leashes in one hand while holding my phone in the other, searching for the information I wanted—needed—to know. But Violet caught a scent on the wind and took off to the right, while at the same moment Peony spotted a woman coming our way and headed left to exchange greetings. When I finally got them under some sort of control, at least heading in the same general direction, they then decided to meet another dog also out for its evening stroll and almost pulled me off my feet in their haste.

"Evening, Gemma," the owner of the approaching dog called to me. "Lovely night."

"Lovely, yes, lovely. Peony, no! Get out of those bushes." I tugged on the leash, and my phone slipped out of my hand. I crouched down, feeling for it in the dark. I dropped the leashes, and the dogs bolted for freedom. When I finally found the phone, dusted it off, checked for cracks (none, fortunately), located both leashes (and attached dogs), I stuffed the phone in my pocket and decided my desperately important business would simply have to wait.

For the remainder of our walk, the dogs trotted contentedly at my side.

Finally, we made it home. Violet and Peony slurped up water while I escaped to the den with my laptop.

Talking to Jayne earlier made me realize I'd made a critical mistake, and thus I'd overlooked a vital component of this case. As the hours stretched on, the street grew quiet, and the dogs snoozed at my feet, the size of my mistake came into focus. I had to do a lot of digging, and at times I ventured into places I probably wasn't supposed to go, but by the time the first rays of the sun were coming through the window, I knew what I needed to know.

I yawned and stretched. "No point in going to bed now," I said to the dogs, who were no doubt wondering why we'd spent the night in the den instead of the bedroom.

I headed for the shower and changed into a fresh set of clothes, and then I padded into the kitchen to put the kettle on. I checked the time: six fifteen.

I needed to speak to Rebecca Stanton, but it was too early to call. Not too early to talk to Ryan, though. I called him and was sent directly to voice mail. Next, I tried Louise Estrada. More voice mail. I left messages for them both.

While the tea steeped, I thought. It wasn't critically important to immediately act on what I'd uncovered, so I could wait for the detectives to call me back.

Then again, I'm not known for being a patient person.

I phoned the police station. "Hi," I said to the voice that answered. "Gemma Doyle here."

"Ms. Doyle. What can I do for you?"

"I need to talk to Detective Ashburton or Detective Estrada, but their mobile phones are not t picking up."

"They've been called out. Big house party ended in a brawl when a couple of college kids who'd been kicked out of the party came back in the early hours with bats and knives and some friends."

"Anyone hurt?"

"A couple of kids sent to the hospital, but looks like nothing too serious. Mess of a scene though; house ransacked, and some valuables appear to have been taken."

"Okay, thanks. I've left messages for the detectives, but if you hear from them, can you tell them I called?"

"Sure."

I prepared my tea in a take-out cup and called to the dogs for their morning walk. I decided not to rush into anything and to wait patiently until Estrada or Ryan got back to me. I'd tell them what I'd learned, the conclusions I'd drawn from it, and let them take matters from there. But as we walked down the tree-lined street, watching the neighborhood (and the local squirrels) come alive, I wondered if that was wise.

If I was right, another person might be in danger.

I turned around and led two reluctant dogs home.

* * *

"You're early this morning, Gemma," Fiona said when I came into Mrs. Hudson's Tea Room.

"Couldn't sleep." Not knowing what the day would bring, I'd driven to Baker Street, parked in the alley, and come into Mrs. Hudson's through the service door.

The bakery was busy at this time of the day. Customers lined up for their morning coffee and bagels or muffins to take to work. A couple of tables were occupied by men and women in business casual clothes, scrolling through their phones or iPads or talking over spreadsheets and binders.

"I want to speak to Miranda, but I don't have her number," I said. "Jayne will have it."

"Speak to me about what?" Miranda came out of the kitchen dressed in the tearoom waitress uniform and carrying a tray of bran muffins.

"You're here," I said. "I thought you might need to take another day off."

"I suggested it, but Aunt Rebecca said she'll be fine. Daniel wasn't her son, remember, and when it comes down to it, they barely knew each other. And what she knew, I'm sorry to say, she didn't like all that much. Neither did I, to be honest."

I stepped to one side of the counter so we could talk while she arranged the muffins. "It was nice of Jayne to give me yesterday off," Miranda said. "Considering she only hired me because she was in a pinch trying to find last-minute summertime help, I would have felt bad leaving her in the lurch again."

"One low fat latte and one caramel macchiato with double whip," Fiona called to waiting customers.

"You're helping in the kitchen this morning?" I asked Miranda.

"Yup. I wanted to see how it's all done. What did you want to talk to me about?"

232

"Have the police had anything further to say to Rebecca about Eleanor's accusations? Regarding what happened to Daniel, I mean?"

"The female detective came to the house again yesterday afternoon. She allowed me to sit with Aunt Rebecca while she asked her questions. Neither of us had anything new to tell her. The detective asked if we'd heard from Mary Moffat again."

"Had you? Heard from her?"

"Not directly, but Bunny, Aunt Rebecca's friend, called yesterday morning while we were having breakfast. She suggested another séance with a new medium. Aunt Rebecca didn't want to talk to her, and I gave Bunny a firm no. Talk about totally inappropriate." She shook her head with so much vehemence her earrings swayed.

"You're not tempted to try it again?"

"A séance? Not in the least. I don't know what I was thinking, Gemma, getting involved in that nonsense. Aunt Rebecca and me. Never mind how it turned out, I would have thought we both had more common sense. My mom's... gone, but that's life, isn't it? She'd want nothing more than for me to get on with my own life, and that's what I intend to do."

"Speaking of getting on with it, what's happening with Eleanor?"

A voice called from the back. "Miranda! "If you're talking to Gemma, bring her in here. If you're talking to anyone else, don't.""

"Oops," Miranda said, heading back to the kitchen.

"Sorry," I said to Jayne.

"You're in early." Jayne pounded a lump of dough as though she were trying to beat it into submission. Both ovens were on, and the kitchen was warm and aromatic with the scent of baking and spices.

"Couldn't sleep. Next time I need to work out some of my anger, can I come in here and do that?"

"Knead bread dough? Any time. As for today, we're fully booked for afternoon tea, so I need you, Miranda, to start on the tea sandwiches while I get these cinnamon buns done. They've been popular this morning, and while I'm at it, I'm going to prepare some smaller ones to serve with tea. The sandwiches will keep in the fridge under a damp cloth until needed. I cooked a chicken yesterday to use for the sandwiches. Recipes and instructions are kept in that white binder. While you're talking, Gemma can peel the boiled eggs."

"I can, can I?"

"Yes, you can."

Miranda rummaged in the fridge for the chicken and passed me the bowl of eggs.

"Eleanor?" I prompted, cracking the shell of the first one. "What's happening with her?"

Miranda dropped the cooked fowl onto a cutting board and reached for a knife. "Considering she accused Aunt Rebecca of killing Daniel, to the police no less, Aunt Rebecca's not inclined to invite her back to the house with open arms. Eleanor spent last night and the night before at the Harbor Inn, at Aunt Rebecca's expense, I might add, but the tap has now been turned firmly off. She's coming around this morning to get the last of her things. And then, I don't know what she's going to do. I suppose she'll stay in town until the police release Daniel's body, but I don't think she can afford to stay at the Harbor Inn much longer."

My nerve ends tingled. I stopped peeling eggs. "She's going to Rebecca's house? Do you know when?"

"She called last night wanting to come around, but Aunt Rebecca was tired and going to bed early, so they arranged a time for today. Aunt Rebecca has a yoga class at nine, so she told Eleanor to come at eight." Miranda glanced at the clock on the oven. "I guess she'll be arriving right about now."

I abandoned the eggs.

Chapter
Twenty-Four

As I pulled the Miata out of the alley that runs behind Baker Steet with a screech of tires, I tried Ryan again.

It went to voice mail, once again. "This is now urgent," I said. "I'm going to Rebecca's home, and I need you or Louise to call me as soon as you can. Better still, join me there."

I drove through town far too fast, and a few minutes later I turned into Rebecca's long driveway. The garage doors were closed, and the rental car I'd seen earlier was parked outside. I parked my own car at the bottom of the steps, stuffed my phone into the pocket of my summer trousers, and jumped out. I rang the doorbell and tapped my foot impatiently, waiting for a response as the sound echoed through the house. I pressed the bell again. Still no answer. Thinking Rebecca and Eleanor might be sitting on the patio and didn't hear the doorbell, I took the path around the house. I listened for voices, but all I heard was birds singing in the trees, the sea crashing against the rocks at the bottom of the cliff as the tide turned to begin coming in, and the low hum of traffic passing on Harbor Road.

I rounded the house. No one was on the patio, in the pool, or working in the garden; no cushions had been laid out on the lounge chairs. The only activity came from bird feeders hanging from branches of trees scattered across the lawn, and the sway of leaves in the soft breeze off the ocean.

It was, of course, entirely possible no one was at home. I didn't know if Eleanor had taken over the rental car after Daniel's death, or it had been left where it sat. Her visit might had been postponed, or ended quickly. Perhaps Rebecca went out early to meet a friend for coffee before yoga.

"Rebecca," I called. "It's Gemma Doyle."

No one answered. I took out my phone, intending to call her.

And then I noticed it: a single mug on the patio table. I walked over to the table. The wrought-iron chairs were empty of cushions, except for one. In front of the chair was the mug, about three quarters full of coffee, fresh enough to still emit that deep, rich scent. I stretched my hand across the top, without touching anything, and I felt the warmth rising up. Someone had been here, drinking this coffee, and no more than a couple of minutes ago.

I walked to the edge of the patio and looked across the lawn. The police had been on the property two nights earlier, disturbing everything. All was now put back to rights. Rebecca kept her house and possessions immaculate; she would have called her gardeners and pool maintenance staff the moment the police let her know they were finished.

Two well-maintained gravel walkways crossed the lawn. One went directly east, toward the ocean; the second headed south, into the woods lining the property. Footsteps marred the gravel on the southern path. I crouched down and studied them. Two sets of prints. One with treads that were likely from trainers, and the other appeared to be left by flip-flops. Both prints were medium-sized, and both went in one direction only. In some places, the mark of the trainers covered the other prints. Meaning the flip-flop wearer had gone first, followed by the trainers.

I stood up, took another look around me, and seeing nothing else of interest, I followed the prints past the perfectly maintained flower beds, a riot of color at this time of year. The gravel path turned into a rough woodland trail when it entered the clump of trees at the edge of the lawn.

The prints carried on into the woods. I did so also.

Fortunately, I'd been here before, and I knew my way around. The forest path ends at a lookout on a cliff above a stretch of rocky beach. It's not a high cliff, but high enough to be dangerous.

I was about to shout to announce myself when I heard a sound. The trace of a voice, carried on the wind, raised in anger. A muffled cry in response.

I broke into a run, pushing aside low-hanging branches and stumbling over rocks. Deep in my pocket, my phone vibrated to tell me I had a call. I pulled it out: Ryan, at last.

"Can't talk," I said. "At Rebecca's. Get here now. I'm leaving the line open."

"Gemma, wait—"

I didn't disconnect the call before putting the phone back into my pocket as I stepped out of the trees onto the bare, windswept rocks overlooking the ocean.

Two women stood at the edge of the cliff. The blue water stretched to the horizon behind them; small whitecaps danced toward shore. A handful of red-hulled dinghies, white sails spread, moved in unison. Rebecca Stanton was facing me, her back to the sea, ready for her yoga class in workout clothes with flip-flops on her feet. "This conversation is over," she said to the person with her. "I told you to get your things and clear out, and I meant it. If I was inclined to give you anything, and I am not, following me down here and making threats isn't likely to change my mind."

She noticed me then, and her eyes blinked in acknowledgement. She wasn't frightened, not yet, only angry and getting angrier.

Eleanor Stanton stood between Rebecca and the woods, her back to me. Her long hair was loose, and the wind whipped it around her head and shoulders.

"Get off my property, or I'll call the police." Rebecca took a step away from the edge, but Eleanor shoved her in the chest, and she staggered backward, stopping only inches before the ground fell away. "What do you think you're doing?" Rebecca cried.

Eleanor said something I didn't catch.

The first traces of fear crept into Rebecca's eyes. She attempted to dodge to one side, but the younger woman grabbed her arm.

"Eleanor Stanton!" I yelled, hoping the phone was picking up my words. "Let Rebecca go and step away from the edge of the cliff."

Eleanor whirled around, but she didn't release Rebecca. Instead, she pulled Rebecca around with her, holding one arm across Rebecca's chest and the other tight around her throat.

"This has nothing to do with you," Eleanor said. "Go away."

I took a step forward. I extended my hands and attempted to appear calm and reasonable, a woman in control of the situation. Rebecca looked at me, fear filling her eyes. She clawed at the arms holding her, but her nicely manicured nails were kept short for gardening, and they had no noticeable effect.

"You know I'm not going to do that," I said to Eleanor. "Why don't we go up to the house and talk this over?" I didn't worry that she'd wonder why I was shouting. The wind threatened to carry my words away from them. "This cliff edge looks dangerous, and you're standing far too close."

"You leave. We'll follow, once Rebecca agrees to give me what I want."

"Sure," I said. "That's okay, right, Rebecca? You didn't mean it."

I didn't want to take my eyes off Eleanor's face, but I chanced a quick look at their feet. Eleanor was so close to the edge, her heels were almost over. The cliff showed evidence of erosion, loose gravel, crumbling rock, and drifting sand. Her hold on Rebecca was tight. If Eleanor went over, Rebecca would go too.

I gave Rebecca what I hoped was an encouraging smile and a nod. She misinterpreted my gestures and attempted to break free with a strangled cry and a sudden lurch forward. Eleanor tightened her grip around Rebecca's throat. Their feet shifted and a section of the cliff fell away. I heard rocks bouncing all the way down.

"Maybe you could come away from the edge while we talk," I said. "It looks dangerous to me."

"That's a good idea," Eleanor said. "I'll throw my stepmother-in-law over. Thanks for suggesting it. Then you can follow her."

"You might be able to make it look as though Rebecca, poor Rebecca, overcome by guilt after murdering her stepson, took her own life, but no one will believe I willingly went after her."

"Maybe you grabbed for her in one last, futile attempt to be a hero." Eleanor shook her head sadly. "Never pays to be a hero."

I could hear nothing coming from my phone. I'd foolishly not waited for Ryan to confirm he'd understood me. Even if he

240

had understood me and come to Rebecca's, if he didn't hear me say we were at the cliff, they'd waste precious time searching the house and grounds. Eleanor didn't look as though she intended to move away from the edge anytime soon. I had to keep her talking.

"Divorce is always a reasonable option these days," I said. "I'm divorced myself. My husband was cheating on me with, of all things, one of my own employees. Best thing I ever did was leave him. I didn't, uh, see the need to kill him."

Eleanor shrugged. "I wouldn't inherit anything from an ex-husband, now would I? I married Daniel because I thought he was going to come into money. He was so sure he'd get his share of his father's estate for his ridiculous business plan. He didn't have a clue about how to manage money or run a business, so I knew his grand idea was never going to fly, but once he had the money he was after, I figured I could control it. Cut myself in for the lion's share, clean and simple. But then it turned out that she"—Eleanor tightened her grip on Rebecca's throat—"had no intention of giving him any. Not while she was alive, anyway." As Eleanor talked, Rebecca clawed at the hands holding her as she struggled to suck in air.

"What makes you think Daniel is mentioned in Rebecca's will? If, as you say, she wasn't going to give him anything for his business. She has family of her own she can leave her property to."

"When we first got here, after their first argument, after he'd stormed out in a childish huff, she told me Daniel would get what was his, but only when it was time. Stupid thing to do, wouldn't you agree, telling someone you have to be dead for them to get any money out of you? I knew Daniel didn't have the guts to do what needed to be done, so I decided to take care of it myself. That didn't happen as I'd planned, so I came up with another plan. For which I had to get rid of Daniel earlier than I first intended."

"You and Daniel came to West London hoping to get Rebecca to invest in your business. You soon realized that wasn't in the cards, so you decided to kill her and hope she'd left him enough in her will to make the killing worth your while. The hat pin was very clever. Lethal yet small enough to carry with you, unnoticed, until you had the chance to use it."

She preened, proud of herself. "I'm glad you think so. I've had that pin for a while. It makes a nice weapon, and tucked into my suitcase through one of my bras, no one's going to confiscate it at the airport. Unfortunately, I was distracted at the séance." At last something approaching emotion moved across her face. When talking about her initial plan to kill Rebecca, the deliberate drowning of Daniel, and threatening to throw Rebecca off the cliff, Eleanor's expression had been unchanging, almost impassive. Maybe even bored. But now, a spark of what might have been genuine fear moved behind her dark eyes. Blood drained from her face, and a visible shudder ran through her. She shook her head to clear it, but she didn't let down her guard, so I dared not make my move. "I was forced to put the pin to another use. I had to shut that medium up."

"Because whoever was speaking through the medium was going to tell everyone around the table, including Daniel, you'd murdered your first husband. That put a fright in you all right. And then, before you got another chance to attempt to kill Rebecca, you started to worry about the amount of police attention focused on this house. And that Daniel might start to put two and two together and wonder what you're up to. Maybe

Daniel even began to suspect what you'd done, and you didn't trust him to keep it to himself."

"Unreliable is the word I'd use to describe Daniel," Eleanor said.

"So you got rid of him?"

"Unfortunately, that proved to be necessary."

"Like you got rid of Eduardo Diaz, your first husband?"

Her burst of laughter was so unexpected, I started. "No harm done. Guy was a waste of space."

"And Jackson Pritchard after him?"

"You seem to know a lot about me."

Despite her terror and shortage of breath, Rebecca's wide eyes slid to one side, and she stared at Eleanor.

"I know enough," I said. "I suspect your father's going to get tired of constantly bailing you out of trouble."

"I am impressed. That connection isn't exactly public knowledge. My mistake for not paying enough attention when Madame Lavalier ordered you out of the room. Too late now. My father's old school. Family's everything, but daughters can't be trusted with business matters or with money. He left me no choice but to try to make my own way somehow."

At last, I heard it. A branch snapped in the woods. Loud enough to have been stepped on by a bear or a six-foot-three detective. Hopefully, the latter.

I was so relieved I almost shouted to let Ryan know where we were. But, if he was moving stealthily, he believed he had reason to not announce his presence.

"Which one of them came to the séance?" I asked. "Eduardo or Jackson? Judging by the accent I heard and the names of your dearly departed husbands, I'm guessing it was Eduardo. Spanish upbringing, I'd say, but he'd been in America for a long time."

She sucked in a breath, and the fear crept back into her face. "Eduardo. He was always jealous and quick to anger. He didn't even have all that much money to leave me, but I needed to get him out of my life. He swore he'd never let me go. I . . . I didn't realize he really did mean never." Her entire body shuddered. "I've been to séances before. My nona took me to a couple of them before she died. She told me the spirits only ever want to help us. After she passed, I contacted her. It was nice talking to her again. I never thought . . . it could turn bad."

I took a slow, cautious, small step forward. I was only a few feet from them now. I was conscious of the complete silence of the woods behind me. No birds chirped and no squirrels rustled the leaves. Rebecca and Eleanor were too close to the edge. Ryan was biding his time. Waiting for me to do something.

Unfortunately, I had no idea of what I could do.

So, I smiled and took another careful step, still holding out my hands in a gesture of friendship. "Difficult husbands. I know how it is. Let's go up to the house and talk about it. I don't know about you, but I could murder a cuppa."

I read the hesitation in Eleanor's eyes. The uncertainty. She threw a quick glance over her shoulder.

"He scared you, didn't he?" I said, attempting to sound perfectly reasonable. "Eduardo? Scared you so much you had to stop Madame Lavalier from continuing to channel him."

I reached out and lightly touched Eleanor's arm, the one she had around Rebecca's throat. I felt the tension in the muscles relax. Slowly, the arm fell away. I took her hand and held it in mine, and I dared to take a peek over her shoulder. It wasn't far to the rocky beach below, but the fall was steep, and the rocks were sharp, and the ocean had just passed the low tide line.

Eleanor released her hold on Rebecca. Rebecca took two steps forward and collapsed to her knees, sucking in great gulps of air.

"I'm a coffee man myself." Ryan stepped out from behind a tree. "But tea sounds good too."

Detective Estrada stood slightly behind him, watching us, her right hand resting on her belt. Uniformed shapes slipped between the trees.

Eleanor gave Ryan the barest glance before turning her head to look directly at me. She gave me the smallest of nods, and her lips said, "You win," although she made no sound.

"Tony Rizzo will get you out of this," I said.

"Perhaps this will be one time too many, as you pointed out," she replied in a low voice. She glanced over her shoulder, and I read the intention in her eyes.

At the school where I was considered to be a problem student, I'd been forced to join the rugby team under the coaching of the legendary and formidable games mistress, Miss White. I hated rugby as much as I hated that school, and I gave the game up as soon as possible. Schoolgirl athletics has done absolutely nothing for me in my life. Until now.

Before Eleanor could jump, rather than grab her and risk her pulling me over the edge with her, I executed a rugby tackle from the side that would have Miss White rising to her feet and cheering. I brought Eleanor crashing to the ground with enough force my brains rattled around inside my head.

I lay on top of Eleanor Rizzo Diaz Pritchard Stanton while she kicked and flailed, rained abuse down upon me, and tried to push me off her.

Then Louise Estrada was holding her down, and Ryan Ashburton was helping me stand up.

245

"I'm okay. I'm okay." I shook my head. Nothing fell out, so I said, "Help Rebecca."

Ryan dropped to his knees next to her and said, "Lie still, Mrs. Stanton."

"I'm okay. I . . . Help me up, please."

Ryan took one arm and Stella Johnson took the other, and together they guided Rebecca to her feet. We stepped to one side and watched as Eleanor, still screaming threats and abuse (and threating to call her father), was handcuffed by Estrada and led away by the detective and a uniform.

"Am I supposed to know who Tony Rizzo is?" Ryan asked me when all that remained of Eleanor's presence was her piercing voice echoing between the trees.

"Look it up in the directory under Las Vegas mob boss. Did you hear our conversation?"

"Snatches of it. I put my phone on Record, so I'm hoping I have it."

"Good. With that, plus Rebecca and my evidence, I don't think even Mr. Rizzo can save Eleanor from herself this time."

Chapter
Twenty-Five

"**I** can be so stupid sometimes."

"Yeah, I've noticed," Ryan said. "I often wonder how you get by."

I punched his shoulder, and he grinned at me.

We were once again gathered in Rebecca Stanton's living room. I'd been here so often lately, I might consider moving some of my things in. News of the police activity had traveled fast, as it does in West London, and Jayne abandoned her almost-baked scones and rising dough. She, followed closely by Miranda, ran out of Mrs. Hudson's Tea Room shouting at Jocelyn and Fiona to manage as best they could, adding she'd pay double time for the remainder of the day. They talked their way past the police at the gate and the front door, and Jayne was now in the kitchen, once again preparing tea and coffee.

Louise Estrada was at the police station booking Eleanor, and Ryan remained behind to speak to the witnesses, namely me and Rebecca. I feared Estrada had a long day ahead of her. Child of a mob family, Eleanor would have been taught, along with her alphabet and the colors, not to talk to the cops without a lawyer.

Miranda sat on the sofa next to Rebecca, one arm wrapped protectively around her aunt. Rebecca huddled under a heavy wool throw, feeling a chill despite the warmth of the morning. It had been suggested she go to the hospital to get herself checked out, but she insisted it wasn't necessary, all she needed was time to collect herself.

Ryan stood at the windows overlooking the garden, watching officers and forensics people come and go between their vehicles and the woods, giving Rebecca the time she needed.

I leaped to my feet at the clatter of the tea tray announcing its arrival and helped Jayne serve. I passed Rebecca a cup of coffee. She looked up at me, blinked in momentary confusion, and then accepted it with both hands. "Thank you, Gemma. Thank you for more, far more, than the coffee. Eleanor. I can't believe it."

"I didn't like her much," Miranda said. "Her or that Daniel. Something was off about the both of them, her in particular. He was openly creepy, but the way she looked at you sometimes when you weren't looking back, it gave me chills."

"You should have said something," Rebecca said.

"You were trying your best to get on with them. I figured you didn't need me interfering."

Ryan took a cup from Jayne and said, "If you're up to it, Mrs. Stanton, I need a brief statement from you about what happened here earlier. I'll get a more detailed formal statement later."

"I'm up to it." Rebecca sipped her coffee as she struggled to gather her thoughts. "There's not much to say other than what Gemma saw and you witnessed. I might have had some sympathy for Eleanor and would have let her stay with me until Daniel's arrangements were finalized, but not after she accused me outright of killing Daniel, and to the police no less. I told her so, and we arranged for her to come to the house this morning to get the last of her things. I met her at the front door. She tried to apologize, but I was having none of it."

Rebecca swallowed. New lines of stress were carved in her face, and dark purple circles had appeared in the delicate skin under her eyes. She said nothing for a long time. Jayne and I sipped our drinks. Miranda held her aunt's hand all the tighter. Ryan turned back to the window, giving Rebecca the time she needed.

"That, I like to think," she said at last, "is unlike me. I hope I'm a forgiving person. Anyone would believe Eleanor spoke in shock and grief, and take sympathy on her. Perhaps my subconscious sense of survival had taken precedence over the instinct to forget about what she'd said. Perhaps I'd noticed something 'off' with her, as Miranda called it, but I hadn't wanted to deal with it. Anyway, regardless of what I was thinking, I told her I'd be out by the pool if she needed anything, but otherwise she was to pack up and take her leave. I took my coffee outside, but I couldn't relax. I like to walk down to the bluff when I've got something on my mind and watch the sea. It was Ron's favorite thinking spot."

"You told Daniel and Eleanor that at some point, I assume," I said.

"I did. When they first arrived, I tried to talk to Daniel about his father, but I soon realized he didn't much care. The boy was nothing but a bundle of anger and resentment. Thus Eleanor knew where to find me when I wasn't by the pool. She followed me to the cliffside. When I first saw her step out of the woods, I assumed she'd come to beg for money one more time. I told her no, and I tried to go back to the house." She shuddered, and Miranda hugged her closer. "Gemma saw the rest."

"Gemma?" Ryan said.

I told them how, when Miranda told me Eleanor was scheduled to pay a visit to Rebecca this morning, I feared Rebecca might be in danger. Then I described all that followed.

When I was done, Ryan said, "Eleanor Stanton wasn't anywhere near our radar. What made you realize it was her?"

I turned to Jayne with a smile. "You started me on that mental path last night."

"Me? What on earth did I have to do with it? We went to my mom's and had dinner and planned Andy's and my wedding."

"You mentioned you have a fear of being undermined as an individual when you get married. When you become a wife."

"Huh?"

"What's that got to do with anything?" Miranda asked.

Ryan let out a burst of laughter. "Got it."

"As did I," I said. "Fortunately before it was too late for Rebecca. Eleanor was Daniel's wife. Because of that, she was on no one's radar. Not even mine. She came to West London as Daniel's wife, not as a person in her own right. Once she was, to repeat the metaphor, on my radar, I started remembering things she'd said and done."

"Like?" Jayne prompted.

"Let's step back a minute. Some of this is speculation, but I think you can build a good case out of it, Ryan. Eleanor married Daniel thinking he was coming into money. He talked a good game about his wealthy father and his father's widow, who was about to cut him in on his share of his father's estate. They came to West London hoping to get Rebecca to invest in Daniel's business plan. They hadn't been here long before Eleanor realized Rebecca had no such intention."

"She got that one right," Rebecca said. "If he'd only talked to me. If he'd discussed his plans in detail. If he'd shown the slightest bit of interest in how I was doing and in sharing memories of Ron with me, I might have. Instead, it was nothing but gimme gimme gimme. The same as he'd always been with Ron. So incredibly sad. Ron deserved much more from his only child."

"Therefore," I said, "Eleanor reasoned, if Rebecca wasn't going to fork out now, better to get rid of her and let Daniel get his inheritance from her will. I believe she kept the hat pin on her, simply waiting for the right time to use it. And then, at the séance, she employed the weapon against a different person, Madame Lavalier. It was Eleanor, not Daniel, who encouraged you to hold the séance, isn't that right?"

"Yes," Rebecca said. "He thought it was nonsense. She was very excited as soon as Bunny mentioned it."

"Because her grandmother had taught her to believe in that stuff. It would appear, however, her beloved nona didn't tell her that sometimes you hear things at these séances you might prefer not to. I suspect she went to the séance with no intention of doing any harm. Not that night, at least. But circumstances changed, and she conveniently had the hat pin concealed on her. A couple of things caught my attention, although I didn't realize their significance until later. That night, when we were all gathered in this room, waiting for Madame Lavalier to summon us, the storm started. Eleanor was standing at the window, looking out. A huge peal of thunder sounded, and the lightning just about lit up the room."

"Gosh, yes," Jayne said. "It was so dramatic. It was as though they'd set the scene deliberately. But what about it? It gave me a heck of a fright."

"You and several other people. But not Eleanor, and that is my point. She turned away from the window, barely reacting, and helped herself to another drink."

I stopped talking and studied the questioning faces staring at me.

"So?" Miranda said.

"And?" Rebecca said.

"That sounds to me like the curious incident of the dog in the nighttime," Jayne said. "You've pulled that one before, Gemma. If I must, I'll play Doctor Watson and ask, why is it significant that Eleanor didn't react to the storm?"

"Because later, after the séance, when the police were questioning everyone about what had happened, she said she'd been frightened by the peal of thunder during the séance, and in her shock, she'd dropped the hands next to her. Which, if I remember the seating arrangements correctly as was described to me, means Ashleigh was on one side of her and Larissa Greenwood on the other. Liars generally talk too much because they believe they need to embellish the story to make it sound more truthful. Instead, they usually accomplish the opposite. Case in point: Eleanor told us she's been terrified of thunderstorms ever since she was a child. That, according to the look on Daniel's face, came as news to him, but he wasn't going to contradict her in front of everyone."

"Wow!" Miranda said. "You noticed all that? And you remembered it?"

"Anyone who was looking at them would have noticed it, and everyone stores tons of seemingly useless information in their brains all the time. It is simply a matter of sifting through the chaff accumulated during the day and coming up with that one grain of wheat when needed. If everyone would—"

"Thank you, Gemma," Jayne said. "We'll conduct a detailed examination of our own memory habits at another time."

Ryan smothered (not very successfully) a laugh. Miranda simply looked confused.

"Very well," I continued. "Once I remembered that minor detail, and thus I realized Eleanor had lied about such an insignificant thing, I started wondering why she'd lie and what else she might have lied about. She needed another explanation as to why she dropped the hands next to hers at the table because the real reason was so she could stand up, slip behind Iris Laval, and kill her with the hat pin concealed on her person. The reason she had such an unusual object on her was that she intended to use it to kill Rebecca when the opportunity presented itself."

"My head's spinning," Miranda said.

"Try spending every day with her," Jayne said.

"I'm not taking all that in front of a judge," Ryan said. "Too much speculation, Gemma. You have to give me more."

"Happy to."

"Wait, please," Miranda said, "before you go on, are you saying Eleanor killed Iris by mistake? That she intended to kill Rebecca?"

"No, I'm not. She killed Iris quite deliberately, although in panicked haste. Rebecca, you heard what she said out on the cliff."

Rebecca snuggled deeper into the blankets. Her face had gone very pale. "I did. I can't credit it."

"Four spirits, including the dog, visited the library that night. Who came last?" I asked.

"Some man," Jayne said. "He wanted revenge for something. He seemed angry. He never said his name though."

"A male voice, sounding as though it was someone between the ages of thirty and fifty, with traces of a Spanish accent.

Spanish from Spain, not the Americas or the southern United States. Eduardo Diaz, first husband of Eleanor Stanton."

"That's—" Ryan began.

I lifted one hand. "There are, as Shakespeare reminds us, 'more things in heaven and earth.' But whether you or I believe the late Mr. Diaz paid us a visit that night or not, Eleanor most definitely did. She feared he was about to name himself and accuse her in front of a roomful of people, including her latest husband, of murdering him. Which is exactly what she'd done. She might have genuinely feared he intended to kill her in revenge. What did he, or whatever it was, say? 'You took my life. I'm here for yours.' In her mind, did she kill Iris Laval or re-kill Eduardo Diaz? I doubt she even knows."

"She was a true believer in the whole spiritualism thing," Rebecca said. "That wasn't an act. Daniel told me he went along with it to humor her."

"For this guy Diaz to appear in front of us all like that," Miranda said, "has to mean it was real. He was real."

"I don't know about that, and I have no intention of speculating," I said. "Mary Moffat, the medium's assistant, told me she and Iris hadn't discussed such a person appearing. But remember, Iris was a con artist. Did she investigate Eleanor's background and realize she had blackmail material? Would the appearance of her late first husband's . . . ghost, for lack of a better word, be a way of softening Eleanor up? Mary and Iris met in Las Vegas, where they were both trying to make a living on the periphery of spiritualism and magic tricks. Eleanor's family lives in that city and is"—I cleared my throat—"highly connected. It's possible Eleanor's habit of ridding herself of unneeded husbands is common, yet unspoken, knowledge in that world."

"Husbands, plural?" Ryan said. "You mean there was another man as well as this Diaz guy?"

"Once I began having my doubts about Eleanor, one thing led to another. She was quick to accuse Rebecca of killing Daniel, so quick he hadn't even been pronounced dead yet. In most cases, the patient's spouse or other relatives initially refuse to accept their loved one has died, despite the evidence. They certainly don't jump the gun. At the time, I thought Eleanor, who can be a bit of a drama queen, had been shocked into assuming the worst. She was quick to point out the possibility that Rebecca killed Daniel, left the house, and then been seen to return. Which, it turns out, is precisely what Eleanor herself did. Once it started to form a pattern, I did a deep dive into her life, and I discovered a great many very interesting things. Eduardo's death was ruled a suicide by the local police, although some questions were raised to the effect that the autopsy was not done as completely as it might have been. Less than six months after his death, Eleanor married one Jackson Pritchard. Pritchard was considerably older than her, and although not extremely wealthy, he had a substantial estate and, most importantly, no offspring or close relatives to leave it to. A year after the wedding, Pritchard was shot to death in an apparent home invasion. No one was ever charged with his murder, and the weapon was never located." I cleared my throat once again. "Questions were raised by Pritchard's friends about the seriousness of the police investigation, but that went nowhere. This happened three years ago. The case was gently shoved into a bottom drawer. The investigating detective retired prematurely and moved away three months later. I was unable to find any record of where he retired to."

"Is that significant?" Jayne asked.

"Probably. Bear in mind, I also learned—and please do not ask me how I know this—that Eleanor was christened Eleanor Rizzo, although her parents never married and her father never publicly acknowledged her. Her mother was a Las Vegas casino hostess, and her father, allegedly, is the head of the Rizzo crime family. Tony Rizzo appears to be a very traditional mobster. He wanted his daughter, born out of wedlock or not, to have his name, but he didn't want her to have anything to do with his, shall we say, business concerns. Eleanor herself confirmed that to me on the cliff. She had to find her own way of making money. And, to her, killing people in order to benefit didn't amount to much of an obstacle. Her father's influence, I suspect."

"You learned all of this because a woman lied about being afraid of thunder?" Miranda said. "I'm sorry, but I find it hard to believe."

"One other thing got me thinking. That was a slip on the part of Eleanor herself. She offered to show me the library in the daylight. She made a big deal of how much she admired it, even to the point of wanting to come back in the winter to see the fireplace being used, and she specifically mentioned she'd touched the wood of the mantle over the fireplace because she liked the feel of it on her fingers."

"So?" Miranda said. "She was a guest in this house. Why shouldn't she go into the library, particularly to see the Chihuly?"

"Fair enough. Except the police didn't find her prints on the mantle. Because she'd wiped them. The fireplace was directly behind Iris's chair."

"You've gone too far with this one, Gemma," Jayne said. "The police didn't find anyone's fingerprints on the mantel. Therefore, the absence of Eleanor's means nothing."

"Nothing. Except she went to pains to let me know her prints might be there, and if they were, they had a legitimate reason to be so. Not something anyone would mention unless they had reason to want me to know it. I suspect at one point she stumbled in the dark and might have put her hand, the one not holding the hat pin and the cloth, on the mantle. She had the presence of mind to quickly swipe at the surface, but she didn't know if she'd been effective enough and had to explain why her prints would be on the mantle, if they were. Once again, she talked too much."

"She said the same to us," Ryan said. "Now I remember. She went to some trouble to make sure we understood she was a guest in this house and had been just about everywhere because she admired the art and furnishings so much."

"Everywhere except in the kitchen," Rebecca said. "She didn't exactly help out."

"I thought she was nervous. I never considered she was covering for something," Ryan said.

"The point being, Eleanor was never nervous, and she never chatted aimlessly. Thus, when she did so, it was out of character and worth my wondering why."

"Unbelievable," Rebecca said. "But I still don't understand why she killed Daniel."

"Because you had to die, Rebecca, for her to inherit. If you were murdered so soon after the death of Iris Laval, in this very house, the police attention would have been intense. And Daniel, because of his barely concealed hostility and his threats, would have been suspect number one. I'm sure Eleanor wouldn't have minded in the least if Daniel was accused of the crime, but she couldn't take that chance. If he was found guilty, he wouldn't inherit. Am I right, Ryan?"

"Yes," he said. "You can't inherit from someone you've been convicted of intentionally killing."

"So Eleanor set Daniel up with the intention of making it look as though Rebecca killed him. Rebecca, you told Eleanor about the meeting at Mrs. Hudson's."

Rebecca nodded.

"Eleanor told Daniel where to find you. I heard him say it wasn't his idea to follow you to the tearoom. If not his, then it could have been only one other person, and that person wanted to engineer a public argument between the two of you."

"That's right," Jayne said. "I forgot about that. I guess I forgot a lot of important stuff."

"I was also watching Eleanor while Rebecca and Daniel were having their confrontation. She was clearly pleased with the way things were going until she saw me watching, and then her self-satisfied expression disappeared. You might remember she goaded him into intensifying the attack."

"Yes!" Jayne shouted. "It was Eleanor who said Daniel had been insulted, even though he hadn't been. She knew he'd react to that."

"Rebecca had told Daniel and Eleanor they were no longer welcome in her house," I said. "Eleanor had to act immediately, or it would be too late. Thus, she engineered a confrontation between Rebecca and Daniel, something very public, which she could later tell the police had embarrassed Rebecca in front of her friends. As they left the tearoom, she pointedly said she was going shopping and Daniel could take the car back to the house. I wondered at the time why she almost shouted that bit of information. You can try to follow the route and timing of her shopping trip, Ryan. I suspect she ran in and out of the shops, establishing her presence and grabbing things to have in the store bags, then hurried through the woods to Rebecca's house. She found Daniel drinking away his anger, as she probably expected, and suggested they have a talk by the pool. One hard shove and he was in the water, unable to get himself out. Back through the woods, grab her shopping bags where she'd concealed them, a hurried walk into town, and hail a taxi on Baker Street to take her to Rebecca's in time for the dramatic discovery of the body in the pool. If you ask the taxi driver where he picked her up, I'll bet it was at the very bottom of Baker Street, maybe even on Harbor Road, rather than farther up the street where the clothing shops are, which would have taken her additional time to get to. If you need proof of my theory, the condition of her hair and trainers when she got out of the taxi here at quarter past seven provides it."

"Trainers?" Miranda asked.

"English word for sneakers," Jayne said. "Okay, I'll bite. What on earth does the condition of her shoes have to do with it? I was there too, remember? If something had been wrong with them, I would have noticed. I mean, I think I would have noticed."

"Some dirt was on her right shoe when they came into the tearoom shortly before four. Later, when she got out of the taxi with her shopping bags at Rebecca's, the shoes were clean. Not only that, but her long hair had been down at Mrs. Hudson's, and later it was tied back. Only when I pondered what had happened at the time of Daniel's death did I realize the significance of those details."

"Sometimes," Ryan muttered, "it's like pulling teeth."

I gave him a big smile. "When on a shopping expedition, a woman will pop into a public loo if required. She will not take the time to wash her shoes and change her hairstyle, not if she's returning to her lodgings immediately after. Eleanor walked through the woods. It had rained the night before, if you remember, and quite heavily. By late afternoon, the streets were dry, but it would have been wet under the trees and in the undergrowth. She would have picked up a fair amount of mud on her feet, and she likely got dead leaves and twigs trapped in that mass of hair she has. She had to remove the evidence, but she went too far. That sort of detail on its own means little to nothing. Put it all together—"

"It's all so logical, once you explain it," Miranda said. "Maybe I should start paying more attention to people's clothes and what they say about them."

"'The world is full of obvious things which nobody by any chance ever observes,'" I quoted.

"No one except for Gemma," Jayne said.

Miranda turned to her aunt. "I've made up my mind. I'm going back to Harvard in the fall, like Mom wanted. I might change my major though. Business seems rather boring after all this. I'm thinking psychology."

"I'm glad," Rebecca said.

Ryan cleared his throat, telling me to get on with it.

I got on with it. "As for the method of the killing itself . . . Who would know a man can't swim? Did he mention it to you, Rebecca?"

She thought for a moment. "No. When they first arrived, I invited them to make use of the pool, but Daniel said, in his abrupt way, he didn't like to swim in chlorinated water when the sea was right outside his door."

"Exactly. Some men might consider not being able to swim a weakness, something not to confess to. Whoever killed Daniel had to know he wouldn't be able to get out of the pool. It's a good-sized pool but not that big. You should check out the clothes Eleanor had been wearing that day, if she hasn't washed them yet. As well as residue picked up in the woods, you might find traces of chlorinated water on her jeans where she knelt at the poolside. I suspect she wasn't content to simply hope he'd flounder and drown, so she held him under with a firm hand on the top of his head. Have the pathologist check again for bruising, Ryan.

"Now that Daniel was dead, you Rebecca were next. You had to die before you had the opportunity to remove mention of Daniel from your will. Your death, however it was arranged, would have been made to look like a suicide committed out of your guilt at having murdered Daniel."

"And Eleanor would inherit as Daniel's widow," Jayne said.

"I'm not entirely up-to-date on the intricacies of the inheritance laws of Massachusetts, and it's possible Eleanor isn't either, but she would have considered such to be a strong possibility."

"That," said a voice from the doorway, "is the most convoluted piece of reasoning I've ever heard. And I've heard a lot of convoluted reasoning since meeting you, Gemma." Louise Estrada came into the room.

"My work here is done," I said. "It's up to you to take what I know for sure, mix it with what I've speculated, and build a solid, unshakable case."

"Easier said than done." Estrada turned to Ryan. "She's lawyered up. One phone call and a mighty big shot attorney's flying in. I recognize the name from my years in Boston. The guy does a lot of work for organized crime figures."

"Then we, in turn, have a lot of work ahead of us," Ryan said. "Gemma, anything else?"

"You'll have no trouble getting her. Eleanor's smart and devious, and she worked it all out with care, but she had to change her plan on the fly after what happened at the séance and unwanted police attention was drawn to this house. As Louise pointed out, the new plan was quite simply too convoluted, and Eleanor couldn't control all the factors, such as the rainstorm. Unlike in *The Sign of Four*, when Holmes remarks it's lucky they've had no rain, we're lucky we did. Poke a hole in one part of her story and the entire edifice will collapse. She'll be expecting her daddy and his pals on the police force to get her out of this one, like they've done before, but he has no influence here. When you're interviewing her, you might mention the séance and Eduardo Diaz's appearance. That truly rattled her, and the memory of it still does."

Chapter
Twenty-Six

When Jayne and I walked into Mrs. Hudson's Tea Room, all conversation stopped. People turned and stared. Fiona froze in the act of pouring a cup of coffee, and Jocelyn almost dropped the tray of scones she was carrying. Even the espresso machine stopped gurgling.

"Carry on, everyone," I said with an imperious wave of my hand.

"Miranda won't be back today," Jayne said, "but I'm sure we can manage without her. Now, what's needed from the kitchen?"

A wave of questions followed me into the Emporium.

"You opened?" I said to Ashleigh. "Thanks for doing that, but you're not scheduled to come in until this afternoon."

"Bunny phoned me to say she heard you bolted out of the tearoom so fast you almost knocked aside a couple of customers as they were coming in, followed not much later by sirens screaming through town and emergency vehicles turning into the Stanton place, and then Jayne also ran out, discarding her apron and hairnet as she went, along with Miranda. Not that she was discarding Miranda, but that Miranda was going with her. So I figured you needed the help." She grinned at me.

Moriarty lay spread across the sales counter, belly up. He did not grin at me but rather bared his formidable teeth and hissed.

"Nicely observed," I said, doing my best to ignore Moriarty. "And I observe you've been busy in my absence."

"Not much Conan Doyle–related psychic traffic this morning. More like the usual tourists looking for books or souvenirs and regulars coming in for the latest releases. Shall I assume Sir Arthur will be back on the main table shortly?" Ashleigh patted Moriarty as she spoke. He turned his head away from me and settled into a loud purr.

"When word gets out of what inspired the murder of Iris Laval, yes. I might have trucks backing up to the loading bay."

"Not that we have a loading bay."

* * *

It was a busy day in the Sherlock Holmes Bookshop and Emporium, and not just with the Sherlock-loving and book-buying public. More than a few people came in to ask what I knew about recent events at the Stanton house. To which I played the innocent and suggested they might enjoy a nice gaslight mystery featuring murmurs of the supernatural. And what do you know, I just happen to have such books in stock.

Irene fell through the doors at 3:35 as I was preparing to go next door to join Jayne for tea. "Okay, Gemma, spill."

I smiled at her sweetly. "I never spill. Might damage the books."

"I was in Boston this morning, so I appear to have missed all the drama. Again! And isn't that just my luck. My sources tell me you were at Rebecca Stanton's house for a long time earlier today, and not only you but a considerable number of West London's finest, as well as vanloads of forensic people, coming and going, and a guard at the gate stopping the curious from entering. The police put out a statement a few minutes ago saying an arrest has been made in the murders of Iris Laval and Daniel Stanton, plus the attempted murder of Rebecca Stanton, but no further details were forthcoming. I cannot believe those three things are not related."

"They are indeed."

"So what—"

I put up a hand. "I can't tell you, and you know that. It's a police matter now, and all will be revealed in the fullness of time."

"The fullness of time. Yeah. Does the name Gordon McRae mean anything to you?"

I thought and came up blank. "No."

"Big shot mob lawyer. Spotted a short while ago getting off a private plane at Hyannis Airport."

"Even big shot mob lawyers go on vacation now and again, I'd guess."

"Okay, Gemma. Keep your secrets. For now. I want first dibs on a statement from you, or at least to get the goods on your inside knowledge, when the time is right."

I was about to say I'd make no such promise when the chimes above the door tinkled and two women I didn't expect to see together came in: Bunny Leigh, in the company of none other than Mary Moffat. Moriarty emerged from his bed under the center table to greet them.

The look on Mary's face could be described as nothing but sheer glee. "So," she announced, "it was a spiritual killing after all!"

Irene swung around. "What? How do you know that? Who are you, anyway? Irene Talbot, *West London Star*."

Mary's eyes gleamed. "The press. I'd be happy to give a statement to your newspaper. I was there. I was a witness to the killing, and I—"

"Hold up," I said. "What do you want, Mary? Bunny, what's going on?"

"Mary called me," Bunny said. "She's had an idea."

"What sort of idea?" I asked suspiciously.

"Mom," Ashleigh said, "this is not a good idea. Whatever it is."

Bunny hesitated.

"I thought you found a new partner," I said to Mary. "Where is she?"

"When she heard Madame Lavalier had accidentally summoned the forces that ultimately killed her, she—"

"Where did she hear that?"

"Everyone knows, Gemma," Irene said. "I mean, that's what people are saying. The paper can't print that as anything more than a rumor, which is why I was hoping to get the solid facts from your side of the story." She smiled sweetly at me.

"Nice try," I said.

"What's going on?" Jayne came into the shop. "Gemma, are we having our meeting?"

"It would seem I have been delayed," I replied.

"Jayne!" Irene exclaimed. "The very person I've been planning to chat with next. You were at Rebecca Stanton's home this morning along with Gemma and the police, I heard."

Jayne's eyes widened in panic. She looked around, seeking escape.

"Leave Jayne alone," I said, "or our deal is off."

"I don't recall you agreeing to make a deal," Irene said.

"I'm mulling it over."

"Bunny," Ashleigh said, "I'm waiting to hear about this idea I already know I'm not going to approve of."

"Mary says—"

"Let me tell them," Mary said. "This is all so terribly exciting. As we all know, Madame Lavalier summoned forces from beyond that ultimately proved to be out of her control."

"We know that, do we?" I said.

"The police department has a leak," Irene said. "I won't mention any names, but one of the civilian clerks was mighty quick to spread the word, saying witnesses to the death of this medium testify she was felled by an unseen force."

"Rubbish," Ashleigh said. "I was there, and I didn't see any unseen forces."

"Exactly!" Mary Moffat said. "Mrs. Rosechild decided perhaps she didn't want to follow in Madame Lavalier's footsteps after all."

"Wise woman," I said.

"She's gone back to New York City to resume her bookkeeping profession."

"Didn't see that one coming," Ashleigh said.

As we spoke, customers began edging ever closer. By now, we were in the center of a good-sized circle. Even Moriarty was listening with rapt attention.

"I've just heard the news." Donald Morris pushed his way into the shop. "Gemma, you put yourself in danger once again. Why didn't you ask for my help?"

"Is it true what people are saying?" a customer asked. "Was Madame Lavalier killed by a ghost, and the same spirit later did in Daniel Stanton?"

"I heard," another customer said, "that there's been an arrest in those cases. The police wouldn't have arrested a ghost, would they?"

I lifted my arms over my head and brought my hands sharply together. "This is a bookshop. We sell books here and other items of interest. Let's return to that, shall we? Donald, no, I didn't put myself in danger, but thank you for your concern. In addition, there's no evidence indicating any spirit from the great beyond killed anyone. Too many people like to overdramatize situations of which they know next to nothing, and I know you people are not among them. Donald, would you be able to mind the shop for a short while?"

His Inverness cape swirled around him as he gave me a slight bow. "I'm always ready to provide what assistance is needed, my dear. You know that."

"Great. Mary and Bunny, upstairs. Ashleigh, you come too. We need privacy before this thing turns into even more of a circus." I headed for the stairs, trusting them to follow.

They did, as well as Irene, Jayne, and Moriarty.

"The poetry of Sir Arthur," Donald said to the assembled shoppers, "is often overlooked by scholars. I myself am currently reading a fascinating treatise on the subject. Shall we see what's on the shelves over there?"

"Fairies," a woman said. "He believed in the existence of fairies, right? I'd like to read about that."

I hustled everyone, invited or not, into my office and shut the door on the babble of questions and breathless speculation coming from below.

"Let's make this quick," I said. "Donald has a tendency to sometimes forget about the minor matter of collecting payment for items chosen."

Mary and Bunny smiled at each other. Mary's grin was broad and self-satisfied; Bunny's not quite so sure. She, I suspected, was being talked into something she wasn't entirely convinced was a good idea. She focused her attention on Moriarty, who'd taken a position in the middle of my desk, and gave him a hearty scratch behind his ears.

"Okay, here it is." Mary paused for dramatic effect and to ensure we were all paying rapt attention. "Bunny and I are going into business together."

Ashleigh groaned.

"What sort of business?" Jayne asked.

"The lecture circuit. Bunny will talk about her life and career and all the famous people she knows."

"And you'll do what?" I asked.

"I'll be her manager, of course. Any number of old pop stars are out there—"

Bunny winced at the word "old."

"So we need to find our niche. What's different about Bunny? What's our angle? I'm thinking the psychic circuit. I have plenty of contacts there, you know. Bunny was at the séance at which a spirit crossed over to kill the medium. That'll bring the ghost hunters in as well as the regular fans who want to meet Bunny."

"That's a terrible idea," Ashleigh said. "Mom, have you thought this through?"

Bunny continued fussing over Moriarty, who is always happy to be fussed over. She spoke in a low voice. "It won't hurt to give it a try, as Mary says. I don't have to commit to anything yet."

"Sounds like a brilliant plan. Not." I pulled my phone out of my pocket and called up a very familiar number. "Except for one small thing. You're not free to travel, Mary."

"Sure I am. I have nothing to keep me here."

I put the phone on speaker and laid it on the desk.

"What's up, Gemma?" Ryan said.

"I'm at the Emporium and with me is, among others, Mary Moffat. You wanted to speak to her, I believe."

Ryan's voice deepened, moving into cop mode. "I'm sending officers now. Can you keep her there until they arrive?"

I smiled at Mary. Her face had gone pale. She shouted at the phone. "You can't detain me, Detective. I told you everything I know about what happened to Iris. If she tried to pull a fast one that night and it went wrong, that had nothing to do with me."

"*I'm* not interested in you, Ms. Moffat," he said, "but the Boston PD are."

Everyone stared at Mary. Bunny stopped paying attention to the cat. Moriarty was not pleased.

Mary's cat-that-swallowed-the-cream look had been wiped away in an instant. She grimaced and shifted her feet.

Ryan continued, "The Boston PD allege that you and Iris Laval conspired to extort grieving individuals with your séance act. I've no doubt you intended to do the same in West London, but that plan ended with the death of your partner. The police in Boston have persuaded several of your alleged victims to come forward and testify."

Earlier today, when we finished at Rebecca's house, Ryan had walked me to my car. He told me Max and Larissa Greenwood had decided to encourage their daughter Laura to take her story to the police. Ryan was confident that once one victim spoke out, others would come forward. I'd realized almost from the beginning of all this Mary was the brains behind their nasty little operation, and I was pleased that ultimately she wouldn't be getting away with it. I glanced out the window onto Baker Steet. Traffic was steady, and pedestrians strolled up and down the sidewalk, popping in and out of shops. People left Mrs.

Hudson's carrying take-out cups or brown bags containing Jayne's marvelous baking. A woman exited the Emporium directly below me, bearing a bulging shopping bag. I hoped Donald remembered to ask her to pay.

"I have suddenly remembered an appointment." Mary opened the door. "Most important. I have to be going."

"What about our partnership?" Bunny asked.

"I'll be in touch."

"Don't count on it, Bunny." I turned away from the window. "Mary, looks like your ride's here." A police cruiser had pulled up in front of the Emporium. Two uniformed officers got out and walked inside.

"There's your story, Irene," I said. "If you want it."

* * *

In the short time Ashleigh and I had been upstairs with Mary and Bunny, Donald had conducted a roaring trade. His impromptu lecture on the poetry of Sir Arthur Conan Doyle, which bored everyone in earshot, turned on a dime to a discussion about the author's spiritualism (including his belief in fairies), and he led the eager customers to the nonfiction section.

Even better, I thought as I surveyed the once-again-almost-empty shelves, everyone had paid!

Chapter Twenty-Seven

I didn't hear from Ryan over the weekend, but I hadn't expected to. He'd be busy gathering the evidence they needed to prepare a solid case against Eleanor Stanton.

On Monday, my phone buzzed as I was going about the closing-up routine after another highly successful day. Apparently news of the death of a prominent medium whilst in the midst of conducting a séance had spread far beyond the Eastern Seaboard, and ghost hunters and spirit chasers were flooding into town. I'd heard some of the tourist shops dragged their Halloween displays out of storage early. Word had also spread that Donald Morris was an expert on Victorian-era spiritualism, and the curious were flocking to hear what he had to say. Donald was definitely not an expert on Victorian-era spiritualism, or any other, but he did know just about all there is to know about Sir Arthur Conan Doyle and his best-known creation, and he led throngs of the curious through our doors.

"Hi," I said to Ryan. "What's up? I'm about to head home."

"I figured you would be. Fancy some company?"

Outside the door, headlights flashed.

"Is that you?" I asked.

"It is. Can I give you a lift?"

"Sure. Are you finished at work?"

"It's been a heck of a long couple of days, but I figure I can sit back and relax tonight."

"I'm glad to hear that. Do you want to go out to dinner?"

"Do you mind if I say no? I'd prefer to stay in tonight, if that's okay with you?"

"Perfect. Give me five minutes to tend to Moriarty and I'll be out. Why don't you order a pizza to be delivered to my place. I don't know that I have much in the fridge."

"Sounds like a plan," he said.

*   *   *

We didn't talk on the drive to Blue Water Place, but once we were settled in the living room, with a beer for Ryan and a glass of wine for me, waiting for the pizza, I said, "I'm pleased we were able to snag Mary Moffat. It had been bothering me, what she and Iris Laval put the Greenwood family through."

"The case likely won't amount to a whole lot, now that Laval's dead. Moffat will try and pin it all on the medium and say she was only doing as she'd been told. I'm hoping the experience might put the fear of the law into her. At least it'll put her out of business for a while."

"What's happening with Eleanor? Anything you can tell me?"

"You were right about her."

I said nothing in response to that.

"Too cocky by half, that one, and overly impressed by her own cleverness. Her big bucks lawyer is having a mighty hard time getting her to shut up. We have her for the attempted murder of Rebecca, considering she did that in front of a couple of very reliable witnesses."

"Meaning me and you."

"Me anyway," he said. "The recording of what I got on my phone's useless. Nothing but a lot of wind and a couple of words from you. But we won't need it. Louise saw how it all went down too. The case around the killing of Iris Laval is getting muddied by all this chatter about a vengeful ghost. I hoped we'd be able to keep that to ourselves, but word got out."

"According to Irene, you have a leak in the police department. A civilian clerk. Want me to drop in one day and have a casual look around. Shouldn't take long to spot the culprit."

Ryan chuckled. "Not necessary. Everyone knows the police chief's niece, who's on a summer placement, has been trying to impress her friends with the depth of her inside knowledge. The chief had a couple of quiet words with her.

"Hopefully that won't matter in court, because we do have two pieces of good, solid evidence to prove Eleanor, not the ghost of whoever, killed Iris Laval." He smiled at me and sipped his beer.

The dogs were curled up at our feet, snoring lightly. Outside a car slowed and turned into my driveway. I stood up. "I'll get the door. You can save your big reveal until I get back, although I suspect I know at least one part of it already."

In the company of Violet and Peony, I opened the door to the pizza delivery guy. I accepted the big box and paid, adding a handsome tip, took the food into the kitchen, also in the company of Violet and Peony, and served it up. I ignored their plaintive looks for one bite—just one tiny bite—and carried the laden plates into the living room.

I handed Ryan his and settled down next to him.

"Okay, so what do you think I was about to say?" he asked.

"That hat pin. You traced it."

"I don't know why I bother trying to solve cases. I can just ask you what happened."

"As we've seen, that doesn't always work out. And, as you're always telling me, you can't take much of what I observe and deduce from those observations to court. The hat pin, I will confess, came as a guess. It's a piece of solid, concrete evidence, which will be absolutely invaluable in court."

"When confronted with it, at last some of that cockiness died in Eleanor. Even her lawyer looked rattled. She was a regular customer at a costume jeweler in Las Vegas, before moving to LA with Daniel Stanton. She bought most of those necklaces and rings she wears there. Because she was a regular, and because everyone in Vegas knows, or suspects they know but would never say, she's Tony Rizzo's daughter, the shop clerks remembered her. They positively identified the pin as having belonged to them. It's not particularly valuable, but it is a nice one, and the young clerk loves old-time jewelry."

"I notice what you're not saying. They can identify the hat pin, but they don't remember Eleanor specifically buying it."

He grinned at me around a mouthful of pizza. "Nope. But I didn't say they did. I put the shop, the pin, and Eleanor in the same sentence and let her draw her own conclusions. She admitted buying it but claims she lost it after she and Daniel came to Rebecca's. She's trying to pin—hey, I made a pun!—the killing on Daniel, but she's slipped up too many times. That won't wash."

"The second piece of solid evidence?"

"She used Daniel's laptop to search for information on the optimal place to stab someone in the neck."

"Good catch."

"I thought so." He beamed. "She deleted the search history, but not many laypeople know how to make sure the history's completely eradicated. When asked about it, she claims she never used Daniel's work computer. Obviously, an attempt to put the entirety of the blame onto Daniel." He paused dramatically.

"But—" I prompted.

"But, we managed to identify a trace of her DNA caught between the keys. A miniscule drop of blood, enough to prove she did use the laptop, at least on one occasion."

"Now that I think of it, she had a healing hangnail on the index finger of her right hand. I noticed it that night but dismissed it as inconsequential."

"Tsk, tsk. I'm disappointed in you, Gemma," he teased. "Didn't someone once say 'the world is full of obvious things which—'"

"I get the point. Thank you."

"When confronted with that piece of evidence, Eleanor suddenly remembered she did use Daniel's laptop a few times. It's all part of building the case, one block at a time. As for the killing of Daniel himself, we have work still to do, but we're putting together a pretty comprehensive time map of where and when Eleanor did her shopping on Baker Street and where and when the taxi picked her up to take her to Rebecca's in time for you to see her arrive. We'll be able to prove she had time to leave town, slip into the woods, shove Daniel into the pool, hold him down, and then get back to town, clean herself up a bit, and hail a taxi. The clerk at the ice-cream shop on the boardwalk remembers a woman rushing in to use the restroom. Eleanor's an attractive woman, and he noticed her. He also noticed leaves trapped in her long, dark hair, and when she came out of the restroom her hair was up.

"Nicely done, Detective," I said.

"I'm glad you're on our side, Gemma Doyle. You'd make a frightful adversary." He stroked my hair.

"I've considered turning to a life of crime, but to be honest, I can't be bothered. It seems far too much like hard work, and I'd be tempted to cut corners. And then you'd pounce."

Violet lifted her head and barked.

"Speaking of pouncing," I said, finishing my second slice of pizza. "Those two vicious creatures need a walk. Want to come with me?"

"Come with you, Gemma?" he said. "Yes, I will. Now. And always."

The two "vicious creatures" heard the magic word, walk, and needed no prompting. They leaped to their feet and ran to the mudroom, nails tapping on the floor. I uncurled myself from Ryan and stood up. I held out my hand and pulled him after me.

Violet barked once, telling us to hurry up.

Acknowledgments

Since starting the Sherlock Holmes Bookshop series, I've gleefully become immersed in the world of Sherlock Holmes and his many admirers. I greatly appreciate all the Sherlockians around the world, the Bootmakers of Toronto in particular, who have enjoyed these books and have accepted them in the spirit in which I've written them.

As always, I'm indebted to Sandy Harding for helping me bring Gemma and Jayne to life and gently pointing out my many plot mistakes. Thanks to the people at Crooked Lane Books for believing in this series and to Kim Lionetti, my super-efficient agent, for her encouragement.